PRAISE FOR

T0248977

Pike I

"The perfect follow-up to Wirt's thrilling *Just Stay Away*, *Pike Island* delivers a breakneck read from the first chapter all the way to Wirt's delivery of the best twist I've read this year. I loved this book!"
—Elle Marr, Amazon Charts bestselling author of *The Alone Time* and *Your Dark Secrets*

"With shades of *House of Cards* and *I Know What You Did Last Summer*, Tony Wirt's *Pike Island* elegantly dances between past and present, gradually cracking open to reveal the 'real' story behind a picture-perfect politician on a meteoric rise and the boyhood secrets he's worked hard to bury. Wirt's immersive writing, clever twists, and layered examinations of loyalty, greed, and ambition's darkest corners will make you want to read this pulse-pounding, utterly satisfying thriller in one sitting."
—Kathleen Willett, author of *Anything for a Friend*

"*Pike Island* is everything you want in a thriller. A compelling plot, great characters, and a storyline that sweeps you along. I devoured it in a single sitting. Absolutely loved it."
—Cate Quinn, author of *The Clinic*

Just Stay Away

"Nobody believes Craig when he insists nine-year-old Levi is the source of the mayhem in his life—which is regrettable, as Levi might be a troublemaker worse than *Baby Teeth*'s Hanna (so says the author of *Baby Teeth*). *Just Stay Away* is a tense page-turner that literally had me reading with my shoulders hunched."
—Zoje Stage, bestselling author of *Baby Teeth* and *Mothered*

"Cancel your plans and find a good chair because once you start *Just Stay Away*, you won't be able to stop. A psychological game of cat and mouse evolves between a writer and his daughter's creepy new friend in this superbly plotted, fantastically immersive domestic thriller. From the characters to the writing to the pitch-perfect ending, Wirt delivers on every level."

—Mindy Mejia, bestselling author of *Everything You Want Me to Be* and *To Catch a Storm*

"A relentlessly creepy and dangerously addictive read, *Just Stay Away* will have you checking your locks and jumping at shadows once you've finished. Using the unique perspective of a stay-at-home dad, Tony Wirt expertly crafts an atmosphere of ever-increasing isolation, claustrophobia, and gaslighting to ramp up from a sinister simmer into a full-blown nightmare. In doing so, Wirt explores gender roles, masculinity, and boyhood in the profound ways you find in the best of the genre. An absolute must read—if you dare!"

—Brianna Labuskes, *Wall Street Journal* bestselling author of *A Familiar Sight*

"In *Just Stay Away*, Wirt flawlessly weaves tension into everyday domestic life. The protagonist, Craig, finds himself in a suspenseful game of cat and mouse with a neighborhood child that will leave you wondering, What would you do to protect those you love?"

—Elle Grawl, author of *One of Those Faces* and *What Still Burns*

A Necessary Act

Underground Book Reviews 2017 Novel of the Year, Reader's Choice

"I literally could not put this book down. As far as thrillers and crime novels go, it ticked every box for me while also managing to be unique in its concept and style. Great characters, genuine bellyaching tension, and an ending that both surprises and satisfies . . . and yet is left wide, wide open . . . I truly hope there is more to come."

—Underground Book Reviews

"*A Necessary Act* grabbed me by the throat and refused to let go—even after I turned the last page!"

—C. H. Armstrong, author of *The Edge of Nowhere*

"This book is filled with creepy and suspenseful moments that are sure to get anyone's heart pumping. Just leave the lights on."

—*Rochester Magazine*

A THRILLER

PIKE
ISLAND

A THRILLER

PIKE ISLAND

TONY WIRT

THOMAS & MERCER

Published by Thomas & Mercer, Seattle

www.apub.com

Amazon, the Amazon logo, and Thomas & Mercer are trademarks of Amazon.com, Inc., or its affiliates.

ISBN-13: 9781662519871 (paperback)
ISBN-13: 9781662519888 (digital)

Cover design by David Drummond
Cover image: © m-agention / Shutterstock; © Cavan Images, © Naomi Rahim / Getty

Printed in the United States of America

To Grandpa Charlie—glad I could tell you about it.
Wish you could have read it.

Chapter One

The fact that anyone of consequence even saw the postcard was pure chance.

There was nothing remarkable about it, so it sat atop a pile of unread correspondence. Krista Walsh paid it no mind because the mail was well below her pay grade. She was very aware of the time, however, as she waited to shuttle her boss to a meeting with the Minnesotans for Better Education. The meeting itself wasn't vital—teachers' groups were easy endorsements for young Democrats like Harrison Leonard—but Krista had built her career (and more importantly, Harry's) on taking nothing for granted. Punctuality was part of that.

"I know." Harry emerged from the back of the office suite with a preemptive apology. "I got stuck on that call with the nurses' union."

"We're fine, but you're gonna have to hustle." There was no hint of exasperation in her voice as she reached back for her briefcase. "You look over those talking points yet?"

"I'll do it on the—" Harry's voice stopped, and it took Krista three steps to realize he wasn't following her. She turned back and saw him in front of the reception desk, holding a postcard. The color had drained from Harry's already light Scandinavian complexion, leaving his face pallid in a way only fear could.

"What?"

The unease reflected in Harry's pale-blue eyes was his only answer as he flipped the card over. Krista made out a faded lake scene with a lone fishing boat in the distance. From across the room, she couldn't tell whether it was supposed to be a retro-style throwback to the days when vacation postcards were used or if it had sat in a wire rack since 1972. Red block letters arching across the top read *Greetings from Cedar Lake!*

Krista wasn't used to being ignored by the man she'd successfully guided from Rochester City Council to the House of Representatives in only a few short years, so she walked over and snatched the postcard from his hands.

The back was blank, which was weird. There was no return address, but Krista saw that the sender obviously knew Harry before that viral video catapulted him from idealistic state senator to the youngest representative in Congress. Before the national media fell in love with him and publications like the *New Yorker* asked questions like Is Minnesota's Leonard the Next Obama?

Whoever sent it knew him before he'd left his tiny hometown for college, where he started going by his middle name.

The postcard was addressed to Andy Leonard.

Krista looked up at her boss. "What the hell is this?"

She had taught Harry from the beginning that successful politicians had to be masterful improvisers, with an answer ready for whatever comes their way. It was a skill that gave Harry an aura of gravitas and control that countered his youthful appearance.

"Huh . . . um . . . nothing."

Krista looked over the top of her glasses, using her dark-brown eyes to pierce through the bullshit. She'd used that look with great success throughout her career, because it's hard to lie to someone who appears to read minds.

"Nothing," Harry repeated. He wiped the fear off his face, replacing it with the affable, approachable politician mask he wore during working hours.

Krista held his gaze for another second before cutting him loose. She didn't like it, but they had a schedule to keep.

"We'll talk later." She reached to drop the postcard on the desk, then stopped and slid it into the back pocket of her bag instead. "You've got to go . . . *Andy.*"

He walked to the door without a word, letting his childhood name hang in the air. Krista turned what she'd witnessed over and over in her head before following him out the door.

The walk down to the reception room was mostly silent. The controlled aura of calm that Krista had drilled into him over the years had returned, but something still poked at the back of her brain. It was her job to know Harrison Leonard better than anyone else, and something about that postcard had rattled him.

It wasn't something she could just sweep away, but it would have to wait.

The voices of a hundred midwestern educators shrank to an excited murmur as soon as Harry walked through the overly elaborate wooden doorway of the Rayburn Reception Room.

A tight smile crossed Krista's face as Harry maneuvered through the crowd to the front, shaking hands where he could, smiling and nodding when he couldn't. The man had a gift, and his magnetic personality felt like it was powering the entire building.

Harry slowly made his way to the podium as the teachers found their seats. His staff had set things up in front of the room's massive portrait of George Washington, ensuring all attendees would see their first president over Harry's shoulder.

Krista made a mental note to address the value of subtlety.

That said, she couldn't fault their enthusiasm. Krista started them on this path because she'd recognized something special in Harry. She had been in charge of Harry's office, his career, and most of his life since she was a lowly intern assigned to keep an equally green and ambitious councilman from embarrassing the party in his state senate race against a five-time incumbent.

Since neither believed in lost causes or moral victories, the duo immediately set out to climb the mountain their colleagues considered unscalable. Krista possessed uncanny political instincts for someone so young and could command respect from anyone with nothing but sheer force of will. She plotted the course and pushed Harry out the door, talking with every voter she could get him in front of. No group was too small and no door too remote to knock on.

When they needed resources, Krista went to the party. When the party wouldn't throw campaign funds at what was considered a lost cause, she improvised.

The first thing Harry did when that initial victory was certified (by a scant 312 votes) was offer Krista a job as chief of staff. Her first official duty was informing him that state senators didn't have a chief of staff. Luckily for Harry, she signed on as his legislative assistant while continuing to fight her way up the party's ladder.

Then someone posted a clip of Harry at a small town hall meeting the day *Roe v. Wade* was struck, and suddenly "STATE SEN OBLITERATES SUPREME COURT" was racking up views faster than any other video on the internet.

That got the party's attention. Suddenly they had campaign funds, prime speaking spots at national conventions, and an invitation to replace a retiring ten-term congressman on the ticket.

It didn't take someone with Krista's political acumen to realize the opportunity in front of them, but doors didn't stay open forever, so she mapped out a path for them. One that could effect real change in the country, as long as nothing unexpected derailed them.

She stood in the back of the room as Harry began his speech. She liked to watch the crowd during these events for reactions, taking note of what resonated and what earned an eye roll, but today she had a hard time ignoring Harry's mediocre performance.

"I probably learned as much from working in the dorm cafeteria as I did in the classroom." Harry remained behind the podium as he told the story of his nose-to-the-grindstone, bootstrap-pulling humble beginnings. They'd added a few embellishments to his origin story over the years, but Harry's natural delivery could make every word sound like truth taken directly from stone tablets.

Krista noticed a nearby teacher pull out his phone and start scrolling. She looked back to the front of the room, where Harry was still rooted behind the podium. Normally he'd pull the microphone free and wander to the edge of the crowd by this point in his story. Harry was definitely off his game. Something had stripped away the polished political veneer she'd spent years developing.

But what, exactly?

An old postcard?

"Education is critical, but as you all know, it doesn't always come from a book. I probably learned as much washing dishes in the O'Hill Dining Room as I did in any classroom at the University of Virginia. Honest work can often be your greatest teacher . . . no offense."

The line got a laugh from the teachers but not the enthusiastic one he usually got. It was the way people laughed at their boss's jokes.

Harry finished the speech and spent another twenty minutes mingling with his constituents. Krista did the same while keeping an eye on her congressman. One-on-one interaction always brought out the best in him. By the time they headed back to the office, Harry seemed to have shaken off whatever had rattled him earlier.

Krista wasn't ready to let it go.

"So, you want to tell me what the hell that was?" Krista's smile dropped the moment the elevator doors closed.

"What?"

She shot Harry a look of annoyance as she jabbed the third-floor button.

"You've given that speech at *least* a dozen times, and that's the best you could do?"

"It wasn't that bad," Harry said.

"You sounded like you were reading it off cue cards." Krista could pick out subtle tics that were imperceptible to most. She'd made a career stamping them into oblivion. "Seriously, what's the matter? It can't be that postcard."

Harry winced as the elevator came to a stop. Krista noticed he waited to confirm the hallway was empty and took a deep breath before answering.

"It reminded me of something. That's all." They stepped through the doors and walked down the corridor. "Something from when I was a kid, no big deal."

Krista's heels clicked on the white marble floor and echoed through the hallway. She preferred flats but wore heels anyway. Not because of an outdated dress code or a halfhearted nod toward expected femininity, but because even though she was already five foot eight, she wasn't about to let anyone on the Hill look down on her. Anyone who told her no had to look her in the eyes, and she'd realized early on plenty of tough guys didn't have the balls to do it.

A small group of people were gathered near a giant Texas flag outside the door to a fellow congressman's office.

Harry approached with a smile. "Make sure you remind your congressman he still owes Representative Leonard twenty-five pounds of brisket from the Salt Lick after that Vikings-Cowboys game."

The comment pulled a smile from a young boy wearing a Cowboys hat. "Yeah, but we beat you in the playoffs."

"Well, yeah, but I've been a Vikings fan my whole life . . . You think I'd ever bet on a *playoff* game?" That got a laugh from the whole group. Harry winked at the mom and slapped the dad on his shoulder as he said goodbye. He'd talked to the kid, but it was a show for the parents. They weren't his constituents, but if things went as planned, Krista would be asking residents of the Lone Star State to vote for Harry soon enough.

"So which one was it?" Krista asked as they left the Texans behind and approached the Minnesota flags bracketing the door to their office suite.

"Which one was what?"

"There are six Cedar Lakes in Minnesota," Krista said. "Which one was it?"

Harry greeted the intern seated at the front desk and made a beeline for his office in back.

"How could you possibly know that?"

"I googled it while you were speaking."

"Seriously?" Harry said. "Weren't you too busy judging my delivery?"

Krista closed the office door behind them. Harry usually kept it open to foster a welcoming atmosphere, not only for his staff, but for the people that came through for meetings or tours as well. But Krista needed his full attention and was beginning to think this was something she didn't want the office to hear.

"I'm doing my job. Are you going to tell me what's going on, or do I have to sit here and pepper you with questions for an hour?"

Harry slipped behind his desk and grabbed a stack of random papers in an obvious attempt to deflect the conversation.

"It's *nothing*, just a place we went to on vacation once."

Krista stood between the two leather chairs in front of the large oak desk that had once belonged to legendary Minnesota senator Paul Wellstone—a fact she required every intern to mention when they brought the weekly constituent tour through the office.

"Your parents didn't have money for vacations," Krista said. "I know that because you literally just told that to a room full of teachers. It's part of the narrative you've built your whole career on. Now, will you please tell me what the hell that was so we can deal with it and move on?"

Harry stared at her across the desk. She was prepared to hold his gaze until he gave up whatever he was holding back.

"It's the lake over by Faribault. I went up with some friends after we graduated from high school. Good friends that I lost touch with over the years. I hadn't thought about it in a long time, that's all. Brought back a lot of memories."

Krista eyed him skeptically, the loose end gnawing at the back of her brain. She forced herself to let it slide. Harry's parents died in a tragic house fire while he was away at college, so there was always some raw emotion in his past. It's one of the reasons they'd crafted a tight biography for him. Something he could stick to that highlighted the useful aspects of his past and glossed over the painful parts.

But while the public didn't need to know every detail, Krista couldn't be left in the dark.

Her phone vibrated a reminder in her pocket. A representative's schedule was an uncompromising overlord that waited for no one.

Not even Krista Walsh.

She let out a breath of temporary surrender and moved on.

"I still think Hatterberg's going to be our best shot." Joe Hatterberg was the five-term Democrat from Colorado's third district, one of the dozen high-ranking members with whom Harry had a meeting in forty-five minutes. "Rumor has it he's looking at the governor's seat in two years, so our bill could be huge for him."

"And not only on his résumé," Harry said. "Automatic voter registration alone will boost the turnout for his base."

After the chaos of the last few cycles, Krista had identified election reform as the sweet spot in American politics. People from across the spectrum yearned for free and fair elections, and she'd made Harry's Election Reform Bill the main plank in their platform. A signature achievement that Krista had staked his (and by extension, her) career on.

If they could pull it off, not only would it change the way government was held to account by voters, but accomplishing something so transformative at a young age would pave the way to any position they desired—up to and including the White House.

But they had to pull it off.

They went over their plan for the next half hour, discussing various strategies and potential concessions. Krista could tell it put Harry back in his element. He was playing the game and helping people.

It seemed enough to push the postcard, and whatever memories it dredged up, out of Harry's mind.

Chapter Two

"But they never specifically said we *couldn't* use the boat, right?" Tall, with the fair Nordic complexion so common to the state of Minnesota, Andy Leonard spoke with the confidence of a trial lawyer who didn't care if his client was guilty or not.

The four teenagers had arrived at the lake the night before, still somewhat amazed their parents had allowed a postgraduation trip to Jake's grandparents' cabin. It had taken him weeks of pleading to get his parents on board, but once they relented, Ryan's and Seth's families agreed. Andy's parents were never a concern, since he rarely seemed to be a concern for them.

But it had been important to the guys, so they'd pushed. They'd been a tight-knit crew since they were kids, doing everything from Little League to debate together. One last week at the lake as a group would be a fitting send-off before they left for college. Jake, Ryan, and Seth were going to state schools, so they'd all be relatively close to home, but Andy was hightailing it out to the University of Virginia. He'd been itching to escape the confines of Ranford, Minnesota, his whole life, but rural towns had an orbit that was hard to break.

Even with Andy on the East Coast, the guys would still be close—bonds of friendship like that don't break easily—but Jake knew things would be different.

That's why the trip to the lake was so important.

"Do you know how to drive it?" Andy asked.

"Pretty much," Jake said with a smile of resignation. "Grandpa Charlie used to let me drive it when I was a kid. It's getting it in and out of the lift I'm not so sure about."

Andy clearly had his sights on a boat ride, and with his combination of charm and dogged determination, Jake knew resistance was futile. Andy was slick enough that, given enough time, he could probably convince Jake it had been his idea. There was a reason Andy was the only one of them to make it to state in debate.

Not that a little cruise around the water was a bad idea. The weather was perfect, and the lake was relatively empty. There would be a lot more traffic come Friday, when the weekenders showed up, so they might as well take advantage of the conditions.

But that didn't stop Jake from worrying about all the things that could go wrong for a group of kids without much boating experience.

"If we have to, we could get in the water and push it in, couldn't we?" Ryan asked, probably looking to bridge the gap.

"I guess so." Jake swallowed his anxiety and pulled the release on the boat lift. The pontoon slowly dropped to the water.

"WOOOOOOOOO BABY!" Seth howled, cracking the serene atmosphere of the lake. He ducked between Andy and Ryan and scampered onto the still-descending boat.

"Dude," Jake said. "Can you at least wait till it's in the water?"

Andy stepped up and put his arm across Jake's shoulders. "Don't worry, man. It's gonna be fine, right?"

"I know, but—"

Andy slid his arm around Jake's neck and put him in a loose headlock. *"Right?"*

Jake laughed and punched his friend in the ribs until he was free. "Yeah, yeah, yeah."

"Seriously, though, is this cool?" Andy's pale-blue eyes held Jake's gaze as Ryan moved to grab the back of the boat. "I don't want you to get into *actual* trouble."

The boys had relatively good judgment for a group of teenagers, which was why their parents had few reservations about giving them a guys' week at the cabin. Sure, they'd probably forget to lock the shed before they left, and somebody might spill grape juice all over the kitchen floor, but there was little worry among the parents about the guys throwing a raging keg party or sneaking a group of girls in.

Jake pointed as the boat settled into the water. "Just grab the front, will ya?"

The boys wrestled the midsize pontoon out of the lift and around to the other side of the dock.

"Whaddya say, fellas?" Seth shouted from the front of the boat. His pale, skinny legs were already propped up on the seat. "Are we gonna hit the water, or did you want to sit around holding our dicks all day?"

"Maybe if you actually did something . . ." Ryan blew a tuft of dark hair out of his eyes as he secured the boat with a loose knot.

"Hey, I'm the only one in the boat ready to go," Seth said.

"Your hard work and sacrifice is truly appreciated." Andy stepped from the dock into the boat.

Jake handed Andy a cooler of pop they'd loaded earlier across the gap. "Grab some life jackets from under the seats."

"Are you serious?" Seth didn't move from his spot.

"We don't have to wear them, but if the DNR stops us, we have to have them out," Jake said.

Andy flipped up the back seat and started tossing out life jackets from the storage underneath. There were a trio of waterskiing jackets and an old-school orange one that had a decent amount of dark mildew growing on it from years stashed in the bowels of a pontoon boat. "Here's yours."

The orange life jacket landed on Seth's lap with a damp thud, and he knocked it to the floor like a dead fish. "Gross."

Andy cackled and piled up the rest on the bench beside him as Ryan pulled the rope off the dock, gave them a push, and hopped aboard.

Jake looked back at the cabin as they slowly drifted out into the lake. He took a deep breath and turned the key. The engine turned over a few times before roaring to life.

"WOOOOOOOOO!" Seth's howl echoed across the open water as Jake eased the boat out onto the lake. The sun hung high in the sky, putting a sharp glare on the greenish lake water surrounding them. There was no breeze, so there was little respite from the heat, but it kept the lake calm. Jake felt a drop of sweat trickle between his shoulder blades as he settled in roughly one hundred feet from the line of docks jutting out from the shoreline and puttered along.

"You gonna open that throttle up or what?"

"It's a pontoon boat, you moron." Andy pulled off his T-shirt and tossed it in Seth's face. He wasn't an athlete, but his lean build was a stark contrast to Seth's scrawny frame beside him. "This is pretty much it."

"Seriously?" Seth leaned back against the bench and folded his arms across his chest. "Weak."

So far, they were the only boat in sight, and the lack of traffic helped calm Jake's nerves.

It was a perfect day to be on the water.

Ryan leaned over the rail to his left. "How deep is it here?"

"Ten, maybe fifteen feet? Most of the lake is in that range, except out there . . ." Jake nodded at one of the two islands in the front section of Cedar Lake. "There's a drop-off that's about forty feet deep. My dad used to take us over there and anchor the boat so we could swim on the sandbar. You can walk way out, and it's only waist deep, but a few steps to the side and WHOOSH! My mom used to freak out about it and always made us wear life jackets. She was completely paranoid that we'd walk out and go straight under. Like we'd forget how to swim or something."

"You guys ever go on the island?" Andy asked.

"Yeah, a couple times."

"What's out there?"

"Nothing exciting. There's a campfire ring by where the sandbar is. People sometimes picnic there and stuff," Jake said. "The rest is just trees. There's some trails that go through it, but nothing back there."

The boat slowly paralleled the shore, passing an increasing number of docks as they approached the Dew Drop Lodge. Situated on the northeast corner of the lake, the Dew Drop was part of the Bourdeau Resort and Campground and the unofficial hub of the lake. It supplied most patrons with their gas, bait, and beer.

"*That's* what we need," Seth said. A massive double-decker pontoon boat was tied up near the small swimming beach in front of the Dew Drop. Bright-red stripes gleamed off the side panels, and the silver pontoons beneath glowed in the sun, either untarnished by use or painstakingly cleaned. A pair of slides hung off the back of the top level and emptied behind the boat.

"Is that a grill on top?" Ryan asked.

"Shit yeah, it is," Seth said. "We could load that sucker up in the morning, take it out into the middle of the lake, and hang out all day. With chicks."

"No girl will ever follow your skinny ass onto a boat, no matter how nice it is," Ryan said.

"Fuck you."

Jake chuckled as he guided their boat past the lodge. He was getting more comfortable driving, and the unease he'd felt earlier was left in their wake.

"How much do you think a boat like that costs?" Andy asked.

"A million," Seth said. "Easy."

"Seriously?" Andy asked.

"It's not that much." Jake knew his grandparents had spent around $20,000 on the boat he was driving, but he didn't feel right telling the guys that. "Probably around $100,000."

"Damn. Imagine having so much money you can drop a hundred grand on a boat," Andy said. "Must be nice."

"You're one to talk, Mr. College Fund." Seth snatched Andy's shirt off the seat and threw it back at him.

Money had always been a little short at Andy's house, but his grandmother had died the previous year and left her only grandchild everything she'd had in hopes of giving him a shot at the best education possible. Having trodden lightly around the topic of money for years and safe knowing Andy had been accepted to his dream school, Seth had needled him about the money all summer like he was making up for lost time.

The only surprise for Jake was that Andy didn't hit him right back, but the gentle churn of their motor combined with the heat of the late-morning sun to create a peaceful vibe as they left the lodge behind.

"What about *that* island?" Andy nodded ahead of them. "Ever go there?"

The smaller island had a much denser forest than its partner to the south, and the trees reached the edge of the water the whole way around. At the far end, an old man stood in a silver fishing boat casting toward a fallen, half-submerged tree that jutted from the shore. He gave the boys the traditional boating salute—a half nod. The guys raised their hands in acknowledgment.

"Nope," Jake said. "Don't think I've ever seen anyone on there. Too many trees and stuff. Everyone goes to the big island. Although we did go to Pike Island once."

Andy turned back to Jake with a furrowed brow. "What's Pike Island?"

"It's where the ghosts of all the fish killed on this lake live," Seth said. "You can hear them calling when the lake is still at night."

Seth started making what he probably assumed were dying-fish noises. They echoed across the water toward the old fisherman, who was surely annoyed at the boat full of damn kids making a racket and scaring his fish away. Ryan chucked a balled-up towel and cut him off midsquawk.

"Seriously, though, where the hell is Pike Island?" asked Andy.

"It's back in—" Jake almost said *Weedy Bay* but was already embarrassed by all the folksy colloquialisms his family used at the cabin. "It's in the back of the lake. There's this little bay out there with an island in the middle. You know that huge northern mounted in the living room back at the cabin? Grandpa Charlie caught that back there a long time ago."

There was no way they could have missed it. Grandpa Charlie's fish was a monster. Forty-one inches long (only two shy of the state record at the time), with a mouth full of razor-sharp teeth frozen agape, the red-and-white Dardevle spoon he'd enticed it with dangling from its jaw. It was enough to give Jake nightmares as a kid, and if he were completely honest, knowing that fish like that patrolled the lake still made him a little nervous whenever he jumped in the water.

"Just to be clear . . . your grandpa caught a fish back in the 1950s, so now everybody calls it Pike Island?" Seth couldn't have put more condescension in his voice if he'd been paid.

"Not everybody." Jake could feel the embarrassment turn the back of his neck red. "Just us. Nobody ever even goes back there, because it's shallow and weedy and stuff. There's no cabins or anything."

"So if nobody can go there, who the fuck cares?" Seth was being purposely antagonistic by that point. It was one of his many charms.

"Because there's some creepy abandoned old house up there." It came out before Jake realized it. Probably a gut reaction to shut Seth up more than anything. He hadn't thought about the house on Pike Island for years. It was just another cabin story.

"Wait . . . what?" Andy, whose interest was clearly piqued, leaned forward. "What do you mean *abandoned old house?*"

Jake felt like he was standing on the high dive for the first time, alone with the sun shining down on him like a spotlight and everyone looking at him.

He'd been so young when they'd gone exploring on Pike Island, it was nothing but a strange memory from childhood that he'd always taken for granted. Looking back under the pressure of his friends' doubts, Jake had to remind himself it was, in fact, real.

"Yeah." It took more than a second to find his voice. "There's this weird-ass house back there that still has furniture in it, clothes still in the closets . . . all that stuff. But nobody lived there. It's like the people just walked away one day, but nobody knows why or who they were."

"I call bullshit," Seth said. "No way."

"I'm serious." Jake was defensive now. Of course it was there. He'd been there and seen it with his own eyes. "I was like five or something when we went, but I remember kid shoes all lined up in one of the bedrooms. It was old, but still . . ."

The last word trailed out and was swallowed by the sound of the motor.

"That's creepy," Ryan said. Jake gave him a little nod.

At least *somebody* believed him.

"Okay, so why are we not there right now?" Seth asked. "You say there's a creepy-ass abandoned house that a whole family disappeared from on an island on *this very* lake, yet I can't help but notice we're still puttering around here like a bunch of fucking old people."

Jake was surprised to admit he was getting curious too. It had to still be there. It was a house, after all. Assuming his brain hadn't just invented the whole damn thing.

"Where is it?" Andy asked.

"Through there." Jake motioned to a small inlet that led to the back section of the lake—what his grandpa had always called Weedy Bay.

"Then let's fucking *go*." Seth turned back to Jake. "You think you can drop an abandoned island house on us and we're just gonna say 'Wow, that's really interesting. Guess we should go home now'?"

"Take it easy, will ya?" Andy dropped his legs to the floor and stepped back toward Jake. "That said—and it pains me to say this—he isn't wrong. Might be kinda cool to check it out."

Seth spread his arms like he'd finished a magic trick. "*Thank you.*"

Andy squeezed Jake's shoulder. "What do you say, Jake? Feel like an adventure?"

"I don't know." He thought back to the time his dad had run aground during a cruise around the lake a few years ago. Jake had learned a bunch of creative words when they got the boat back on the lift and saw a big chunk of propeller missing. "It's really shallow back there, you know? Grandpa Charlie would kill me if we hit something."

"Then we'll take it slow." Andy crouched down next to the captain's chair so he didn't block Jake's view of the lake. "Tell you what, let's head back there and check it out. If it's too weedy or there's no place to tie up the boat, we'll leave."

Jake looked to the back of the lake. It was a straight shot to the inlet, and there were no other boats around. That little bite of curiosity surprised him by itching a bit more. It would almost be worth the risk just to shove it in Seth's face.

He glanced at Ryan. He was always the steady hand who could be counted on to pump the brakes when Andy and Seth tried to drag them into places where trouble resided.

Ryan gave a little shrug.

"All right," Jake said. "But you guys need to keep an eye out the front of the boat. Make sure there aren't any logs or rocks or anything under the surface."

"Hell yeah, we will." Andy smiled and leaned in closer as he stood up. "And if we do hit something, we'll blame it on Seth."

Jake forced a chuckle and took a deep breath, then turned the steering wheel toward the inlet and pushed the throttle forward. The engine growled to life and earned a whoop from the front of the boat. Andy reached back and squeezed his shoulder.

"Attaboy, Jakey!"

Chapter Three

Krista understood the congressional hierarchy, but always bristled at the way these meeting rooms were set up. Members occupied most of the seats around the long wooden table, while chairs were lined up on the wall behind them for the support staff. They often did the majority of the work but were relegated to the kids' table. She was tempted to commandeer one of the empty chairs next to Harry, but that could upset the established order. If there was one thing old congressmen loved, it was protocol, and they needed leadership on their side today.

So Krista stayed in her chair, notebook in her lap and folder full of documentation at the ready, should Harry need it. A few other staff members had joined her along the wall, but not as many as she'd hoped such an important meeting would bring. Representative Hatterberg's chief of staff was the most notable absence. Krista did her best to ignore the snub, but it hovered in the periphery of her thoughts like the first pangs of a coming migraine.

"Well, I think we're all here," Delaware representative Alan Porter said. He'd served as house majority leader for the past eight years and was the heaviest of heavyweights in Washington. "What do you have for us, Representative Leonard . . . or did you want to wait for a few cameras to show up?"

The swipe pulled a chuckle out of the old men at the table and reminded Krista of why she'd dedicated so much to election reform.

It wasn't only politicians on the other side of the aisle that had gotten a little too comfortable camping out in their safe congressional seats.

"I'm ready if you are, Representative Porter." Harry deflected the dismissive slight with a smile. "When we're done, my chief of staff can give you a list of talking points for your slot on *Meet the Press* for when we're ready to announce."

She studied the majority leader for a reaction and was encouraged to see a flash of respect. They had to see Harry as someone who could stand on his own two feet, not simply a flash-in-the-pan lightweight, if there was any chance they'd back his legislation.

They'd all heard Harry talk about election reform in speeches and interviews. It had even gotten some national attention late in the election cycle with a few strategically placed stories that Krista still owed favors for. Now he had to convince them that his plan for election reform wasn't just campaign bluster; it was a serious and attainable goal that would fundamentally improve the way the country was governed.

She'd prepped him for this meeting the same way they'd prepped for debates during the election. He'd done speech club in high school, and Krista treated this as the same, drilling Harry on his lines until they sounded unrehearsed.

He was a natural performer.

Krista watched in awe as he calmly and competently walked the congressmen through his plan.

"This is all pretty substantial," Representative Porter said. "You're inching toward constitutional-amendment territory."

"We've looked into it and believe Congress can make these changes through the normal legislative process," Harry said.

"But anything that big will get challenged in the courts," Representative Clinton Davis said. Krista had singled out the seventy-eight-year-old congressman from upstate New York as one of the biggest obstacles. He'd been a lawyer an eon ago, before he decided to become a congressional lifer.

"Then we defend it and win." Harry pushed back in his chair and walked to the head of the table. He was in full campaign mode and pulling out all the stops. "Legal standing aside—and I'm fully confident in the constitutionality of these changes—these reforms are going to be *wildly* popular. This is what I campaigned on, and people across the political spectrum are hungry for this. Even if their guy doesn't win, they want to know their vote counts for something."

Harry let the words hang in the room, making Krista feel like she was watching a live-action remake of *Mr. Smith Goes to Washington.*

"Are there any more questions I can answer for you?"

The summer after Krista graduated from University of Minnesota Duluth, a few of her friends convinced her to join them in one of those Spartan mud races. Already a runner, Krista wasn't worried about a few obstacles and figured it would be fun. Even when she discovered her friends had opted for the twelve-mile Beast Race, she wasn't overly concerned. Then an emboldened thirty-one-year-old man directed a condescending comment disguised as a come-on toward her at the starting line. Krista's plan of pacing herself alongside her friends was immediately discarded in favor of leaving his smug face in her muddy wake. Unfortunately for her, he'd trained for that specific race, which forced Krista to use every ounce of strength and willpower she had to keep ahead of him for two and a half hours.

She used the same amount of effort to keep from screaming during the last five minutes of their meeting with party leadership.

Harry nailed his presentation, but they might as well have addressed it to a brick wall.

An old white brick wall.

"This is all interesting, but our agenda is set for this session. Has been for a while," the majority leader said. "I know you're new and have a lot of ideas that get a lot of attention on the stump, but you have to understand how things get done here. You can't expect us to upset the applecart like that."

If Harry was as irritated as Krista, he was doing a better job of holding it back. "I absolutely understand, sir, but I feel that this—"

"You've got a bright future, Harry." The condescension in Porter's voice was a taunting rattle on the cage in which Krista hid her growing fury. "You know it, and we do as well. And your ideas for election reform are legitimately intriguing. It's something I could see happening someday, and I think you should keep talking about it on TV, on the . . . internet."

Krista bit her cheek hard enough to draw blood.

"Start paving the way now. After a few more sessions, a few more election cycles, you get some experience under your belt, and it may be something we can seriously look at."

They'd planned for every potential response, but before Harry could open his mouth, leadership ended the meeting and got up to leave. It wasn't merely a dismissal; it was a pat on the head. The numbness of defeat flowed through her, and she had to force herself to stand up. She shared a look with Harry as she stuffed folders full of rebuttal information they never got to use, but his calm face offered no answers or comfort. Just as she'd trained him to do.

She kept her frustration at bay until they were out the door.

"Fucking scared and comfortable."

"Take it easy," Harry whispered. He looked around to make sure none of the congressmen or their staffers were within earshot. "It's a setback, that's all."

"It's a pretty big fucking setback." Krista's voice was still louder than either of them had wanted, but she was mad enough she didn't care. Mad at the crusty politicians, sure, but more so at herself for not seeing it coming. They were the new blood, and she'd entered that room underestimating the powerful's propensity for the status quo.

"I don't care," Harry said. "No matter what Porter says, this isn't done yet. There's interest there. Nowhere in the constitution does it say

I need the majority leader's blessing to introduce a bill. Hell, I bet I can get two-thirds of the people at that table to back me on this."

"They sure as hell didn't back you just now," Krista said.

"I can get them."

They took an elevator down to the underground tram that connected congressional office buildings and the Capitol itself. The subway halls were full of tourists, ending their conversation but allowing Harry to try a few of his state-specific jokes as they waited for the train.

Krista watched Harry work the small crowd of vacationers. It was impossible to tell he'd just had the entire focus of his congressional career casually swatted down by his own leadership. His ability to compartmentalize such a massive setback was impressive, but also a little unnerving.

This wasn't a tiny setback. It was going to take more than a good speech and some schmoozing to get them back on track from this. If Harry couldn't deliver on his biggest campaign promise, there would be some serious blowback from voters in the next election.

A burst of laughter pulled Krista out of her thoughts. Harry was in his element, connecting with whoever stood in front of him. It was a real gift, and she couldn't let it go to waste.

She took a deep breath and blew it across the fire of frustration that smoldered in her gut. They'd come here to make real change, and she wasn't about to let a few political fossils stand in their way.

If they couldn't get around a few geriatric roadblocks, they might as well go home.

Chapter Four

The boys peppered Jake with questions as they motored toward the small isolated section of the lake, but he didn't have any good answers. He was clinging to fuzzy memories from his childhood. Memories that, when he tried to shine the light of logic on them, made no sense.

But it wasn't only him—his family had mentioned the house plenty of times. It *had* to be real.

Maybe that's why he'd bypassed his better judgment and taken his grandpa's boat back to the part of the lake he'd always been told was a no-go area.

Jake pulled the throttle back as they approached the narrow inlet that led into the bay.

"Why are you slowing down?" Seth asked.

Andy jumped in before Jake had to explain himself. "Did you not hear him say it was shallow back here? Now, look out over the front and make sure we don't hit anything."

His friend's backing helped sweep away the wisps of doubt that grew around the margins of his brain like stubborn mold.

Ryan leaned over the port side as they approached. "Looks okay over here."

Andy peered over the right side and said the same. "If you stay in the middle, you should be fine."

The boat slowly glided through the skinny channel. Jake raised the prop as high as he could while still keeping it in the water.

Pike Island sat in the far corner of the cove. Jake pulled the boat in a slow left turn in that direction. Cattails stuck up from the water along the north shoreline, buffered by a huge strip of water lilies. There probably were a lot of fish under there, but most fishers wouldn't put up with the snags trying to get near them.

The island was smaller and more densely forested than the other two in Cedar Lake. The trees were thick and tall and extended all the way to the edge of the water. Fallen trees dotted the shoreline, the half-submerged branches looking like bony zombie fingers reaching out from the soft dirt in front of a gravestone.

"That's it," Jake said. He slowed down even more as they approached and gradually turned right to parallel the shoreline.

"You can't see anything back there," Seth said. "Too many trees."

Jake glanced over the railing to his right and saw weeds floating just below the surface.

"You guys see any place we can tie the boat up?" Andy asked. "What did you do when you were a kid, Jake?"

"I don't know." Jake scanned the shoreline for anything that would jog his memory. "I feel like there was a path that led up to the house. Dad said it was where the people had the dock back whenever, but there was no dock when we went. I think he tied the boat to a tree or something."

As they continued around the back side of the island, the weeds carpeted the top of the water all the way to the far shoreline. Any thicker and Jake worried they'd have to turn back.

"See anything?" Andy asked.

"Nope," Seth said. "Although I am detecting the distinct odor of bullshit."

Jake bristled at the suggestion. Like he would make up some stupid story just so he could drive them all back to this weedy, shallow part of the lake.

"It's up there," he said. "Trust me, I—"

The boat jolted as the motor churned harder. Jake felt panic shoot through him. If he messed up the boat, his parents would kill him well before Grandpa could.

The motor straightened out for a second, then jerked again before dying entirely.

"Shit," Jake said. He killed the throttle and turned the key to the off position. "No-no-no-no-no . . ."

"What is it?" Andy called from the front.

Jake looked up and caught Seth struggling to stay calm. He shot him a look that dared him to say something stupid as he tried the key again. The engine turned over repeatedly without catching.

"Goddammit."

"Out of gas?" Ryan asked from the copilot's seat.

"No." The gauge behind the steering wheel was low, but not empty. Jake reached out and tapped it a few times, like that would do anything. Of course, nothing changed.

"Think we hit something?" Andy glanced over the side.

"I fucking hope not," Jake said.

Jake tried the ignition again, dropping it quickly after it didn't start. He didn't want to flood the engine on top of whatever had stopped it in the first place. Jake hit the trim button to bring the prop out of the water.

"Go back there and check the propeller, will you?" Andy got up and joined Ryan at the back of the boat. Their momentum had slowed, and there was no breeze to push them anywhere, but Jake felt he had to stay in the driver's seat. The shore looked a lot farther away than it had seconds before.

Ryan leaned over the back. "It's full of weeds."

"Yeah, there's weeds all over back here," Andy said. "Totally wrapped around the prop. Can you raise it a bit more?"

Jake thumbed the up button again, and the motor made a whining sound that confirmed it was as far out of the water as it would get.

"The propeller looks fine," Andy said, standing back from the edge and turning toward Jake. "It's just tangled up. If we get the weeds off, I think we'll be okay."

Relief flooded through Jake. Weeds could be dealt with. They might be a pain in the ass, but they did no damage that would require an explanation.

"Can you reach down there and get 'em off?" Jake asked.

Ryan leaned farther out from the end of the boat before standing back up.

"No." His eyes searched the front of the boat. "Is there anything we can use to scrape them off? An oar or something?"

The guys did a quick, fruitless search as the boat continued its imperceptible drift.

"We'll have to get in the water and pull them off by hand," Andy said.

"I can go," Ryan said. "Shouldn't be too hard."

Andy looked up at Seth, who still hadn't moved from his perch in the front of the boat. "You gonna help?"

Seth propped his legs up on the bench and put his hands behind his head. Whatever worry he'd cooked up was long gone. "You guys go ahead. You still have your swimsuits on."

"So do you," Ryan said.

"That's true, but I'm, you know . . . pretty comfortable here. I trust you guys to handle it."

"God, you're a dick," Ryan said, but there was no malice behind it. Seth smiled.

Andy climbed over the back seats and used his foot to flip the two-step ladder attached to the back of the boat into the water.

"Want a life jacket?" Jake called back.

Andy jumped into the water. It only reached halfway up his chest.

"Nope, probably gonna be fine." Andy walked around the end of the pontoon to the motor. It felt like an optical illusion seeing him standing in water this far from shore. No wonder they'd gotten tangled up, at barely four feet deep.

Ryan slid into the water to help as Andy started pulling threads of milfoil from the propeller and discarding them behind the boat.

"Prop looks fine," Andy called up from the water. "But do me a favor and don't start the motor yet, okay?"

Relief flooded through Jake's veins. "You want me to start it now, you say?"

"Fuck you."

"You're welcome."

Jake got up to check on Ryan's and Andy's progress when the sound of another motor came across the water.

"I think we're getting company, fellas," Seth said.

A gray speedboat roared in and stopped about twenty feet from them. The boat was unmarked, but the woman driving it wore an olive gray uniform with the maroon shoulder patch of the Minnesota Department of Natural Resources. The DNR was mostly known for their work in wildlife conservation in the state, but on a lot of lakes where police presence was unavailable, they served as water patrol as well.

"You boys having a problem?" The officer's voice projected over the still-running motor. Her dark hair was pulled back in a tight ponytail. She wore mirrored sunglasses and a tanned complexion earned from a career on the lake.

"No ma'am." A drop of sweat trickled down the back of Jake's neck. He fought the urge to shudder. The wake from the DNR boat rolled under the pontoons on its way to shore, and a queasy feeling shot through his stomach. There was no need to be nervous, but his dad's voice already echoed in his head—*Why did the DNR stop if you weren't doing anything wrong?*

"We got tangled up in some weeds, that's all." Andy cut in as he climbed back onto the boat with a stream of lake water dripping from his swimsuit. "It killed the engine, but the prop's fine. I think we'll be okay as soon as we get them all off."

The officer had a firm grip on the steering wheel, which pushed her sleeve up just enough to show a pale tan line around her taut biceps. She kept the boat right where it stopped without cutting the engine. Even with the lake as still as it was, Jake would never have been able to control his boat that well.

"What are you doing back here in the first place?" Her tone almost brought an unnecessary apology to Jake's lips, but once again Andy answered before he could say anything.

"We were just taking a cruise around the lake, Officer . . ." Andy squinted at the name badge pinned on her uniform. "Schroeder. We didn't mean to get hung up like this, although we do appreciate you checking on us."

The way Andy could flip into his Adult-Schmoozing Mode was always impressive. The guy had an uncanny knack for gaining the trust of adults without wading into brownnosing territory. It was a useful skill, certainly, and had gotten them out of a few jams in the past. And if Jake were honest, it was at least partly responsible for getting them up to the lake that weekend.

People trusted Andy, which made it even more surprising when the woman in the boat did not look impressed.

"This your boat?"

"No ma'am, it's mine." Jake found his voice, not quite trusting his friend wouldn't make the situation worse. He was still fairly confident that they hadn't done anything wrong, but the nerves were there none-theless. "I mean, it's my family's. We have a cabin over on the southeast side."

"How old are you?" she asked.

"Eighteen." That made him a legal boater in the state, but he worried she wouldn't believe him. At five foot six he wasn't necessarily short, but between his height and the little bit of baby fat that hid around his face, he often looked younger than his years.

"Got your driver's license on you?"

Shit.

Jake's license was back in the cabin, tucked into his wallet like those of 95 percent of the boaters in the state. He hadn't even thought to bring it.

"No ma'am, I don't. It's back at the cabin, but we can run back and get it if you want."

She gave a quick shake of her head. Jake fought to keep his unease from sliding into the early stages of panic as he imagined telling his parents about the citation he'd gotten on the boat he'd never asked if he could take out in the first place.

He blinked, and he concentrated on his breathing.

"You boys have life jackets?"

"Absolutely, ma'am," Andy said before Jake could respond. He snatched the mildewy orange jacket off the floor and held it up for the officer to see. Ryan, who had followed Andy up the ladder, held up a pair of life jackets they had pulled out earlier. The DNR officer lifted her head so she could see inside the boat and do a quick mental count.

"You haven't been drinking, have you?"

The four guys blurted out denials in a way Jake hoped sounded earnest.

"We were taking a loop around the lake. That's all, ma'am," Andy said.

Her expression changed enough to show she still wasn't charmed by Andy's efforts. She reached down to her throttle and brought her boat alongside the pontoon for a better look inside.

"Then what's in the cooler?"

Jake's eyes snapped down to the little blue Coleman sitting on the deck between the bench seating in front.

"Just pop," Jake said. He snatched it off the floor and flipped the lid to reveal the Mountain Dew nestled inside. "See?"

"It's getting to be a hot day," Andy said. "Would you like one?"

She ignored his offer and kept talking to Jake. "You get your prop clear?"

"I . . . uh . . . I believe so." He looked back to Ryan for confirmation and got a nod.

She switched her gaze back to Jake, and it took a few embarrassing seconds before he realized she was waiting for him to try the engine. Jake's nerves spiked as he turned the ignition, then fluttered away with the exhaust when it started. The DNR officer sat back in front of her steering wheel and put the throttle in reverse. For a second Jake thought she looked disappointed she hadn't been able to slap a ticket on them.

"This section of the lake is choked with weeds, along with a lot of other crap—that's why we recommend people stay out of here," she said. "I don't expect I'll have to come back and get you boys again, right?"

Jake nodded, content to ignore the fact that she'd done nothing to help them get up and running again. He saw the beginning of movement from Andy and smacked him in the shoulder before any words could escape his mouth.

"And don't forget your driver's license if you go out again." Her boat slowly backed away as she spoke. "By law you have to have it on board, but I'll cut you some slack this time."

"Absolutely," Jake said, relief shooting through his veins as he let out a breath he didn't know he'd been holding. The DNR boat's engine roared as it took off toward the front section of the lake. "Thank you so much."

Jake watched her shoot through the inlet without slowing down, as their boat lolled in the fresh wake. She'd probably given them a hard time for no other reason than they were a boat full of teenage boys. Simply a preemptive warning, letting her presence be known before they tried anything stupid.

"I don't know about you guys, but I thought she was kinda hot." Seth's words broke the tension and brought a moan from the guys.

Jake settled back into the captain's chair and eased the throttle forward. Andy reached down and grabbed a side rail to keep himself upright.

"We're headed back?" he asked.

"Did you not hear her?" Jake asked.

"Yeah, but we aren't doing anything illegal," Andy said. "It's a public lake, and we have the right to go anywhere we want on it, right?"

Jake ignored Andy's technically factual argument and turned them back to the inlet. He wasn't about to risk a citation, bogus or otherwise, by pissing off a self-important DNR officer.

"Did she sound like she was interested in discussing the Bill of Rights?"

Andy sank onto the bench in defeat. "I know, but . . ."

"You know, Andy's right." Seth stood up in the front of the boat like a coach rallying his team for a late-game comeback. "If we leave—if we go back now like a bunch of cowards—what does that say about us? Are you going to be able to wake up every morning from here on out, look yourself in the mirror and say . . ."

Seth took a pause and stepped onto the seat for dramatic effect. Jake was genuinely impressed by the passion his friend showed over this, especially while he was obviously holding back an obnoxiously gigantic smirk.

". . . that you did everything you could to get that woman to go out with me?"

Andy raised a questioning eyebrow at Jake, who responded with a nod. He bolted out of his seat and shoved both hands into Seth's chest, sending him toppling back into the water.

The laughter from Jake, Andy, and Ryan lasted longer than Seth's soggy stream of swear words, which continued through his climb back onto the boat and half the ride back to the cabin.

Chapter Five

Harry had a list of scheduled phone calls waiting when they got back, so Krista headed to her office to chart a new course.

It was true that they didn't need the leadership to introduce a bill, but the painful reality was they needed Porter's blessing if they expected any chance of success. The thought of that old man lording over them all, handing out his official blessing like royalty gifting stale bread to the peasants, was a squirt of lighter fluid on her anger.

Krista took a deep breath and slowly blew it out into her empty office. Rage wasn't going to get anything done.

They needed a plan—a novel approach that sidestepped the land mines that littered their path.

A tentative knock on the doorframe pulled Krista back from her frustrations. She looked up to see their newest intern—Emma? Amelia?—looming outside.

"Hi . . . um . . . Ms. Walsh?" The intern's lean six-foot, two-inch frame took up most of the doorway. It was a wonder she could find suits that fit properly, although maybe that was why she seemed to rotate the same two.

"What can I do for you, Emily?" The kid's height was what had made the name click for Krista. Emily Kohan. She'd started a few weeks ago and played volleyball at the University of Minnesota.

"Julia said you wanted to know if we got any weird mail or anything."

Everything before their meeting with leadership felt like a lifetime ago, and it took Krista a second to remember the text she'd sent their legislative correspondent while Harry was speaking. Back when a mediocre speech had seemed like a big deal to her.

"What did you find?"

"Just this." Emily held out a manila envelope. The top had been neatly cut open with a letter opener, and it felt empty when Krista grabbed it. She looked inside and pulled out a single sheet of paper.

A topographical map of Cedar Lake. Krista recognized it from her earlier googling escapades. It looked like a lumpy number eight that had too much to drink. The large section at the bottom had a pair of islands, surrounded by various rings and numbers stating how deep the water was.

In the small section—the one that was cockeyed and looked like it was about to fall over—there was a triangle-shaped island tucked away in the corner.

Whoever had sent the map circled it numerous times with a red marker.

"The envelope caught my attention because it was addressed to Andy Leonard," Emily said. "I didn't even know that was the congressman's real first name until Julia told me."

Krista nodded as she studied the map, then flipped it over to look for anything written on the back that might explain what the hell she was looking at.

"Did you show it to anybody?"

"Only Julia," Emily said. "She said to bring it to you. What is it?"

Krista turned it back over and stared at the island. There were no other markings aside from the red circle.

"I don't know."

Emily loomed over the desk awkwardly as Krista searched the map for any type of meaning.

"Thanks for bringing it, Emily," Krista said. "If you guys find anything else like this, make sure you bring it to me. And I want to see anything addressed to Andy Leonard, okay?"

Emily smiled and turned to go back to her workspace.

"Hey, Emily, don't mention this to anyone." Krista didn't know why she'd said it, but her instinct told her this might be the start of something weird, and they didn't need weird floating around the office.

———

Krista expected to spend the night stewing over their party leadership's lack of vision—thinking of ways to rally support from the rest of their caucus while occasionally being sidetracked by an elaborate revenge fantasy that resulted in a new majority leader.

But as the sounds of the street filtered through her bedroom window, Krista was shocked to find her thoughts on the map. That island, circled in red, had set up camp in her mind.

She eventually tossed her covers aside and walked into the living room. Unlike Harry's office, which was filled with Minnesota-based kitsch, Krista's place was modern and efficient. A few carefully curated pieces of art adorned the white walls of the living room, keeping watch over the angular black couch and small flat-screen TV. The place was small, but small was the only option for someone who wanted to be close to the Hill. Living alone, Krista didn't need much space. Most of her life was spent in the office anyway.

Krista sat down and stretched her legs out on the couch while booting up her laptop. She opened an internet browser and typed *cedar lake minnesota faribault island*.

The results came up quickly and unimpressively.

The first three were Realtors listing cabins and homes for sale at the lake, then a website for the Bourdeau Resort and Campground.

A click brought up a satellite view of the lake, and she zoomed in until the small triangle of land in the back half of the lake filled the screen. As the picture cleared, Krista saw an odd, gray-brown spot directly in the middle of the textured green canopy, as if all the trees at the center of the island had died.

She zoomed in as far as her computer would allow and studied the screen. The resolution of the image was low enough it was impossible to tell, but it almost looked like there was some sort of rubble on the ground between the trees.

Like a building had been there a long time ago, but something had destroyed it so completely that nothing ever grew back.

Chapter Six

The moon danced across the water in the distance, while the sounds of the lake—crickets, the steady lap of the waves against the shore, an occasional loon—drifted in. Andy slouched next to Seth on the wicker couch inside the large screened porch that ran the length of the cabin on the lake side, while Ryan slumped deep in the patio chair to their left. After a cursory attempt at cleaning up their dinner mess, Jake plopped into the other chair.

"There's not really a house up there, is there?" Andy asked.

"What do you mean?" Jake said. An afternoon of swimming in the hot sun, followed by a dinner of burgers and junk food, left him too worn out to sound defensive.

"On that island," Andy said. "There's no house up there, right? You were just shitting us."

"Swear to God," Jake said. "Ask my parents when we get home. They'll tell you."

"Screw that," Seth said. "Let's go back tomorrow and find out."

The request hung over the four tired boys on the porch, getting neither an enthusiastic endorsement nor a flat rejection.

"What about the DNR lady?" Jake asked.

"Fuck her," Seth said. "We can go back there if we want. She doesn't like it, she can kiss my ass."

"I thought you were in love with her." Ryan chuckled.

"Not my type. Too much attitude." Seth stretched his legs out on the old porch coffee table in front of him. "Seriously, though, what's she going to do if we go back? It's not like she's a cop. She's fucking DNR. Her job is to check fishing licenses and give boring-ass presentations about owl pellets to third graders. That's it."

"Easy, tough guy," Ryan said. "I don't remember you saying anything when she was right in front of you."

Legal or not, Jake would rather not test the authority of the DNR. That said, while the thought of taking the boat back there made him nervous, he couldn't shake the curiosity his memories had brought up. On his own it would probably be gone by morning, but with the guys talking about the house . . . well, hopefully they'd forget too.

"What if we tied up the boat on the back side?" Andy asked.

Seth sat forward on the couch before looking from Andy to Jake. "Oh, yeah?"

"When we were digging the weeds out of the motor, I saw an open spot behind a fallen tree back there. Nobody would see us unless they came all the way back."

"What about the weeds?" Jake surprised himself by not dismissing it out of hand. "I don't want to get stuck again."

"There actually weren't that many in the water where we got in," Ryan said. He wasn't the guy Jake expected to be making the case. Seth and Andy were always the instigators, but Ryan was a steady hand. His stamp of approval went a long way to winning Jake over. "I think we just went through a few big patches before that."

"And we made it out fine, anyway," Seth added.

Jake hated to admit it, but he was right. Once they'd gotten turned around, there was a fairly clean stretch closer to the island. Some weeds, sure, but not enough to clog the prop. If there was, in fact, a place to tie the boat up on the far side, nobody would know they were there.

That nugget of curiosity had grown exponentially since they'd first brought it up. Either there was an inaccessible island with a giant house full of stuff whose owners walked away without any explanation, or his juvenile mind had somehow gotten confused and misremembered the whole thing.

Either way, Jake realized he had to see for himself.

"Fine. I'll prove to you dicks I'm not making this up."

———

Jake started a slow turn as they approached the lodge, then killed the engine as they drifted in. Ryan and Seth leaned over the front and grabbed the poles jutting up along the dock and eased them alongside. Andy jumped out and tied them up.

"Good?"

"Yeah," Jake said, getting up from the driver's seat. A small white shed stood a few feet from the water on the shore ahead of them. The gas pump was in front, while the inside was full of minnow tanks and night crawlers. An ancient-looking man emerged from the bait shack and squinted at their boat.

Crazy Larry.

Jake couldn't think of a single time he'd been down there and not seen Larry Bourdeau. The old man had owned the Dew Drop so long he probably pissed lake water. Jake had no idea why he was called Crazy Larry, but the nickname was ingrained enough that he'd heard people call him Crazy Larry to his face. Then again, the guy had looked at least one hundred years old for as long as Jake could remember, so there was a legit chance he'd never heard any of them.

Crazy Larry adjusted an Orvis fishing hat that looked as old and worn as he was and eyed the boys. His beard was long and white, with a patch on the side of his mouth stained brown from decades of Old Gold cigarettes.

"Hi, Larry," Jake called out, dropping the *Crazy* to soften the disapproving you-kids-get-off-my-lake vibe the old man was putting out. "Can I get some gas? Ten bucks' worth."

Larry nodded and turned back to the pump without a word.

Seth sidled up next to Jake as Crazy Larry pulled the nozzle toward the boat.

"Morning, sir." Seth's voice was slathered in fake congeniality. "How are you today?"

The baked-in wrinkles around the old man's eyes folded together. He'd fill up their tank, but Crazy Larry certainly wasn't the type to enjoy a nice chat with some random kid.

"How's the fishing out there?" Seth plowed forward despite the cold response, and Jake noticed his friend focusing on something over the old man's shoulder.

"Fine."

It was a juvenile game they had been playing for years. They'd pick a spot behind the guy they were talking to and keep glancing at it during the conversation. Eyes shift to the background, then snap back. Get that person to look back and you win.

Somehow, it never got old. The guys usually only did it to each other, and it was amazing how successful they were. Plenty of times Jake knew exactly what his friend was doing, but something in the far reaches of the brain just couldn't let it go.

Eventually, everybody looked.

"That's great. Any hot spots we should check out?" Seth's eyes snapped back, but once again drifted to the background as the old man answered. Oblivious to what was going on, Crazy Larry spun around while Seth did his best to keep cackles of laughter from erupting.

Jake elbowed Seth in the ribs. "Dude."

Crazy Larry turned back at them with a scowl. "You can pay my grandson Blake, behind the bar."

Andy strolled down the dock past them. "I'm gonna hit the pinball machine."

"Hold up." Jake dug the ten-dollar bill he'd brought for gas out of his pocket. "Pay for the gas while you're in there, will ya?"

Seth bolted toward the Dew Drop. "I call first game."

Andy snatched the ten out of Jake's hand and ran off in pursuit, leaving him to deal with the surly lake veteran who was now much more agitated than confused.

———

Jake stared at the entrance for the Dew Drop Lodge as his grandpa's pontoon boat gently bobbed beneath him. Crazy Larry had re-capped the gas tank and retrieved the hose at least five minutes ago, but Seth and Andy had yet to reemerge from the lodge.

"Want me to go get 'em?" While others were usually oblivious, Ryan could always tell when Jake was getting anxious.

Crazy Larry poked his head out of the little white bait shed and didn't attempt to hide his annoyance that they were still tied to his dock.

"I'll go," Jake said. "Stay with the boat, will you?"

Jake hopped onto the dock and jogged toward the lodge. Crazy Larry was still staring at him when he stepped ashore. "Thanks again. We'll be out of here in a sec."

He bounded up the four concrete steps to the lodge and pulled the screen door open.

Even at 10:00 a.m., the inside of the Dew Drop Lodge was dark and oozed Minnesota. Jake scanned the mishmash of old photos and posters pitching beer, many including out-of-date calendars, that covered the walls. A stuffed northern pike—almost as big as his grandpa's—hung behind the bar to the right, lording over a small variety of liquor bottles with a disproportionate number of fruity schnapps.

Jake's nose picked up the stale smell of spilled beer, and it reminded him of Andy's house.

They didn't hang out there often, mostly because it was painfully obvious Andy didn't want his friends anywhere near his father. Back in sixth grade they'd been at Andy's house one Saturday afternoon when his dad came downstairs absolutely plastered. He stumbled off the last step, knocking a photo from the wall and startling the group of boys hanging out below. Andy tried his hardest to usher his friends out and away from his father's slurred ramblings, but the man was having none of it. He told them to stick around. When Andy insisted they leave, his dad got combative. Bill Leonard mocked his only son mercilessly, and Jake remembered smelling the booze on his breath when he invited the three friends join in. It was even stronger when he insisted.

Andy had fought back tears as he sat there, taking every drunken barb and drowning in the potent brand of shame a twelve-year-old saves for their parents. When Bill finally felt he'd made his point and staggered off, Andy ran out the door. The guys caught up to him in the backyard, insisting it was no big deal and offering whatever comfort boys of that age could.

The three of them had promised they'd never tell anyone what had happened, but it wasn't enough for Andy. He dug up a knife and put a small cut on each of their fingers, making each shake hands and swear on their own blood they would never breathe a word of what they'd seen.

He'd called it a blood oath, and it worked because that story never seeped into the oral encyclopedia of small-town gossip that kept tales like that around for generations.

But it was more than just keeping a secret. The group dynamic had changed that day. If Andy's family wouldn't be there for him, then his friends would be.

It's probably why Jake tended to defer to him. It was a way of offering support.

"DAMMIT!"

Seth's voice erupted from the back of the room where the pinball machines were.

Jake headed that way and stepped up behind Seth right as he dropped another quarter in the slot.

"Come on, guys, let's go."

Seth pulled the plunger back and sent the little silver ball careening into the playfield. "I just started a game."

43

Jake rolled his eyes and looked out the window toward Ryan and their boat. He turned to Andy. "You pay for the gas yet?"

Andy's eyes went up to the ceiling with a grimace.

"Give me the money," Jake said.

Andy handed the bill back, and Jake walked up front. The guy behind the bar had the same angular nose and lack of chin as his grandfather, leaving no doubt he was a descendant of the crotchety owner. But while Crazy Larry had a gut that made him look like he'd swallowed a buoy and a beard worthy of a ZZ Top cover band, Blake Bourdeau was scrawny with scraggly patches of facial hair. He was watching a fishing show on the old television hanging in the corner and didn't acknowledge Jake until he gave a little excuse-me cough.

"Um, we got ten bucks in gas out there."

Blake reached up and took the money without a word.

"Thanks." Jake turned to leave and jumped when an arm locked around his shoulders. It was Seth. Jake had underestimated how fast his friend could lose three balls on that old machine.

"Hey, you ever heard of a house on that back island?" Seth asked across the bar.

The question pulled the first sound from Blake.

"Huh?"

Seth kept one arm around Jake and slapped him on the shoulder with the other. "My buddy here says that there's an old house on the island in the back part of the lake. Just abandoned—furniture, clothes, everything. Like the people simply walked away fifty years ago and never came back."

Blake sat back on his stool and turned toward the television.

"I don't know nothing about no abandoned house."

Seth chuckled and shook Jake by the shoulders. "Yeah, that's what I thought."

Andy walked up behind Seth and flicked him in the ear. "Come on. Let's go."

Blake looked back at them. "I wouldn't mess around back there. It's choked with weeds and stuff. Can't get around much."

"Yeah, we got hung up when we were back there yesterday," Andy said.

Blake stood back up and put his hands on the bar. His gray, blood-shot eyes trained down on the boy standing in front of him. His voice lost the ambivalence it had earlier. "There's lots more than weeds back there, kid—lots of submerged logs, sandbars, and even a few rock piles. There's no reason to go back there, and all you'll do is fuck up your prop. Trust me, stay outta there."

Jake thought the tone of his voice went beyond helpful advice, but figured he was being paranoid.

"Good to know." Andy grabbed Seth by the shoulder and pulled him toward the door.

Jake stood in front of the bar, trying to shake the look Blake Bourdeau was giving him.

"How's the south end of the lake? Anything to avoid over there? We'd talked about doing some fishing." They hadn't mentioned fishing, and Jake wasn't sure why he said it. Maybe it was his simmering anxiety over ignoring the advice of two separate adults that heading back to Pike Island was a bad idea.

The bartender kept his gaze on Jake for a second, then softened it.

"Should be smooth sailing that way," he said. "In fact, that's some of the best walleye fishing in the county. There's an underwater bluff that runs all along there about fifty feet out. Just fish a slip bobber or a drop shot on the drop-off, and you'll pull them in all day. Need some minnows?"

"No, we've got some." Another lie, but it got Blake to nod and turn back to his show, so it was worth it. Jake hustled out the door. It snapped behind him with a metallic bang.

"Let's go!" Seth shouted from the boat, prompting Jake to burst into a jog. Crazy Larry stared at him with an old man's snarl as he passed the bait shed and headed down the dock. Ryan untied the boat as Jake stepped across and plopped down behind the steering wheel.

Ryan and Andy pushed away from the dock as Jake started the motor. He hit the throttle and pulled out into the lake.

Seth had his feet propped up on the bench in the front of the boat. "It's nice they have a work release program for the crackheads up here, don't ya think?"

Jake felt a tingling at the nape of his neck and glanced over his shoulder at the Dew Drop. Blake Bourdeau was standing out front, watching them motor toward the back section of the lake.

Chapter Seven

Krista jogged to a stop at the base of the Lincoln Memorial. The accumulated beads of sweat on her forehead surrendered to gravity and rolled into her eyes. She wiped them away and squinted back at the Capitol Building, where the morning sun glowed in the background. Not only was she sucking wind after ten minutes, but she'd felt the impact of every step. The effortless stride she'd developed over the years was nowhere to be found.

"Outta gas?"

Krista turned to see Renna Marin tying her shoe on the third step.

"One of those days, I guess," Krista said. The sight of Joe Hatterberg's legislative assistant blew a fresh puff of oxygen on the angry embers that had been in the back of her head since yesterday's meeting. Not that she had anything against Renna personally. She'd been friendly the few times they'd bumped into each other around the Capitol. A mutual friend had even attempted to set them up when Krista first arrived in Washington, but her brutal work schedule made it too easy to push any potential relationships to the back burner.

"I heard about your meeting with leadership yesterday." Renna pulled the white earbuds out of her ears. Her black hair was pulled back in a tight french braid that shone in the sunlight. "Sounds like you guys are bringing up some interesting ideas."

Krista put her leg on one of the steps and leaned forward to stretch her hamstring. "Thanks. I wish your boss thought the same."

Renna's eyebrows lifted slightly. "Don't be so sure he doesn't."

Krista straightened and looked down at Renna. She did her best to keep her face neutral. "He say anything about it?"

Renna nodded to the spot beside her. Krista instinctively glanced around for eavesdropping ears and slid onto the granite step.

"He said your guy made a hell of an argument, and that probably spooked Porter more than anything," Renna said.

"What do you mean?"

"You don't keep the position for as long as the majority leader has without recognizing who has the juice to take your spot," Renna said. "Guys like that aren't going to let someone come in and lead the way on a signature piece of legislation—especially something like you guys are proposing. A freshman gets that done and suddenly they've got to answer questions about what the hell *they've* been doing all these years."

The idea threw another log on the fire inside Krista. "Fuck that guy."

Renna chuckled. "Porter wants the freshman representatives like children—seen but not heard."

Krista's short fingernails dug into her palms. "We didn't come here to be stuck at the kids' table."

"Oh, I don't think you will be." Renna stood up and shook her legs out. "I guarantee Porter is already looking for a spot to stick your boss that's high profile but doesn't have any real power behind it. Something that makes the party look young and fresh without having to change a damn thing."

Renna reached her hand down to Krista.

"Don't sweat it too much," Renna said. "Porter will retire someday. By that time, this town will have stamped all that pesky idealism out of your guy and he'll be ready for leadership."

The sarcasm drew a frustrated laugh from Krista. She grabbed Renna's hand and pulled herself up.

"Thanks."

Renna tucked her earbuds back in her ears.

"Don't let this town get to you," Renna said. "I love your passion. There needs to be a lot more of that around here. And keep me in the loop on what you guys decide to do. Never know where you'll find a few allies."

She smiled a goodbye and jogged off. Krista watched her disappear in the direction of the Vietnam Memorial.

She and Harry hadn't talked about contingency plans before their big meeting, and the lack of support from leadership admittedly caught them off guard. Harry mentioned going around party leadership to try and pass the bill on his own, but he'd need some big names to get behind him to have a chance. Hatterberg would've been big, but if he was truly running for governor in two years, he wouldn't be around to help anyway.

She thought of Renna following Hatterberg back to Colorado and was hit with a pang of jealousy. Not that things had been easy when Harry was a state senator, but all the obstacles they'd faced back in Minnesota were pebbles compared to the boulders that littered the road to progress in DC.

Maybe the state level was the place to kick off real reform. A big fish in a small pond could actually get things done.

Krista pulled her phone from the thin black waist pack she wore and pecked out a message to Harry before abandoning her run and heading back to the Capitol.

I've got our Plan B.

———

Krista's dark-brown hair still had a wet sheen from her shower when she burst into their office suite. She'd been excited enough about her epiphany she almost skipped the locker room altogether and went to the office in her running clothes. Their office manager and a pair of interns were laying out pastries on a long table for that morning's constituent breakfast.

"He in yet?" Krista blew past them toward Harry's office, not waiting for an answer. She wove past their IT guy and bumped directly into Emily, who was carrying a box of paper plates from the back.

"Ope, sorry about—" Krista watched as their tallest intern's face went from apologetic to eager as she realized who she'd run into. "Ms. Walsh, um . . . I need to speak with you."

In the euphoria of her new plan, Krista briefly forgot the instructions she'd left with Emily after she'd shown her that map of Cedar Lake.

"Later, okay?" Krista said, barely breaking stride. An intern's report on weird mail could wait. She wove through a few more bodies on her way back and pushed open Harry's office door.

He was behind his desk, cell phone plastered to his ear. His jacket was off and the coffee cup on his desk was already empty, so it was obvious he'd come in early. Harry waved her in with a broad campaign smile.

"Absolutely, sir." Harry's voice was calm and laced with optimistic confidence.

The chairs in front of Harry's desk made Krista feel like a kid summoned to the principal's office, so she never sat in them. She dropped her bag on the nearest one and leaned against the corner of his desk.

"Uh-huh . . ." Harry held up a finger and mouthed *Almost done.* "That won't be a problem . . . thank you, sir."

Harry ended the call and dropped his phone on the desk with a triumphant clatter, but Krista didn't wait for him to tell her about the conversation.

"We're running for governor," she said.

Harry's eyebrows shot up.

"What?"

"If leadership isn't going to let us get anything done here, fuck 'em," Krista said. "We go back to Minnesota and pass election reform there. We show how effective it can be—then, after a few terms, they're going to be begging you to run for president."

Krista had expected Harry to share her excitement, but he leaned back in his chair and smirked. "That's interesting. And all in all, not a bad idea. But . . ."

Harry gave her the look of a guy slow playing a winning poker hand. It raised Krista's hackles more than her curiosity.

"That was Representative Davis. He wanted to let me know that ever since our meeting, he's been talking with Porter and Russi about me. They're considering pushing me for vice president in the next election."

"What?"

"Yep. V-fucking-P."

The news tore a hole in Krista's plan, and all the excitement she'd been running on spilled out. Renna Marin's warning echoed through her mind. The vice presidency was certainly high profile, but had famously been described by someone who held the job as "not worth a bucket of warm piss" in terms of power and influence.

"Are you kidding?" Krista asked.

"Nope." Harry didn't seem to realize she wasn't sharing his enthusiasm over the news.

"The election is two years away," Krista said. "They don't even have a nominee yet. How can they promise you the VP spot when they don't even know who's running?"

"They vet candidates for the nominee," Harry said. "I've been assured they have a lot of influence over the final decision."

The grand plan that had promised to solve all their problems less than an hour ago was unraveling at Krista's feet.

"They're only dangling this in front of you to keep you in your place," Krista said. "Even if you do get that spot, you can kiss any chance of election reform goodbye. If you're going to do that, why the hell did we even come here?"

"What are you talking about?" Harry's frustration crept into his voice. "We'd be in the White House, for God's sake, and eight years later I'd be the favorite for the nomination. Isn't that the goal?"

Krista suddenly realized the office door was open and walked over to close it. She tried to quickly organize her thoughts before turning back to Harry.

"The whole point has always been to shake up the system, to take on the entrenched power structure," Krista said. "That's everything you ever campaigned on. It's why people voted for you."

"I can do that when I'm VP."

"Oh, please." Krista knew the amount of disdain in her voice wouldn't help her argument, but it was there anyway. "If they won't listen to you as a voting member of Congress, they certainly won't give a damn what you say when you have no official duties. It would be eight years of attending state funerals and speaking to groups deemed not important enough for the president. You'd be reduced to nothing more than political arm candy."

She couldn't tell if Harry was hurt or confused or angry, something he rarely was. He'd probably thought she'd be as excited as he was.

"But if we go back to St. Paul, you can make a difference," she said. "You'll still get to the White House eventually, but you'll get to do it on your terms. You've got to trust me on this. I haven't led you astray yet, have I?"

Harry stood up and grabbed his suit jacket from the chair in front of his desk. He slipped it on and reached back for his phone.

"We worked so hard to get here," he said. "I'm not going to leave and go home right when things are starting to pay off."

Krista stepped aside as Harry crossed over toward the door. It hit her that for the first time, he was going against her counsel. After her game plan had taken him from city council to Congress, he was ready to abandon the path and chase the first shiny object dangled in front of him.

"Come on. You don't really think they can just stick me in a corner, do you?" Harry smirked with confidence and walked out the door.

Chapter Eight

The woods that covered Pike Island were almost supernaturally thick, more a camouflaged wall than a shoreline of trees. Jake peered into them from behind the wheel of the pontoon boat, but couldn't see more than a few feet in through the dense foliage that spread all the way to the water.

Andy stood waist deep next to the fallen tree he'd mentioned the night before, about ten feet out from the shore. Ryan tossed him a rope, and Andy lashed it tightly around one of the thicker branches.

"We should tie the back too," Jake said, reaching for the stern line. "I don't want it swinging all over if the wind picks up."

"What wind?" Seth asked. "There hasn't been any—"

"Toss it down," Andy said. Ever since Jake relented and agreed to take them back to Pike Island, he'd noticed Andy going out of his way to be amenable. Even though it was fairly transparent, Jake didn't mind. It was nice having someone listen to him, even if it was almost certainly for selfish reasons.

Andy grabbed the rope and secured it to another branch. "There you go, buddy. She's not going anywhere."

Ryan and Seth were already in the water, shoes in hand, by the time Jake got to the front of the boat. Andy climbed past the fallen tree and out of the lake while the other two waded over toward him.

Jake looked at the spots where the lines were attached, mentally checking their security. He sat down on the rear platform of the boat and slid into the lake.

"Damn, it's cold," he hissed.

"Quit your whining," Seth hollered as he pulled himself ashore.

Jake reached back into the boat and grabbed his flip-flops, then waded over to the island.

A few feet from the tree, something brushed against Jake's shin and sent a jolt through him. The sharp, needlelike teeth jutting from the mouth of his grandpa's northern crystalized in his mind. He could almost feel them sinking into the fleshy part of his calf, tearing away a chunk of muscle and turning the muted green lake water red around him.

A sheen of sweat broke out on his skin and immediately turned to goose bumps in the cool air. The flip-flop he'd dropped bobbed in front of him, fading in and out of his vision.

Ryan sat on the trunk of the fallen tree, waiting for him. "You okay?"

Jake focused on his breathing until he was able to wrestle it under control.

"Yeah . . . fine." Jake snatched his rubber sandal off the top of the water and looked up at Ryan with what he hoped was a normal face. "Just brushed up against a branch or something. Gave me the skeeves."

Ryan stood up and stepped over to the island, making room for Jake. He grabbed a branch with one hand, braced his other on the trunk, and pulled himself out of the water. Jake looked back to the boat, then toward the lake. The carpet of weeds still covered most of the water between the back of the island and the shore across the way.

"You're sure you're cool with this?" Ryan asked.

"Yeah." Jake looked back over his shoulder. "Just hope that DNR lady doesn't see our boat, you know?"

"She's not going to see it," Andy said as he followed Seth and disappeared into the woods.

Ryan offered a hand and pulled Jake over to the island. "As much as it kills me to say it—they're right; we aren't doing anything illegal."

"I know, but I don't want her to give us a hard time. 'Cause we're kids or whatever."

"Who you calling kids?" Ryan said with mock outrage.

"To *her* . . . you know what I mean."

A crash filtered through the trees, followed by Seth's unmistakable brand of creative swearing.

"It'll be fine." Ryan smacked his friend on the shoulder. "Besides, she'd have to come all the way back in the weeds to even see the boat. I wouldn't worry."

Jake pulled a pair of saplings aside, and they stepped farther into the underbrush. The branches above filtered out a good amount of sunlight and cast weird shadows all over. The island was thick with mature trees, while younger ones—scrawny from lack of light—stuck up from the forest floor. The rest of the ground was covered in ferns and smaller bushes that could handle the low-light conditions.

"Where'd they go?" Jake asked. He stepped over one of the many fallen logs littering the ground.

"You donkey dicks coming or what?" Seth's shrill voice filtered in from the woods. It took a second before Jake saw him and Andy waiting behind a huge fallen oak tree about fifteen yards ahead.

"Doesn't matter if the DNR lady can't see the boat when she can hear that dickhead from across the lake," Jake muttered as they made their way through the underbrush. The branches scratched at his legs. He scanned the ground for the three-leaved signature of poison ivy, but saw none.

"Check it out," Andy said. "There actually kinda looks like a path back here."

A giant bush grew around the base of the log, but Jake could make out a little ribbon of dirt that cut through the ferns and fallen logs covering the ground.

"Whoa. Maybe Jakey isn't full of shit after all," Seth said.

"Let's go." Andy stepped over a log and onto the dirt. The island sloped up like a pyramid, and the woods thickened as they made their way uphill.

Jake paused and looked back down the path. They hadn't gone far, but the trees had already filled in behind them and swallowed up any view of the lake. A mosquito buzzed in his ear, and he tried to flick it away. The ground felt damp around Jake's flip-flops, and little ferns that lined the old path reached for his ankles as if they wanted to pull him back into the thickest part of the woods. He stumbled over a fallen branch and fought to keep up with the guys ahead of him.

Seth's voice seeped back from the front of the line and told Jake his memories had been right.

"Holy shit."

They'd found the house.

Built in a small clearing on top of the hill, the house on Pike Island was a two-story monstrosity. A rickety set of steps led to a small front porch, while a massive six-sided turret pointed up past the roof on the right side. It had a strange layered wooden siding that looked like the scales of a dead walleye. Whatever flakes of paint that remained might have been white at some point, but decades of rain and mildew had washed it all out in an aggressive gray. A giant picture window in front was spiderwebbed with cracks and opaque from years of dirt. The ground surrounding the house was surprisingly bare of vegetation, as if the ferns and bushes were afraid to approach.

Seeing the house gave Jake a strange case of déjà vu. Memories of it had been flittering around the back of his brain for the last twenty-four hours, but had spurted away like cottonwood fluff whenever he'd tried to grab them. Now the house was here, right in front of him, crystalizing the memories he'd had and bringing a few others to the front.

"That is freaking creepy," Ryan said.

"Oh yeah," Seth said. "It's like the cabin in *Evil Dead 2*."

"It's way bigger than that," Ryan said.

"Would you two shut up?" Jake's chest should have been full of vindication, but instead he could feel it tightening.

"Oh, are we *scaring* you?" Seth asked.

"No," Jake shot back so fast it didn't sound convincing.

"You can stay out here if you don't want the boogeyman to find you."

Jake pushed down the swirling mass of worms that had crept into his stomach and set off up the front steps. The old boards had some give to them, but held. Jake couldn't help but wonder how they'd get a guy with a broken ankle back into the boat if one of the steps gave way. He turned back with all the bravado he could muster and gave Seth the finger before pushing the door open. "You coming, tough guy?"

Seth, Ryan, and Andy bounded up the steps. "Just remember, don't touch any dolls, put on any necklaces, or read any weird spell books." Seth wore his I'm-trying-so-hard-to-be-serious face. "That's how the spirits attach themselves to you."

Andy pushed past Seth through the open door. "Thanks. That's really helpful."

Seth backed out of the way with his hands held in mock surrender. "Hey, I'm just giving advice. Don't come crying to me when you're possessed by the ghost of a nine-year-old girl. She *was* murdered here, you know."

Jake and Ryan left Seth on the porch and followed Andy through the door.

"*YOU HEAR THAT, MURDER GIRL? I WARNED THEM, SO DON'T COME AFTER ME. I'M ON YOUR—*" Seth's performance abruptly ended when he got inside.

The house was musty, dusty, and had a weird smell that Jake couldn't place. But for a house that had been abandoned half a century ago, it was remarkably intact.

And that was the most unnerving thing about it.

A large wooden staircase stretched up in front of them, a faded and tattered carpet runner leading up to a platform before making a right turn and disappearing onto the second floor.

Old wallpaper sloughed off the walls in random strips, while floating specks of dust glowed in the little bit of light that filtered through the cracked and faded windows. Jake stepped across the worn and warped hardwood floor into the dining room and ran his fingers across an old hutch, carving three lines into the dust that had settled on top.

He popped open one of the cabinet doors and jerked back as a spider the size of a silver dollar skittered away from the light. Jake's breath buried itself in his chest and refused to come out. He waited for the guys to rip him for his reaction, but nothing came. They were either too busy checking out the house or scared themselves.

"Check this out." Seth's voice came from across the front hall.

Jake doubled back into the family room with Andy and Ryan. A large braided rug covered most of the floor, with a tattered couch in the middle of the room and a giant old console radio in the corner. The far wall of the room was covered in floor-to-ceiling bookshelves, the cracked spines of countless hardcovers and paperbacks staring out.

"You were right." Jake wasn't sure if he'd ever heard those words slip from Seth's mouth, and that alone helped calm his nerves. "It's like they just up and left one day. Disappeared."

Seth pulled a random book off the shelf. The yellowed paper crinkled as he flipped through it.

"Careful," Ryan said. "You'd hate for it to be one of those possessed books, right?"

"Those are all in the *P* section," Seth said. "But seriously, though . . . old books can be worth something, right? Like, a lot."

Jake stepped beside him and scanned the titles. Old books *could* be worth a bunch, assuming they were in decent condition. His mom was a voracious reader, and Dad bought her an antique copy of her favorite book, *Pride and Prejudice*, for their twentieth anniversary last year. He wouldn't say how much it had cost, but Jake could tell it was a heck of a lot more than something pulled off a shelf at the mall.

There was nothing like that here. It was mostly reference books—multiple encyclopedia sets, dictionaries, and cheap paperbacks whose pages were fanning out due to the humidity seeping through the broken windows and walls.

"Don't take anything," Jake said, suddenly feeling protective of the house. He'd been there only one other time and had no idea whose place it had been, but since he'd brought the guys here, he felt a responsibility to treat the place with respect. "Wouldn't want to get possessed, right?"

Seth tried to keep a straight face but couldn't hold back the smirk. "Absolutely."

Jake stayed in the little family room looking over the books while the others fanned out around the house. He had expected much more rot and decay, with plenty of rooms unexplorable due to unsafe conditions. Heck, he wouldn't have been surprised to find nothing more than a crumbling foundation providing the only evidence that, yes, there had been a house here at one time, but it was now relegated to nothing but vague memories.

But here it was, the house on Pike Island, intact and hopefully ghost-free.

Jake caught up with Ryan and Seth, who were back in the kitchen, rummaging through the cabinets. The door swung closed behind him, cutting off the light coming from the front of the house. A large window facing the backyard was boarded up, and Jake's eyes took a few seconds to adjust.

"You guys find anything cool?" he asked.

"Meh. Bunch of normal crap," Seth said. "Some broken dishes, pots. Nothing exciting."

"You know what gets me?" Ryan said. "There's no graffiti."

"Huh?"

"You know, people spray-painting their names, giant dicks on the wall, *ROONEY EATS IT* . . . that kind of stuff." Ryan turned toward

Jake. "You guys came here when you were a kid. I can't imagine you were the only ones who knew about it, so there had to be others coming out here, right? And you know how people are. Like under the Root River Bridge. That place is nothing but graffiti. I guess I'm just surprised there isn't any of that here."

Jake looked around the bare walls of the kitchen. Ryan was right. For as long as this place had been supposedly abandoned, it seemed like at some point a group of teenagers would have shown up and trashed the place just for kicks. But there was no spray paint. No holes kicked into the walls. A few cabinet doors were missing or hanging off a single hinge, but most were still attached and closed.

The place was almost supernaturally intact, and the thought sent another chill through Jake.

Andy's voice echoed in from the front of the house, jolting Jake from his thoughts. It was loud, but still subdued. Almost a shouted whisper.

"Hey, guys . . ."

The door swung open again, and Andy's dark silhouette stood in the frame.

"Somebody else might be here."

Chapter Nine

After Harry dropped the vice president bomb on her, Krista secluded herself in her office. Like any duo, they didn't always agree, but they had always known when to trust the other. Krista couldn't let the lure of a spot on the Democratic ticket pull Harry off the path she had so painstakingly laid out for him. She had to figure out a way to get him to see the bigger picture.

A knock on her door broke the silence.

"Come in."

Emily opened the door, and an eerie sense of déjà vu crept through Krista. Their fight with leadership and Harry's VP drama had pushed any worries about weird mail aside.

The manila folder in Emily's hand brought them raging back.

Krista waved her in, and Emily closed the door behind her before sitting down.

"I saw this in a pile of letters when I got in today." Her voice was low as she placed the folder on the desk.

Krista pulled the cover back to reveal another idyllic scene from the state of Minnesota.

Greetings from Cedar Lake!

She picked up the corner of the postcard like it was a snake's tail. She flipped it over and saw it addressed to Andy Leonard in a now-familiar script.

But unlike the first one, this card wasn't blank.

I know what you are.
You can't hide from your past.
Justice is coming.

Krista stared at the simple, stilted handwriting.

"Jesus." The word slid from her mouth like air from a punctured bike tire as she flipped the postcard over. The photo was different from the first—a water-skier had replaced the fishermen—but the arching font was the same. The red letters that had once looked friendly now jumped off the card like an ominous warning.

"We're supposed to bring anything threatening straight to Julia, but you said you wanted to see anything addressed to Andy Leonard, so I thought you should see it first."

Krista had briefly forgotten the intern was still in the room.

She pushed the shock away and pulled on an aura of confidence. "No, that's good. Exactly what I wanted you to do. I'm sorry I didn't see you sooner."

That Emily was the intern on mail duty today was a stroke of luck. Krista still didn't know how much she could be trusted to keep to herself, but the fact that she'd bypassed her supervisor to bring the postcard to Krista was a good start.

"How much unopened mail is sitting back there right now?"

"A decent amount," Emily said. "Lee is supposed to be on correspondence this week, but when I saw this, I offered to swap with him. He's out helping with the constituent breakfast—then he's going to give my tour. He'll be gone at least another hour."

The interns all shared a workspace in the back of their office suite, and Krista could picture the box of letters waiting for someone to sort them. "Go back and look through it all to see if there are any more postcards like this."

"There aren't," Emily said. "I looked through it all after I found that. No postcards. Nothing else addressed to Andy Leonard."

The fingers on Krista's right hand drummed on her desk with the pace of a tiny racehorse as she stared down at the postcard on her desk. Congressional offices were supposed to report any threats to the Capitol Police.

She read through the words multiple times in a fruitless attempt to uncover some benign meaning. A blank postcard could be written off as random. A map could be considered weird. But *justice is coming?*

This was a threat.

Krista closed the folder and looked up at Emily. "Thanks for bringing me this. I'll talk with Representative Leonard, and we'll figure out how we're going to handle this. It's probably just some troll out there looking to stir things up, but I guess that's for the Capitol Police to figure out. I would appreciate it if you kept this to yourself, though. I don't want to scare anyone around the office before we know what's going on."

"Of course," Emily said. "I'll make sure I sort the mail every day for now to keep an eye out for anything more. If anything comes, I'll bring it straight to you."

Krista thanked her again and sent her back to her workstation. She was impressed by the young woman's ability to take direction while still being proactive. Probably why her volleyball coach made her team captain. Krista made a mental note to hire more athletes.

A steady murmur of conversation streamed back from the weekly constituent breakfast in the front room of their office suite. Krista picked up her cell phone to check the time. Harry would give a little talk to the visitors before he left for a committee meeting and the interns led the group on a tour of the Capitol Building.

Normally she'd be out there with him, mingling with dozens of Minnesotans visiting their nation's capital. But the folder on her desk had made the day anything but normal.

She knew she should put in a call to the Capitol Police and report the postcard, but she pulled up an internet browser instead.

A search for Cedar Lake brought up the same results she'd seen before. She scrolled down past Realtor listings and DNR maps and clicked through to the next page.

Still nothing.

Their office had accounts with a few different newspaper-archive sites for research, so Krista pulled one up and logged in. Harry said he'd been to Cedar Lake after his high school graduation, so she looked up the *Faribault Daily News* and started scrolling in May 2003.

She'd gotten through June when a headline jumped out at her.

ISLAND DRUG LAB DISCOVERED

DNR Officer, Two Others Killed in Explosion

A hidden methamphetamine lab on an island in Cedar Lake exploded early Saturday morning, killing three people, including a Minnesota Department of Natural Resources officer.

Officer Kim Schroeder, 32, was pronounced dead at the scene, along with Blake Boudreaux, 26, and Jeffery Gonsalves, 20. Schroeder is the daughter of Rice County Sheriff Dean Schroeder.

"Officer Schroeder was a highly respected member of the Department of Natural Resources and a wonderful ambassador who will be greatly missed," DNR Spokesperson Matthew Weitzel said. "Our thoughts and prayers also go out to Sheriff Schroeder and all of Kim's loved ones."

An investigation into the fire is ongoing, but according to sources inside the Rice County Sheriff's Office,

> Officer Schroeder was responding to reports that
> Boudreaux and Gonsalves were operating a drug lab
> in an abandoned building on the island. The remains
> of items consistent with the manufacture of metham-
> phetamines were found in the rubble.

Krista opened another window and called up the satellite picture of the island she'd found during her midnight googling the previous night. She zoomed in on the island and stared at the rubble in the middle. A burned-down drug shack certainly fit the image, but she still couldn't imagine how Harry was connected.

She found a few more articles printed over the following weeks, mostly focusing on the fallen officer's heroism and assurances from the sheriff's office that there was no lingering drug problem in the area. There was no mention of Harry's name or anything that could remotely connect him to what happened.

Krista looked through the rest of that summer's archives, but nothing else newsworthy happened out at Cedar Lake. She leaned back in her chair and tried to fit together the oddball puzzle pieces that had piled up over the last week.

I know what you are.

You can't hide from your past.

Justice is coming.

ISLAND DRUG LAB DISCOVERED

Only one thing was clear. Before she reported anything to the Capitol Police, she needed a conversation with Representative Andrew Harrison Leonard.

Chapter Ten

"I found some stuff upstairs." Andy stepped into the gloom of the kitchen, and the door swung shut behind him. "In one of the bedrooms."

Every bit of anxiety Jake had suppressed since he'd stepped on the island bloomed into something just short of panic. The mildewy air felt like it dropped ten degrees as nervous sweat broke out on his forehead.

"Fuck you." Seth's voice contained none of the sarcasm that usually infected everything he said. "You're full of it."

"Hand to God," Andy said. "I went upstairs and was looking around, and there's stuff in one of the bedrooms. A mattress, blankets—"

"There's stuff all over the house," Ryan said. "That's what makes it creepy."

"But this isn't old shit," Andy insisted. "It's an air mattress and a lantern and magazines and stuff. It's not left over from whoever the hell lived here. Somebody *brought* it out and left it."

Jake glanced back at Ryan, who was looking analytical. As for Seth, Jake couldn't tell if he was confused or intrigued.

Maybe both.

"Show us," Ryan said.

Andy pushed the door open and headed out through the dining room. Ryan caught it on its swing back and stepped through, holding it for Seth and Jake. Andy turned around at the foot of the stairs, his hand resting atop the ornate banister.

"The first room was normal—I mean, it's what you'd expect." He turned up the stairway and led their climb. The first step squealed and bowed slightly under their weight, but held. The air thickened in the narrow stairway, and the smell Jake had noticed earlier got stronger with every step. It reminded him of his great-aunt Martha's house. Musty and old with a side of cat pee.

"The second one's door was closed," Andy said from the front of the line. "That's where I found all the stuff."

The narrow stairway darkened as they climbed to the second floor. The guys regrouped at the top, the only light creeping in from the open doors that lined the hallway. Jake squinted against the gloom as whatever hung in the air crept into his sinuses.

There were two doors on each side of the hall, but the ones facing the front side of the house cast out more light.

"Down there." Andy nodded toward the end of the hall.

The floorboards creaked, and Jake pushed away the thought of them breaking through to the dining room below. Cobwebs lined the ceiling and collected in the doorframe of the first room he glanced into. Like Andy had said, it matched the rest of the house. A large four-poster bed with a tattered mattress full of holes dominated the near wall. Generations of mice had probably lived there in rodent luxury.

On the other side of the hall, a similar bedroom stood with its door open. A small bed frame, probably a child's, was in the corner. A wooden hobbyhorse lay on its side next to it. Broken tufts of straw were all that were left of the mane, and faint lines of paint formed a sickening smile below. The room's lone window loomed above it, and Jake could barely make out the trees outside through the dirt and grime caked on it.

Andy was standing in a doorway down the hall like the guy that rips tickets at the movies.

Seth and Ryan stopped next to him and looked inside. Jake crept up behind and peered over their shoulders. Andy hadn't lied. It was obvious the stuff in there hadn't belonged to the people who'd originally lived here.

An old wooden bed frame had been flipped on its side and pushed into the corner, its mattress missing. A large beach towel hung over the window, a frame of light surrounding it and making the room brighter than the one next to it.

An inflated air mattress lay in the middle of the room with a pair of tangled blankets on top. A blue battery-operated Coleman lantern sat next to the bed alongside a pair of *Cycle World* magazines and a copy of *Guns & Ammo*.

Ryan slipped through the doorway and approached the mattress. Jake fought the urge to reach out and grab him—to pull him back and get them the hell out of there. It was a fight he barely won.

"There's no dust or dirt or anything on it." Ryan looked back toward the guys piled in the doorway. "Somebody's been using it. Recently."

"Who?" Jake knew it was a stupid question as soon as it left his mouth. Who cared who it was? Somebody was sleeping in a room on the second floor of an abandoned house on a remote island in the back section of a lake.

A room they were all currently standing in.

"Could be a homeless guy," Ryan said. "Like a squatter or something."

"What if this is a crack house?" Jake said. The thought of people coming here to smoke crack or shoot up—lying around on an old air mattress, eyes glazed over in a zombielike haze—was creepy as hell. Jake had no idea what an actual crack house looked like, but an abandoned house in the middle of nowhere would fit all the ideas he'd gotten from movies and commercials paid for by the Partnership for a Drug-Free America.

Seth walked around the mattress, scanning the floor of the bedroom. "As much of a pain in the ass as it was to get here, I highly doubt it."

"What then?" Ryan asked.

"I don't know," Andy said. "But nobody's living here. There isn't enough stuff like clothes and food, you know. More likely whoever it is just comes out every now and—" Andy froze midsentence. He knelt and pulled something from under one of the blankets that had spilled off the mattress onto the floor. A cheap-looking broken gold chain. Something clattered to the floorboard as he stood up to examine it. He stooped down again and grabbed it.

"Is that a key?" Ryan asked.

"Yep," Andy said, holding the little silver key up so the guys could see it.

"What for?" Jake's imagination provided plenty of answers he didn't want to consider.

"Your ass," Seth interrupted. "How the fuck should he know? Probably a lock somewhere, genius."

Seth tried to snatch it from Andy's hand, but he pulled it away and knocked the Coleman lantern over with a clatter that felt like it echoed through the entire house.

"Put it back," Jake said.

Seth kept grabbing at the key, but Andy held it behind his back, eventually tossing it over to Ryan.

Jake remained rooted in the doorway, fingers clinging to the frame. Fear had staked out a spot on the perimeter of his brain and was probing the fence, looking for a weak spot to break through.

The guys ignored him.

"You see anything with a lock on it?" Andy spun away from Seth and scanned the room. He stepped over to the closet and opened the door to a lone bar stretched under an empty shelf. No hangers dangled from the bar. Nothing littered the floor.

Jake remained in the door, fighting to keep his breathing under control, helpless as the other guys skimmed over the far corners of the room.

"Seriously, guys, put it back, okay?" Jake wrestled for control of his voice. "It's probably time to head out anyway."

Seth backed up from the bed frame. "Dude, we just got here. What are you worried about?"

"If there's a guy staying here, I don't want to be here when he comes back."

"What's he gonna do?" Andy asked. "It's not *his* place, right? We've got just as much right to be here as he does."

"Yeah," Seth said. "Just because he likes a private place to spank it doesn't mean he owns the place."

It was a losing cause. The fever had gripped them—even Ryan, who Jake could usually count on to be the levelheaded one, was searching the room for something locked. It was clear they weren't going anywhere until the guys had explored every inch of the house.

Jake backed away as Seth and Andy slipped past him into the hallway. He stepped into the bedroom and walked past the mattress to join Ryan at the dresser.

"Find anything yet?" Jake tried his best to keep the worry from his voice.

"Nada," Ryan said, then lowered his voice so only Jake could hear him. "You okay?"

Jake moved the makeshift curtain aside and looked down on the backyard. The trees had encroached a little more than in front, and the grass was in much worse shape. There was a large dead patch near the back, and the plants surrounding it looked fairly wilted as well. Ten feet to the right was a black spot full of ash. Whoever came out here must have had a campfire every now and then.

But that would have been a huge campfire.

"Yeah, fine," Jake said. "I'm just being paranoid, probably. But it *is* creepy, you know?"

Ryan closed the last empty drawer and stood back up.

"I hear ya," he said. "But you gotta admit, it's also pretty cool. And don't worry about that guy. Like Andy said, even if he shows up, it's not like he can do anything to us."

Chapter Eleven

Krista took a long pull from the old-fashioned sitting on the mahogany bar in front of her. The only person nearby was a middle-aged man in a rumpled suit at the far end of the bar. He'd been there when Krista arrived, and if he kept drinking, he'd be on the floor when she left.

She checked her watch for the fourth time and glanced back at the door.

Krista sometimes met Harry for an evening drink when schedules kept them apart at the office, and this bar was her favorite. It was dark and quiet, and the patrons were more concerned with alcohol than eavesdropping. The faint odor of cigars that had been smoked long ago still hung in the farthest corners of the room.

Harry walked through the front door and wove past the empty tables with the confidence of a guy about to cross the finish line. The sight of him still riding high off that bullshit offer was another needle in Krista's gut.

"How's it going?" Harry slid onto the stool next to her. The bartender approached, and he ordered a gin and tonic.

"You seem chipper," Krista said.

"Porter asked me to cosponsor a bill he's working on."

Krista picked up her drink off the bar and took another sip. She savored the burn, then replaced her glass on the coaster in front of her as the bartender delivered Harry's.

"What's the bill?" Krista fought to keep the annoyance out of her voice.

"It's a telecom-regulation thing. Nothing major, but it'll pass easy." Krista rolled her eyes.

"Come on," Harry said. "Not everything we do is going to tear down the walls of inequality and reshape the world. Passing legislation is a good thing, remember? It's literally what we were sent here to do."

"Is it?" Krista snapped before calming herself down.

Harry shrugged and took a drink.

"Sometimes you have to play their game now to get what you want later," Harry said. "You know that as well as anybody."

A dozen responses raced into Krista's head, but she swatted them all down before they could exit her mouth. If Harry couldn't yet see how Porter was attempting to politically neuter him, her snark wouldn't help. He'd see through his bullshit eventually; then they'd be back on the right path.

Assuming those postcards didn't turn into something major.

"We need to talk about that postcard you got the other day," Krista said.

"I told you it was nothing." Harry's face showed none of the shock that had struck him when he'd seen it sitting on their reception desk. That was somewhat comforting, although the fact he knew exactly what she was talking about meant he hadn't completely swept it from his mind.

"We've gotten more."

The flash of panic behind Harry's eyes was fleeting but noticeable to someone who knew him as well as Krista did. "Who else knows about this?"

"One of the interns found them going through the mail." The fact that Harry asked about who knew instead of what it said poked at the back of Krista's brain. "Someone sent a map of Cedar Lake with one of the islands circled in red. Like the first postcard, the envelope was addressed to Andy Leonard. And a second postcard came today.

Different design, but from Cedar Lake and again addressed to Andy Leonard. But it wasn't blank."

Harry glanced over his shoulder at the bartender, then back to Krista.

"What did it say?"

Krista had read it enough times that afternoon to have it memorized. *"I know what you are. You can't hide from your past. Justice is coming."*

She could see Harry connecting dots in his head, like someone asked to solve a riddle.

"So just you and the intern have seen these?" Harry's normally genial voice had lowered. Krista was glad to see he was taking it seriously.

"So far," she said. "Julia saw the map, but by itself it wouldn't mean much. I think we should have a talk with her before we contact Capitol Police, though."

Harry looked over his shoulder again. "Hold on, now. I don't think we're at that point yet, do you? I mean, it's only a couple of weird postcards."

"You know we're required to report any threats to Capitol Police," Krista said. "Technically, I should have called them this afternoon, but I wanted to give you a heads-up before I did."

"Yeah, but who's to say that's a real—"

Krista cut him off. *"Justice is coming?* You can blow off a blank postcard and a map as just weird stuff, but *justice is coming* is a threat. We have to report it."

Harry picked up his gin and tonic and drained it. He dropped the empty glass on the bar and signaled the bartender for another.

"I get what you're saying," Harry said. Krista could feel the pull of his tone, trying to drag her over to his side. "But we've got to figure out if this is the right time for a big investigation, because that's what it'll be. Capitol Police will want to talk to everybody, monitor our correspondence, everything."

Krista agreed it would be an annoyance but argued that would be a relatively minor inconvenience.

"You think nobody is going to talk?" Harry asked. "What happens when the press gets wind of it?"

"I don't know, we get some free publicity?" Krista said. "If I'm being honest, having someone threaten you gives us sympathetic coverage. It gets your name out to people who don't keep up on who's sponsoring the latest telecom bill. Frankly, it makes you look like a big deal."

The bartender delivered Harry's drink. Krista declined an offer of another as Harry grabbed his and guzzled half of it. He set it down and stared into the long mirror that hung behind the bar in front of them.

"Harry." He didn't look at her, so she repeated herself. "What is this Cedar Lake stuff about?"

"Nothing. I was literally there one time in my life."

As smooth as Harry could be, the fact that his words were so unconvincing alarmed Krista more than anything.

"That island that was circled . . . there was a meth lab out there. I figured that out with barely two minutes of googling. Biggest drug bust in the area at the time. Now, I'm not gullible enough to believe you were somehow involved in that as a teenager, but don't for one second think there aren't people out there who are willing to believe anything they read on the internet. If we let this thing fester, who knows what can grow out of it? And you better believe your opponents will weaponize this the first chance they get."

Krista felt herself getting worked up and took a calming breath. She had to be the steady hand at the wheel.

"Look, I know what the end goal is. But what you have to realize is that no matter what path we choose, there are about a million land mines between you and the White House. My job is to defuse them before you come strolling by, and I can, but only if I know where they are. Did you buy something from them? Get caught holding something? High school drug use is something we can handle easily, but the only way I can do my job is if I know all the facts. If I'm flying blind, I may end up steering you right into a fucking mountain. You understand that, right?" Krista put her elbow on the bar next to her empty glass and leaned into Harry. "Why are you fighting me on this?"

It was only a few seconds, but the silence hung between them long enough for Krista to have her first real doubts.

Who exactly had she dedicated her life to these last eight years?

"We were up there for the week." Harry's voice was so low Krista almost didn't notice he had started talking. "One of the guys . . . Jake. It was his family's cabin. He tells us this story about an abandoned house out on an island in the back of the lake, so, of course, we've got to check it out."

Harry described the trip there in intricate detail, the story flowing as if from a direct spigot to the past.

The boat ride.

The weeds.

The smell of the place that should have tipped them off immediately.

Chapter Twelve

Seth and Andy were standing at the end of the hall, where a skinny wooden door had stopped their exploration.

"I think we found what the key is for," Andy said, flipping a large padlock that held the door shut about two feet above the handle. The sound of the lock slapping against the wood echoed down the hallway like a gunshot.

Jake blinked. Hard. It was the second time he'd noticed it, but he told himself it was only the dust they were kicking up around this old house. It had to be, because he'd had his tics under control since middle school.

He anxiously tried to remember the calming exercises he'd learned back then.

That made him blink again.

"You all right?" Ryan whispered.

Jake nodded and headed down the hallway. Ryan knew about the tics because back in eighth grade Jake's doctor suggested holding secrets wasn't helping his anxiety. He picked Ryan because Seth was incapable of taking anything seriously and would've just made fun of him, and Andy had enough of his own problems. Looking back, maybe it would've made him a sympathetic ear, but Jake hadn't wanted to put anything more on his plate.

"Give me the key," Andy said.

Jake put as much false nonchalance in his voice as he could. "What's back there?"

"Gee, I don't know," Seth said. "If there was only something we could use to open the door and find out."

"Don't be a dick." Ryan stepped up between Seth and Andy and examined the lock. "It's gotta be the tower, right?"

"There's only one way to find out," Seth said. "You gonna open the door, or should we stand here and make a few more guesses?"

Ryan inserted the key into the bottom of the lock and gave it a turn. He pulled the door open with a stiff creak. The air that wafted down into the hall was heavy and sour.

"Hold on," Jake said. The three boys turned from the door and stared down the hall at him. He couldn't think of anything that wouldn't make him sound paranoid, so the words hung in the weighty air of the house.

Andy broke the silence.

"Dude, we've got to see what's up there. It's a freaking turret tower in an abandoned house on an island. It's locked. Some dude is camping down the hall. You telling me you aren't at all curious about what's up there?"

Jake was surprised to discover that, yes, there *was* a part of him that wanted to see it. Although *wanted* wasn't the right word.

Needed?

His nerves hadn't gone anywhere. In fact, he was as anxious as ever. But a deep-seated curiosity—one that had been lurking there since he was a kid—had made itself known. At that precise moment, it was stronger than any paranoia. The house had been a mystery for too many years.

Jake leaned forward and looked up to where the stairs disappeared into the dark.

He didn't blink.

"Okay, but quick."

Andy slapped him on the back of the shoulder and looked over at Seth. "Run and get that lantern."

Seth ducked back into the bedroom and returned before anyone changed their mind. Andy took the lantern from Seth and headed up the steps. Unlike the ornate staircase leading up from the front hall, these weren't much more than boards.

Ryan followed, but Seth held back and turned to Jake. "Didn't mean to give you crap, man."

They'd been friends long enough Jake knew Seth's biting humor could morph into frequent obnoxiousness, but it was harmless. They were guys. Among good friends, feelings were made to be hurt. But an apology was completely out of character, and suggested Seth was more nervous than he let on.

More than anything, that made Jake feel better about exploring.

"Don't worry about it. I know you're a shithead." Jake smiled and stepped by him onto the first stair. "Let's check this out before that guy comes back and kills us all, eh?"

Seth snorted out a clipped laugh and followed Jake up the stairs.

The weird stench of ammonia Jake had noticed earlier got worse as they climbed. Could the original owners have kept their pets up here? And if so, why did it still smell like pee all these years later?

Ryan and Andy were blocking the way at the top of the stairs, so Jake gave a nudge and squeezed by. The windows had been blacked out, and the lantern sent a circle of light around the top of the tower, illuminating a huge stash of seemingly random goods.

Two rows of shelves were filled with dozens of boxes of cold medicine, wooden matches, and yellow bottles of antifreeze. At least twenty cans of camp stove fuel were lined up in neat rows beneath them.

On the other side of the room, a long, skinny table ran the length of the wall. Four huge glass bottles, like the ones atop an office water-cooler, were in a row on top.

"What the hell is all this?"

Jake scanned the room, and suddenly a nightmarish face peered out of the darkness and locked eyes with him. He stumbled back into Andy, who grabbed the top of the railing to keep from careening back down the stairs.

"Jeezus!" Andy pulled himself back upright. "What is it?"

Jake looked back at the black gas mask hanging from a nail in the wall. Two massive eyes stared out at him above a pair of short cylinders that jutted out from the bottom.

"Nothing . . ."

Seth joined them at the top of the stairs. The air felt like someone had run a humidifier filled with vinegar. The lantern continued to cast disconcerting shadows around the room, making even the normally benign household products look sinister.

Andy stepped over toward the table. The others followed closely, not wanting to be left behind by the room's only source of light. Jake saw tubes sticking out the tops of the bottles before disappearing somewhere in the darkness.

"Seriously, what's all this?" Jake said.

"It's drugs." Ryan's voice was soft enough it practically disappeared in the darkness. "He's making meth."

"What?" Jake asked. His visions of zombied crack addicts stumbling through the house came shuffling back, instinctively making him look around all the shadows of the room. He felt himself blink twice in rapid succession.

"Remember Coach Hansen talking about it in health class? They make meth out of all these household chemicals." Ryan grabbed Andy's wrist and pulled the lantern back toward the shelves across the room. "Cold medicine is a big part of it, and look at this. *Tons* of it."

"Are you sure?"

"What the hell else could it be?" Ryan said.

Andy walked alongside the table, running the light over it. A box of coffee filters sat open on the end, while random jars and smaller bottles were scattered between the tubes.

"Okay, now we've got to get out of here." Jake's resurgent curiosity had been completely chased away.

"Yeah, let's go." Seth's voice had lost all comic bravado, which assured Jake he wasn't overreacting. They needed to get out of there, and fast.

Andy continued past the end of the table, holding the lantern out in front of him. The walls had been stripped to the studs, and the hexagonal angles they formed cast strange shadows.

A large metal cabinet loomed in the darkness at the far end of the room. It was slightly tarnished, but still looked solid. Jake's dad had a similar one where he kept his power tools in their garage.

Another padlock held the cabinet doors together, identical to the one that barred the stairway. Andy stepped in front of the cabinet and gave the lock a tug.

"Gimme that key," Andy said, examining the bottom of the lock.

"Why?" Seth's voice held the same fright that Jake felt rising inside his own brain. "Let's get the fuck out of here."

Still holding the lock, Andy turned to the three other guys behind him. The lantern's light cast shadows across his face like on a kid telling ghost stories around a campfire.

"It's the same as the one on the stairway," he said. "Same key may work."

"That's not how locks work." Jake knew nothing about padlocks and the keys that opened them, but his brain convinced him he was right. It had to be, because he needed to convince Andy to stop exploring and hightail it back to their boat.

Where the drug dealers may be waiting . . . if they aren't in the house already, ready to grab us the second we descend the stairs.

Jake blinked. Then he blinked again. Hard.

"Let me see it." Andy was only talking to Ryan, who stood silently next to Seth and Jake on the periphery of the lantern's light. Andy's body cast a shadow that left Ryan in near darkness, so Jake couldn't get a read on what his best friend was thinking. But he didn't need to. Andy could always talk them into anything. It's most of the reason they were there in the first place.

"Dude," Andy insisted, holding out his hand in expectation. Ryan's arm flicked out, and Jake saw the broken chain the key was threaded on glint as it flew through the light. Andy snatched it out of midair and turned back toward the lock.

"We should get out of here." Seth's hot breath hit Jake's ear with his whisper. Jake agreed but said nothing as he watched Andy stick the key in the bottom of the lock and give it a turn. The sound of the shackle popping free sent a fresh wave of fear through Jake.

"Told ya it'd work," Andy said, pulling the lock free and the doors apart.

"Come on," Jake said without much conviction. He knew it was a lost cause. Andy could be as agreeable as the others, but also had a dogged determination when he wanted something. If Andrew Harrison Leonard thought he was right about something, nobody could change his mind. The course was set, and they weren't leaving until Andy's exploration was done.

He held the light in front of the gray metal box, his silhouette like a human eclipse.

"Holy shit." Andy's voice sounded like a tire with a slow leak.

"What is it?" Ryan stepped forward and peered over Andy's shoulder. Jake heard him gasp before his voice drifted back through the dark. "Oh my God."

"What?" Jake asked, but made no move to see around Ryan. His friend glanced back over his shoulder, then stepped aside to allow Seth and Jake a look into the cabinet.

A few notebooks sat on the top shelf, along with a collection of random tools. Just under the shelf, a white plastic grocery bag was stashed in the corner. Rolled bundles of cash were stuffed inside. Jake saw tens, twenties, fifties—all randomly piled in and held together with rubber bands.

Stacks of envelopes were lined up next to the bundles, each about an inch thick. Andy reached out and picked up one off the top.

"Don't . . . ," Jake said, despite knowing it would have no effect. Andy placed the lantern on the shelf and fanned open the envelope. His thumb ran over countless hundred-dollar bills.

Jake's brain was in full short-circuit mode and couldn't do the math on how much money was sitting in front of them.

"Holy fucking shit." Andy's voice was a whisper of restrained excitement. He handed the envelope to Ryan and grabbed another off the stack. "Can you believe this?"

"How much is in there?" Seth asked, stepping past Ryan for a better look.

"A metric shit ton," Andy said.

The only experience Jake had with denominations like that was the yearly hundred-dollar bill Grandpa Charlie gave him at Christmas, but a quick guesstimate said each of those envelopes held around $10,000.

Andy stuck his hand into the cabinet and ran his finger down the stacks of envelopes. The tip of his fingernail ticked past each one.

"I bet there's at least $100,000 here." His voice was giddy. "Holy shit."

Jake reached up and put his hand on Ryan's shoulder. "Let's get the hell out of here, okay?"

Ryan stepped back from the cabinet, but it was Andy who responded.

"All right," he said. "Let's go."

Jake tried to shut the cabinet door, but it banged against Andy's wrist with a metallic gong and wobbled back open.

Andy pulled out a pair of envelopes and reached in for more.

"What are you doing?" Jake asked. It was the first time his voice had risen above a concerned whisper since they'd ascended the stairs. Andy ignored the question and held a pair of envelopes out toward Jake, who reacted like he'd thrust a snake at him.

"What?" Andy asked. The envelopes of cash hung between them.

"Put that back so we can get the fuck out of here," Jake said.

The light behind him left most of Andy's face in shadows, but Jake could sense the disbelief.

"Put it back?" Andy repeated Jake's words like he'd spoken them in German.

"Yeah, man." Seth's voice was without snark for a change. "Let's just go."

The confusion drained from Andy's face and was replaced by resentment. Money had never been an issue among the four of them, although it would be fairly obvious to anyone who paid attention that Andy's family had less than most. But the money in those envelopes was life changing, even for middle-class kids.

"What the fuck are you guys talking about?" Andy said. "There's no way I'm leaving this much money here." He shifted the extended envelopes from Jake to Ryan, who took them without saying anything.

"No way, man," Seth said. "That's fucking crazy. That's *drug* money."

Andy spun away from the open cabinet. "Exactly. These are drug dealers. Bad guys. Why would you want to leave them all this cash? Fuck 'em."

"But what if they catch us? Holy shit, man . . . I'm not ending up at the bottom of this fucking lake," Seth said.

Andy took a deep breath to try to cool the rapidly heating conversation down. "Dude . . . there's no way they're going to find us. Nobody knows who we are, and nobody knows we're out here."

He paused and made eye contact with each of his friends. He wore a calm expression, like a guy who could be trusted. "They'll *never* find us. Hell, if it makes you feel better, we can leave tonight. Go home, never come back. They'll never know we were here."

"What would our parents say?" Ryan asked in a low voice.

"Our parents?" Andy said. "We can tell them anything. Tell them I got sick or something . . . anything. That's no problem at all."

Ryan shook his head. "About the money. You can't hide that much cash. And besides, you don't think your mom is going to notice a new stereo or TV or whatever? They'll find out—then what are you gonna say?"

Ryan reached back into the cabinet and placed the envelopes he was holding on the shelf.

"You're right. This is a shitload of money," Andy said. "So we'll have to be smart about it. We'll have to be very low key—"

"What the fuck are you talking about?" Seth said. "Think about it, man. People get killed over this kind of stuff."

"But—"

"No, he's right," Ryan said. "Put it back and let's go."

Jake peered through the gloom at Andy, trying to get a read on how his friend would react. Even in the darkness he could see the conflict behind his friend's eyes.

"I mean, I guess you're right, but . . . fuck, man. This is life-changing money right here."

Andy held the silence for a moment, then shocked Jake by putting the envelopes back in the cabinet.

"Thank you." Relief pushed the words out of Jake's mouth.

"All right, can we get the hell out of here, please?" Seth said. Seeing his usual manic energy morph into fear had been as unsettling as anything. It would be nice when he was back to fart jokes and movie quotes. But Jake knew that might not be until they were back home with this whole thing a few days and a hundred miles behind them.

Andy and Ryan evened out the stacks of envelopes as a bundle of twenties fell out of the plastic grocery bag and rolled to the edge of the shelf. Andy restored the cabinet to what they assumed was the exact way it had looked before they opened it, then swung the doors shut and replaced the lock.

Seth reached forward and rubbed his shirt all over the handle of the cabinet.

"You worried they're gonna dust for prints?" Andy's sarcasm was sharpened by his disappointment.

"Shut up."

They retreated down the steps and put the lantern back next to the air mattress.

They stashed the key in the tangle of blankets where Andy had found it and made their way out of the house and back to the boat without incident.

———

When they finally emerged from the cover of trees and waded into the water, Jake felt exposed in a way that wouldn't abate until they'd climbed aboard the boat, pulled away from the island, and made their way through the inlet to the main part of the lake.

The tension eased the farther they got from the island, but they were halfway back to the cabin before Jake took a full breath.

As always, Seth broke the silence. By the time they pulled up to the dock, the four of them were laughing again.

Andy was first off the boat. "What say we get some beer tonight?"

Jake heard a whoop of agreement from Seth before he looked up from the captain's seat and saw a roll of cash in Andy's hand. Somehow, it took a second before he realized where it had come from.

Andy wore a self-satisfied smile as Seth hopped onto the dock and snatched it from Andy's hand. "Holy shit."

"You didn't . . . ," Jake said.

"It's one bundle," Andy said. "Fuck 'em."

"But—"

"You saw that bag with all those rolls tossed in," Andy said. "There's no way they could ever notice it's gone. Even if they did, they'll probably just think it got lost. Who would break in and leave the rest of the cash?"

Jake opened his mouth for another, more strenuous objection but then felt Ryan's hand on his shoulder.

"He's right," Ryan said as Seth counted the bills out loud a few steps away. "There's no way they'll notice it's gone, but more importantly, there's no possible way they'd know we were out there."

"Exactly." Andy smirked. "I mean, you saw Seth wipe the fingerprints off the handle, right?"

"Shut up."

Jake wanted to say something, to make them take it back anyway, but Ryan was probably right. Besides, returning it would only increase their chances of getting caught out there. It still felt like a mistake, but Jake knew there was nothing to be done about it now. It was just one roll. It couldn't be that much money, so he swallowed his worry and forced himself to go along.

"How much we got?"

Chapter Thirteen

Harry had yanked the tablecloth out from under everything Krista had built over the last eight years. She had been fully confident she knew everything about Harrison Leonard's past. Even the little embellishments they'd sprinkled into his bio had been committed to memory long ago. But she'd demanded from him full transparency. It was the only way she could do her job effectively.

"You stole money from a drug lab." It wasn't a question. Krista was processing the idea, running scenarios over in her head. Gauging reactions from party officials, opponents, pundits, voters. It was worse than she'd expected, but it could still be navigated. They were kids, and it wasn't like they stole from Sister Helen's Home for Blind Orphans.

Krista shook off the shock and flipped her switch to battle mode.

"All right, we can manage this, but I need you to be completely honest with me." She glanced behind her to make sure nobody had sidled up to the bar without her notice. "How much did you take?"

"It was barely more than beer money, and we spent most of it that night." Harry's voice bordered on defensive. "It was the first time in my life I got drunk. It was the first time for all of us, I think."

Krista turned that over in her head. Youthful indiscretions were not uncommon among politicians, and plenty had survived worse and gone on to higher office. But the stink of drug money wouldn't be easy to shake, and just because it wasn't a major scandal didn't mean it couldn't be a thorn in their side for years to come. Most people ignored politics in general, but stolen drug money was the kind of story that could stick like a burr in even the most apathetic voter's memory.

"So what do we do?" Harry asked.

Krista swallowed hard and tried to keep her voice down. She was glad the place was mostly empty, but that meant no background noise to give their conversation some cover. "I think we go public with the threats and cop to it. It's early in your career, and we've got a year until the next election. It will certainly be an issue there, but if we get through that first reelection, we can probably put it to bed. Hell, if we frame it as blackmail, maybe we can even get a little sympathy out of it."

Harry sat back on his stool and ran his hands through his hair. It was his go-to move when he was flustered. She first noticed it when they used to kill time with staff poker games on the campaign trail.

"I doubt it," Harry said. "I mean, I know it's no big deal, but it'll still be catnip for the press. Why get my name anywhere near drug money if we don't have to?"

"Because it shows you aren't afraid to admit past mistakes. If you aren't hiding it, it seems like less of a big deal. Besides, there's a decent chance it leaks after we report it to the Capitol Police anyway. This allows us to control it somewhat."

"*That's* why I don't want to report it to the Capitol Police," Harry said.

Krista looked up from her empty glass. She wanted another one but wasn't about to bring the bartender within earshot. "We have to report it. Proper procedure aside, what if this person decides to come after you? We have no idea who this is or what's going through their head."

"Oh, come on, don't be dramatic," Harry said. "They aren't threatening anything except to talk. They don't want to hurt me; they want to hurt my career. Why give them what they want? I'd bet you that it isn't even some random dude, but that somebody on the other side of the aisle is behind this." A bolt of realization flashed across his face. "What if it's somebody on *our* side? Someone looking to dirty up a potential VP pick before he gets any steam? Fuck . . ."

No matter what she thought of Porter's bogus offer, Krista couldn't simply disregard what Harry said. Politics was a dirty business, and the timing was a little suspicious.

Harry leaned in with a low voice. "We can handle this ourselves. If we can find out who sent it, maybe we can find a way to keep them quiet."

"Easier said than done," Krista said.

"Nobody said it was going to be easy," Harry said. "But if we don't take care of this, the VP spot may be gone. They won't let anyone with even a whiff of scandal on the ticket."

Krista stifled her thoughts on that possibility. She might be the one steering the ship, but when it came down to it, Harrison Leonard was the captain. If he wanted to ignore the advice of the person who had built his career, it was his choice. Krista's job as chief of staff was to support him in any way she could. She was his fixer, and sometimes she had to be morally flexible to serve the greater good.

She would fix this.

"All right, you need to think of everyone who could possibly know about this."

"You're the first person I've ever told."

"What about the others who were there?" Krista asked. "The story had to come from one of them. Any of them have a problem with you?"

"I don't know. I mean, I don't think so," Harry said. "The trip was after graduation, and we all kind of went our separate ways after that. But I can't think of a reason any of the guys would have to bring this up—especially after all these years. We were really good friends."

Krista thought back to the newspaper articles she'd found.

"So, if you guys were up there after graduation, that probably wasn't much before the place got busted. You're lucky you weren't out there when it went down."

Harry nodded and sipped from his glass. "Yeah, that would've been awkward. Although I'm pretty sure they would figure out quickly that a group of dumb kids had nothing to do with it."

"I mean when it blew up."

The thick bottom of Harry's tumbler made a sharp rap on the bar. "What?"

"The lab exploded during the bust," Krista said. "A couple of the guys running it and a DNR officer died. Seemed like it was big news at the time. I figured you would've heard."

"Wow, no. I mean, it's not like I read the paper or watched the news back then. Man . . . I guess we dodged a bullet out there."

Krista watched Harry's eyes as he considered what could've been. Behind him, the guy at the end of the bar had put his head down and appeared to be passed out. The bartender had the drunk's phone in hand, probably requesting him a ride home. Maybe grabbing an extra tip from his Venmo.

"Yeah, well, let me see what else I can dig up," Krista said. "But we're going to have to work fast. Understand this—if we keep getting mail, there's going to be no choice. It can't get out that we knew about this but didn't report it. If we get any more weird shit, we'll have to talk to the Capitol Police."

Harry didn't look happy, but he nodded. Krista swiveled on her stool so she could face him directly. She waited to speak until he lifted his gaze to meet hers.

"If I'm going to do this, we've got to be on the same page or it doesn't work. Is there anything you haven't told me?"

Harry didn't hesitate. The unconvincing trepidation she'd seen in him at the beginning of their conversation was nowhere to be found, which was comforting. She wasn't overexaggerating. If she went into this without all the facts, it could be an unmitigated disaster.

"No."

Chapter Fourteen

"Do you guys think we should call the police?"

The group had skipped the screened-in porch and eaten at the kitchen table. They'd left no trace, no breadcrumbs to follow, but the porch still felt a little too exposed after the sun went down.

The roll Andy had grabbed added up to $440 in twenty-dollar bills. Not a huge sum, but enough to put a pair of large pizza boxes on the counter.

"No way," Andy said. He placed tall glasses of fizzy brown liquid in front of Jake and Ryan before turning back to the counter for the remaining two. The pizza joint they'd carried out from was a few doors down from a liquor store. Somehow, while Jake and Ryan were picking up the pizza, Andy had convinced a guy in a camo fishing cap to buy him a bottle of Captain Morgan.

Because that's what Andy did. He got people to do things.

"We need to stay out of it," Andy said, handing Seth his rum and Coke before plopping down into a chair at the head of the table. "Forget about it."

"But what if there's a reward or something?" Seth said. "That looked like a pretty big operation out there."

"All the more reason to stay out of it," Andy said. "Seriously. Nothing good can come from getting involved at this point."

Jake took a sip of his drink and felt it singe his sinuses. He didn't have much experience with alcohol and had no way to know if Andy had even made it right. Jake held in a cough while the burning sensation trickled down his throat.

"He's probably right," Ryan said. "Something that big isn't just a bust and a ticket either. There'll be a trial and all kinds of stuff."

"We'd probably have to testify or something," Andy said.

A rack of coughs came from across the table, and Seth almost dropped his drink. Some splashed out as he struggled to keep his glass from hitting the table. "Jeezus."

"Take 'er easy." Andy reached over and slapped Seth on the back. "You can't chug it, man. You gotta sip."

Seth's face was red as his coughs turned to laughs. "How much did you put in here?"

"I don't know. You don't like it, make your own next time," Andy said. "Seriously, though, Ryan's right. It's not like we can call in a report and leave it at that. They're gonna want to talk to us. Why were we out there? What did we find? All that shit. And if we have to testify . . . man. Those trials take a long time. Like a year or more sometimes."

"Seriously?" Seth said. "I can't be coming back up here to testify or anything. Shit, by that time we'll be at college."

Jake hadn't considered what they would have to do if they called the police. It seemed like the right thing to do, but he knew Andy would be unwilling to risk anything getting in the way of his plans. The University of Virginia had always been his ticket out. His light at the end of the tunnel.

That said, it still felt wrong to forget about what they'd seen.

"What if we gave an anonymous tip?" Jake asked. "We could call the police and not give our names."

"And what happens when they trace the call?" Andy took two huge pulls from the glass in front of him. No throat burn there, apparently. He wiped his mouth with the back of his hand. "They'll still try to figure out who you are, if only to figure out how you know all that."

"We could do it later," Seth said, taking another, smaller sip. "We could stop at a gas station on the way home. Use a pay phone. That way even if they do trace it back, there's no way they would know it was us."

The table considered it, and it seemed like a good compromise. The dealers would get put away, and the guys' consciences would be clear. They'd know they did something to help, but wouldn't get pulled into a huge drug bust.

It also served to keep them anonymous from whoever put that meth lab out there. None of them had mentioned what could happen to witnesses in drug cases. With the amount of cash they'd seen, it was obvious this wasn't just some hick cooking up crank for his buddies. It had to be a fairly sophisticated operation, which meant the people involved would probably do whatever they had to in order to keep it going. Jake had seen enough movies to never want to get between a drug dealer and his business. He glanced around the table. The looks on the other faces said they were thinking the same thing.

"Okay," Andy said, finally breaking the silence. "If it makes you feel better, we'll do it. We can call Sunday."

"Where from?" Seth asked.

"Like you said, we can find a gas station on the way back." Andy got up and walked back to the counter. He held his and Ryan's glasses, empty save for some melting ice. Andy grabbed the bottle of rum and poured. "Want me to top you guys off?"

Jake glanced down at his drink, still half full. Next to him, Seth tilted his head back and drained the remaining liquid in his cup and handed it over. Jake took a long drink of his own. It went down much smoother. Maybe all the rum had been at the top and the remainder was mostly Coke?

"Sure," he said.

Putting together a plan to report the lab without having to identify themselves seemed to loosen the night up for the guys. Or maybe it was the rum. They had migrated into the living room, where Seth was intent on proving he could recite every *Kids in the Hall* sketch verbatim.

"*ERADICATOR!*"

It was definitely the rum.

Jake couldn't stop laughing. Seth was funny. *Really* funny. He could probably grow up to be a comedian someday. Because he was funny. Like, *REALLY* funny.

Jake was laughing so hard he almost dropped the drink Andy handed him. He must have gotten better at mixing them as the night went on because Jake couldn't even taste the alcohol anymore. Just like drinking a . . .

". . . plain ole Coke."

"Huh?" Ryan said from the couch beside him. He was slouched in the crook of the arm. "Whaddya say?"

Jake tried to answer, but he was laughing so hard he was shaking. He raised his glass above his head in a mock toast. A decent-size glug sloshed out and landed in his lap.

"PLAIN OLE COKE!" Jake yelled. The guys exploded at their brand-new inside joke that none of them understood, aside from the fact that it was hilarious.

"Plain ole Coke," Seth cackled. "Hey! Go make me another plain ole Coke."

Andy chuckled and headed to the kitchen again. He'd been their bartender all night.

Jake laughed so hard he had to put his head down on the back of the couch. All that laughing took a lot out of a person. At the other end, Ryan's eyes were three-quarters closed. It must be really late.

"All right, guys, I'm going to bed."

The voice came from way far away, but it must have been loud because it cut through the black fog that enveloped Jake's head. He tried to open his eyes, but they were the heaviest things in the whole universe, so what the heck was he doing trying to open them up?

"You guys hear that? I'm going upstairs to go to bed."

That voice again. What was it doing?

Sounded like Andy, probably, but maybe Jake was dreaming. Kinda hard to tell with all that fog.

Jake gathered all his strength and was able to open his eyes.

Whoa.

Bad idea.

The room was spinning like that ride at the fair. The one that goes round and round and then the floor goes down and all the people are, like, stuck to the wall? How did that ride happen? Centrickamal force or something?

Jake closed his eyes again, but he kept spinning. Probably because the centrickamal force in the room had gotten into his head.

Whatever.

"Okay, I'm going to bed."

That was definitely Andy's voice. Even spinning, Jake could tell it was Andy's voice. But why was it Andy's voice? Who cared? *Quit making announcements, and just go to bed.* Jake was going to bed right there on the couch, and he wasn't yelling it to the world. Besides, Jake was trying to sleep, and Andy kept yelling at him, and how could he sleep right here on the couch if Andy kept yelling at him?

Jake pried his eyes open again.

The room was still spinning, but Jake could see all the way across it this time even though it was really far. Andy was turning back into the kitchen, not going up the stairs like he said he was. He wanted to ask Andy where he was going, but all his energy was being used to keep his eyes open, so he let them fall, and the room slowed down.

Jake heard something that sounded like the bang of the screen door on the porch, but the black fog rolled back in and enveloped him before he could figure out what it was.

Chapter Fifteen

Krista's schedule was jammed and kept her in meetings for the next few days. It was enough to push Cedar Lake out of her consciousness. Well, almost.

She had squeezed in some basic internet research on the guys Harry was with at Cedar Lake.

Ryan Kelter was quickly cleared of suspicion. His obituary from last year was vague, but it gave enough hints to make it clear he died of an overdose. Jake Nelson's name was common enough that it would take some serious digging to sift through all the others and find the one she was looking for. Unfortunately, her schedule left little time for anything beyond basic web searches.

Luckily, Seth Meloy had a large online presence. With a public Facebook page full of pictures of smiling kids and family vacations, Seth didn't come off as the bitter stalking type. Krista knew better than to trust somebody's social media image, though.

She glanced at the clock. Her lunch meeting was in fifteen minutes, and she'd have to hustle to get there on time.

Krista was a block away from the Capitol when her phone buzzed. She pulled it from the inside of her suit jacket and checked the screen. The crowd of pedestrians she walked among slid past her as she stopped.

It was Maggie Wander, the Minneapolis *Star Tribune*'s political reporter.

"Hey, Krista, you got a second?"

Maggie was well respected and widely read, so Krista had made a point of cultivating a good working relationship with her over the years.

"Headed to a meeting, but I've got a few. What's up?" Krista approached the crosswalk and punched the button. A small bead of sweat formed on her left temple, a sign that DC's brutal summer was bearing down on them at a full sprint.

"I got a weird letter this morning."

Krista closed her eyes as a shiver went down her spine despite the heat. The light changed, and the flock of suits that had gathered flowed around her like she was a boulder in a stream.

"Oh, yeah?"

"Somebody says he's got dirt on your boy. Proof that he's unfit for office."

The alarm bells in Krista's head blared into full-fledged air raid sirens and kicked her into crisis mode. When reporters got involved—especially good ones like Maggie Wander—the DEFCON level went up.

"Sounds like somebody signed up for updates from the Republican National Committee." Krista fought to keep the worry out of her voice. "Seriously, though, what did it say?"

"Just that Harrison Leonard wasn't the man people think he is and that he must be stopped," Maggie said. "The letter told me to look into Cedar Lake. That mean anything to you?"

Shit.

The numbers on the crosswalk counted down to zero, and the glowing red hand stopped all but a final few who bolted across the street against a salvo of honks. Krista was still on the curb, the next batch of pedestrians already queuing up behind her. She swung her head around, mentally counting the number of ears in position to pick up anything she said.

Krista doubled back into the shadow of a grand marble staircase that led into one of the countless federal buildings dotting the Hill, away from the steady stream of staffers, tourists, and other DC denizens.

"Are we off the record?" Krista asked even though she knew the answer. It was one of the first things she drilled into every person who worked in their office. No matter what anyone says, never say anything to a reporter you wouldn't want to see on the front page.

"You tell me." The tone of Maggie's voice changed. She was a fisherman who felt a small tug on her line—but she still didn't know if it was a tangle of weeds or a trophy.

"It's honestly not a big deal, but it's not something we want out there for . . . reasons. Not even on deep background."

Krista knew off-the-record comments were a last resort for reporters, but she could tell Maggie's interest was piqued. She hoped to dangle enough to satisfy Maggie's curiosity without putting her on the scent of what was actually going on.

"Agreed," Maggie said.

Krista scanned the sidewalk ahead of her before continuing.

"We've gotten some stuff too. Nothing we're overly concerned about, just some weird mail. But we think it's all coming from the same guy."

"Leonard has a stalker?"

Krista was thrilled to hear Maggie use that term. Stalkers were crazy. Stalkers lied, would say anything to hurt whomever they were obsessed with. If she thought it was a stalker, she'd be that much less likely to believe whatever came out of that person's mouth. Or letters.

"I wouldn't say that." Deliberately cagey, to keep Maggie interested.

"What did the letters or whatever you got say?"

"I can't tell you that," Krista said. "But I can say it wasn't anything overtly threatening or anything."

"Okay. What's the Cedar Lake stuff about?"

Krista pulled her phone away and wiped the sweat from her ear. "Honestly, no clue. Can't say I've ever heard of it."

"Huh." Maggie let the conversation hang for a few beats, probably hoping the awkward silence would prompt Krista to offer up some nugget of information to break the tension. All it did was give her time to regroup.

"It mean anything to you?" Krista asked.

"I did some digging but couldn't find anything. There's lots of Cedar Lakes out there."

The fact that Maggie hadn't uncovered anything about Harry's trip to the lake was encouraging, but Krista knew it was most likely temporary. If she kept digging, the story would come out. Krista leaned against the wall behind her. Her hair was pulled up in a dark bun, and the stone felt cool on her bare neck.

"Yeah, I bet there is," Krista said. "Any chance you could send me a copy of that letter?"

"If there is an official investigation, I'd be happy to show them the letter," Maggie said.

"I doubt it'll come to that," Krista said. "Like I said, the stuff we've got has been more weird than threatening. We've just got to be extra cautious."

"Especially if your boy is getting looked at for the vice president spot."

Krista pushed herself off the wall and almost dropped her phone. "Where did you hear that?"

"Is it true?"

It took a few seconds for Krista to formulate an answer. She was stunned that word of Porter's not-quite offer had made its way back to Minneapolis already, although she shouldn't have been. Porter's office probably leaked the rumor to generate buzz with the younger voters who loved Harry, even if they eventually decided to go another way.

"We're considering our next move." Just because Krista hated the idea of Harry as vice president didn't mean she couldn't use the story to distract a curious reporter.

"Will one of those moves be accepting the nomination for vice president?"

Krista glanced down at her watch and saw she had four minutes to get to her meeting. She stepped back into the pedestrian herd and headed through the crosswalk.

"There's no offer to accept, so I can't officially comment on that."

"But can you confirm he's being vetted for me?"

A guy in a pin-striped suit shouldered past her as she reached the far curb. Krista resisted the urge to stick her leg out and send his self-important ass sprawling.

"Will you keep that letter out of your story?"

The pause was long enough she thought the answer might be no.

"I can do that," Maggie said as Krista rounded the corner and caught sight of the restaurant she was headed to. "But if it happens, I want to know *before* you officially announce the VP spot. And a one-on-one with him the day of the announcement. Exclusive."

Krista cut her way through the gaggle of lobbyist-looking men gathered around the entrance. The restaurant's air conditioner was working hard enough to send a sheen of goose bumps across her shoulders.

"I can't give you an exclusive on something that big, but I can make sure you're the only newspaper with a one-on-one interview." Their press secretary wasn't going to like it, but she'd deal with him later.

"Deal," Maggie said. "One more thing, though. If this stalker thing turns out to be something real, I'll be calling you again."

———

Krista paced the living room of her apartment, her personal cell phone in hand and a UMD mug of chamomile tea cooling on the coffee table. The call from Maggie Wander that morning had drastically accelerated her timeline. Even if she could temporarily distract her with the VP rumors, Maggie would eventually take another look at Cedar Lake.

Which meant Krista had to take care of it immediately.

"Hello, is this Seth Meloy?"

"Yes, who am I speaking with, please?" His voice had all the patience and respect most people reserved for telemarketers. Krista glanced at the clock and realized it was 6:00 p.m. in Kansas City. Seth was probably sitting down for dinner with his wife and two daughters.

"My name is Krista Walsh. I'm Representative Harrison Leonard's chief of staff here in Washington, DC, and I was hoping I could talk to you for a minute."

She could have simply said she worked for Harry Leonard, but made sure to add the words *Representative, chief of staff,* and *Washington* to add as much gravitas as she could. Most people were less likely to lie to a government official than somebody who worked with an old friend.

"Oh, yeah, um, I've got a minute . . . sure." Seth paused, and a rustling sound came over the line. Krista could picture him heading away from the commotion of the kitchen for a quiet place to talk. "What can I do for you?"

"You grew up with Representative Leonard, correct?" It was a pointless question to get him started. Krista had been researching Seth online since she got home from the office, and there was no question she had the right Seth Meloy. He'd graduated from Ranford High School in 2003, then went to St. Cloud State. After college he'd worked for Southern Minnesota's Home of the Hits 99.1 KEEZ as a morning DJ, then got married and moved to Kansas City, where he was currently a media and digital sales representative.

"Yeah, Andy . . . we called him Andy back then. I guess he changed his name to sound more congressional or something, right?" There was a pause, and Krista wasn't sure if he was expecting a laugh. "But, yeah, I knew him. We were friends. Good friends. Haven't seen him in a long time, though. He's probably a little too busy to hang out with old dorks like me."

"Seth, we're doing some background research, and I was hoping you'd be able to answer some questions for me." Krista softened her tone. She could already tell Seth was a talker, and she'd probably get more out of him if he thought of them as friends. "But before we go any further, I need your assurances that this will remain confidential."

"Absolutely." His immediate response said his curiosity was piqued. "What do you want to know?"

Krista picked up her tea and took a drink.

"Well, Seth, like I said, we're doing some background checks with people who grew up with the representative, just to make sure there are no . . . surprises out there that we don't know about."

There was a telling pause before Seth answered.

"No, nothing I can think of."

"Nothing that may have not been a big deal back then, but may look bad if someone brings it up now? You know how cutthroat politics can be these days."

"Nope." His voice projected the fake confidence of a morning-radio DJ. "We were just normal kids doing typical stuff. Never got arrested or in trouble or anything like that. I mean, we did stupid teenager crap like throw toilet paper in our teachers' trees for homecoming and that kind of stuff, but nothing major or anything."

"Did you ever go to Cedar Lake with Representative Leonard?" The question was met with silence. She heard a door close in Kansas City and the muffled pause of someone trying to figure out a way forward.

"Yeah. We went up there one time. Why are you asking about that?"

Krista didn't respond immediately, hoping the awkward silence would soften up Seth's reticence. She took another sip of tea and savored the warmth. Some claimed a hot drink in summertime actually cooled you down, but Krista liked the ritual of it. It helped her decompress.

"Seth, I'm going to be honest with you. Harrison Leonard is being looked at for the vice presidential nomination, but before that, we need to know everything about him. Absolutely everything. My job is to make sure there are absolutely no stories that will pop up at the last minute and derail a presidential campaign."

"Holy shit," Seth said. "Andy's gonna be vice president?"

"That all depends." Krista was happy to hear some excitement creep back into Seth's voice at the suggestion of Harry as VP. For as much as she'd hated it, the idea was repeatedly proving valuable. Everybody wants a connection in the White House. "You can help out a bunch by answering my questions."

"Yeah, sure, I can do that," Seth said. "I mean, we didn't see Andy much after he left for college out East, and after his mom and dad died, he didn't have any reason to come back for holidays or anything. Besides, we all knew he was looking to get out of Ranford the first chance he got. It was all he ever talked about, even before the accident. I was already down here when he ran for state senate, but my mom would send me newspaper clippings about him. She always loved Andy. I think everybody's parents did. Everybody kind of assumed he'd be a big shot in greener pastures someday, but when that video of him cussing out the Supreme Court got out . . . crazy. That thing was *everywhere*."

Listening to Seth gush about his old friend made it easy to eliminate him from suspicion, but hopefully he could still have some useful information if she could keep him on track.

"We know about the island on Cedar Lake. About what you guys found out there," Krista said. "What I need to know is who else knows."

"Nobody," Seth said. "I mean, Jake and Ryan . . . they were the other guys with us, but you probably know that already. I never told anyone, though. I swear to God."

The answer was quick and convincing.

"What about the others?" Krista asked. "Any idea if they ever talked to anyone?"

"I guess I can't say for sure, but I highly doubt it," Seth said. "And I'll say this—the way stories get passed around in Ranford, if either of them had said anything, the whole goddamn town would've heard about it. There's no secrets in a small town like that."

There'd better be.

"So you guys never talked about it? Not even with each other?" Krista asked.

"We had an . . . agreement. Honestly, I've done what I could to forget about it."

"Did you keep in touch with the others over the years?"

"Ryan and I roomed together at St. Cloud State and hung out a decent amount for a few years after that," he said. "I didn't see him near as much after we moved to KC, though. And then, well, you probably know he passed last year."

Krista thought back to the obituary she'd found online.

"I read that. It was an overdose, correct?"

She could hear Seth breathing over the line.

"Ryan had been in a car accident a few years before," Seth said. "Messed up his back, and it always bothered him after that. I guess he got addicted to the painkillers they gave him."

"I'm sorry to hear that," Krista said. "What about Jake Nelson? Have you had much contact with him over the years?"

"Not really," Seth said. "Jake went to college for like a year, but he partied pretty hard and ended up flunking out and moved back home. We'd see him around when we were on break or whatever, but he always had a chip on his shoulder. Like he was jealous that we didn't get stuck back home like he did. Eventually he just kind of faded away, you know? I don't even think I have his phone number anymore."

That caught Krista's attention. "When was the last time you saw him?"

"Ryan's funeral, actually," Seth said. "It was back in Ranford. Apparently Jake's living at his grandpa's old farmhouse outside of town. I talked to him for a little bit, but not much more than *how ya doin'*."

"How was he doing?"

"He looked kinda rough, if I'm honest," Seth said. "I mean, it was a funeral, so it wasn't like I expected to share a lot of laughs or anything, but . . ."

Whatever Seth wanted to say remained on the other end of the line, but Krista couldn't let him hold anything back.

"But what?"

Her words hung between them long enough Krista wondered if the call had dropped.

"He seemed upset," Seth said. "I know it was a funeral and all . . . it's hard to explain. I don't know . . . he seemed more mad than sad. Like he was looking to blame somebody for Ryan's death. And I could smell booze on him."

Krista flipped open her computer and pulled up the shared master schedule their executive assistant updated daily. "People all grieve differently."

"Yeah. I guess," Seth said, but Krista was busy scrolling. Harry was headed back to Minnesota for a round of meetings and appearances around the district that weekend. It was mostly photo ops and public relations with no need for a chief of staff, so she had planned on skipping it.

They were scheduled to leave the following afternoon.

"Any chance you could give me directions to Jake's place?"

Chapter Sixteen

Jake opened his eyes, but a blinding flash of pain forced him to clamp them shut again. He could feel every beat of his heart in his temples, which told him he was still alive.

Even if death seemed more appealing.

He cracked his eyes open again, doing his best to limit the light pouring in. He saw Ryan slouched on the other end of the couch, in the exact same position where he'd passed out last night.

Jake looked back into the fog of the previous night and came up with little more than a series of clips. Everything had been hilarious. Now, he felt like laughter would kill him.

He sat up and felt a fresh wave of pain slosh through his head. His neck was stiff from using the couch's arm as a pillow. His movement rousted Ryan, who looked as green as Jake felt.

"Hey," Jake said. The only response Ryan gave was to keep breathing. He slid up into a sitting position and immediately put his head between his knees.

Jake glanced at the clock—8:48 a.m.

It took him a second to realize he and Ryan were the only two in the room.

"Where's everybody?" Jake's mouth felt like someone had stuffed it with cotton balls.

As if answering his question, a retching sound came from the bathroom.

The two remained silent for the next few minutes. Eventually they heard the toilet flush, and Seth padded back into the living room.

"Well, that was fun," Seth said, shuffling toward the love seat. One of the throw pillows was on the floor next to the coffee table. Instead of sitting back down, Seth dropped to his knees and lay straight down on the floor, face buried in an old, musty pillow.

"How's it going, Cabbage Head?" Ryan asked from his end of the couch.

Seth's voice was muffled, but his response was unmistakable: "Fuck you."

Jake chuckled. It was enough to send a wave of nausea rocketing from his stomach to his throat. He clamped his lips shut in a herculean effort to keep from puking right there. The feeling passed, and he let out a careful breath.

The room smelled like a combination of night sweats and booze. A glass sat on the coffee table with two inches of melted ice at the bottom. Crumbs of chips Jake didn't remember eating were still on the front of his shirt, the open bag on the floor.

He craned his aching neck around the room.

"Where's Andy?" Jake had a fleeting thought that Andy had left, but the throbbing behind his eyes quickly pushed it aside.

"No clue," Seth muttered without lifting his face from the pillow.

Jake gathered his remaining strength and stood up, using more energy to keep from vomiting than to walk. He stepped around the coffee table and over Seth on the way to the kitchen. It was in a similar condition to the living room. Two blue ice trays lay side by side on the counter, one empty and the other a third full of water.

A two-liter Coke bottle lay on its side next to the empty bottle of Captain Morgan spiced rum. The sailor who'd sent them on their drunken voyage grinned mockingly from the label.

Jake closed his eyes as the taste of the rum washed through his mouth again, this time tinged with whatever junk food he'd downed with it the night before.

He turned and passed the bathroom on the way back to the living room. Seth had pulled himself up onto the love seat, his head on one arm and legs dangling over the other.

"He's not in there," Jake said.

Neither Seth nor Ryan offered any response. A vague memory of Andy's voice flittered around the back of Jake's head.

. . . *going upstairs to go to bed.*

But for some reason Jake didn't remember him doing that. Then again, did he have a single memory from last night that wasn't blurred by the booze?

Jake walked over to the stairs. The squeak from the old wood was a familiar sound, but it felt like knitting needles going into his ears as he climbed. He looked over the railing to the guys below and wondered if they would stay in that position all day.

There were two bedrooms on the second level, separated by a bathroom. All were on the left side, while the right was open and looked down on the living room. Jake held tight to the wooden railing, not trusting his rubbery legs to keep him upright.

He pushed open the door to the first bedroom. A king-size bed took up almost the entire room, leaving no space for furniture other than a small bedside table. It was so crowded that the door barely cleared the corner of the mattress when you opened it.

Andy lay face down among a swirl of blankets.

Jake opened his mouth to say something, then snapped it shut when a torrent of rum and BBQ chips made a run for the hatch. He clamped his hand firmly over his mouth and took two deep breaths through his nose with his eyelids squeezed shut. A wave of sweat crested over his skin, quickly chilling into goose bumps.

When Jake finally opened his eyes again, Andy had stirred. He hadn't left, and he was alive. Missing friend found, Jake backtracked out the door and down the steps.

The nausea had passed by the time he rejoined the guys in the living room, allowing his headache to retake center stage.

"Find him?" Ryan asked.

The sound of footsteps on the stairs answered before Jake had to say anything.

"Goddamn," Andy said, taking each step deliberately. He hit the bottom and walked over to the guys in a pair of pajama pants and a North Stars T-shirt. "How you guys doin'?"

"Fucking peachy," Seth said, not moving from the love seat. Without a place to sit, Andy stood in front of the coffee table.

"That was . . . an experience, huh?" Andy said.

"Probably," Ryan said. "Can't say I remember a whole lot of it."

"You guys don't remember anything?" Andy asked.

"I remember Seth saying he was going to swim down to the Dew Drop to get one of those frozen pizzas," Ryan said. He pushed himself up on the couch once again and looked over at Seth. "You didn't, did you?"

"God, I hope not."

"What about you, dude?" Andy laughed, but Jake couldn't imagine laughing ever again. He wanted to drink something to wash the taste of gas station bathroom floor from his mouth, but worried anything he ingested would come back up twice as fast as it went down.

"I don't know when I passed out, but I woke up here," Jake said. "Seth was puking in the bathroom—"

"*Allegedly*," Seth interjected, his finger pointed up in objection from the love seat.

"—and then I went and found you."

With the fog slowly clearing in his head, Jake realized something felt weird about Andy sleeping up in the king bed. That room had always been Grandma and Grandpa's bedroom. The first two nights, Andy had slept in the downstairs bedroom while Jake, Ryan, and Seth took the far bedroom on the second floor. Heck, even his parents left that one empty when they came up.

The thought brought back a hazy echo of Andy announcing to the group he was going to bed. "Why did you go upstairs?"

Andy looked back over his shoulder to the open hallway above. "I don't remember going up there at all. Like you guys, I must've been hammered. I just woke up when you came in."

"I mess my neck up passed out on this stupid couch while this guy goes up, puts freaking pajamas on, and gets into bed," Seth said. "That's a quality drunk right there."

"I'm lucky, I guess," Andy said. He stretched his arms above his head with a massive yawn. "Should we make some breakfast?"

Seth and Ryan both groaned. Jake couldn't fathom how Andy could even talk about food at this point. Like Seth said, everyone reacted differently, apparently. By the time Jake was able to pull himself off the couch and head into the kitchen, Andy already had a full pan of bacon on the stove and was whipping a bowl of eggs.

———

While initially unappealing, the smell of breakfast eventually pulled the boys from their hangover fog, and a layer of bacon and eggs settled their stomachs. The guys compared notes throughout the morning, doing their best to piece together the puzzle of the night before. The haze of alcohol made it impossible to get a clear picture, so they had to be content with the basics.

They drank. They passed out. They woke up.

Around noon Andy suggested they head down to the water, where the day was already shaping into a beautiful one. The sun was high in the sky, and an occasional cloud cut in front to keep the temperature from rising too much and give a little relief to hungover eyes.

They took the boat off the lift and tied it to the far side of the dock. Just sitting in the boat was enough. Jake wasn't ready for a trip around the lake yet. Seth and Ryan also seemed perfectly content to hang out on the boat, slightly bobbing with the waves while their insides recovered.

The low-key approach to the day didn't seem to appeal to Andy, who grabbed a fishing pole from the shed upstairs and sat at the end of the dock, toes in the water, repeatedly hooking crappies from a few feet out.

"This is crazy," he said, pulling in another. It wasn't what Jake's dad would have called a lunker, but it was a decent size for bobber fishing. "I've never caught fish like this in my life."

"They hang out under the dock," Jake said, stretched out in the front of the boat. Ryan lounged on the opposite side, while Seth lay across the bench in back. "It was awesome when I was a kid. Couldn't go ten seconds without a bite."

"Still can't." Andy dropped the crappie back into the water. The worm on his hook had been chewed down to a stump, but would probably still work with the feeding frenzy that was going on below. He plopped his hook back into the water and watched the tiny red-and-white bobber jerk under almost immediately. Andy let out a small whoop and pulled another crappie out of the lake.

"Crazy. You guys have to try this."

"I've caught enough fish sticks in my life, thanks," Seth said. "I'm good."

Andy twisted the hook out of the fish's mouth and released it into the water. His worm was officially gone, so he reached back for the light-blue Styrofoam container they had picked up at the Dew Drop the day before. He looked over at Jake.

"You ever catch anything big here?" Andy asked.

"Off the dock? Every now and then you can hook a bass or something, but you've got to cast by those weeds over there. You're not going to get anything under the dock but those little crappies and bluegills."

Jake thought back to when he was a kid, fishing down here with his cousins, when a northern pike had come by for a bite. It was a young one—nothing close to the one mounted on the wall in the cabin—but still the biggest fish any of them had ever seen. When that thing dove, it bent his kiddie pole well past what Jake had assumed was the breaking point. With no landing net, he'd grabbed a hold of the pole and held on while his cousin climbed into the boat lift and honked the horn until the adults showed up. There was a picture of them with the fish on the wall of Grandma and Grandpa's bedroom upstairs.

The bedroom Andy had ended up in last night.

"Hey, I think that cop is coming," Andy said.

Jake slid up along the backrest and saw the DNR boat coasting up to their dock again. It was the same woman who'd stopped them the other day, wearing the same mirrored sunglasses and ponytail.

Jake's queasy stomach did a flip.

What does she want?

They hadn't been out on the lake, and with the way he felt, he doubted they'd do more than float in the sun all day. They certainly weren't making any noise, thanks to the pounding still residing in the back of his skull.

Heck, even Seth had been quiet.

"Hello, boys," Officer Schroeder said as her boat crept toward them. Unlike last time, she killed the engine and allowed her patrol boat to slowly float in. "How are you all feeling today?"

Jake stood up while both Ryan and Seth straightened in their seats. The silver pontoons on their boat floated much higher in the water than the little DNR speedboat, so Jake actually looked down on the officer as she drifted in alongside them.

"Fine." He wanted to ask if there was a problem, but felt like an elementary school kid sent to the principal's office, so he let it stand at that.

"You have fun last night?"

Shit. Jake should have known that was what this was about. He didn't remember much, but the flashes he could recall were obnoxiously loud. Surrounded by trees, with no immediate neighbors, their cabin was fairly isolated—at least in comparison to others on the lake—but sound traveled well across the water. Especially on a quiet night when you are being anything but quiet.

"Oh my God, we're so sorry," Jake said. Seth and Ryan nodded along solemnly, while Andy had stood up from the dock and was leaning on the pole where their boat was tied. All shared his look of guilt and remorse. "We were just . . ."

. . . drunk off our asses on rum we paid a sketchy construction worker to buy us with money we took out of a drug lab?

"Being stupid," Andy jumped in. "Honestly, we were stupid. But I can promise you this, Officer Schroeder, if you knew how we felt right now, you'd know that there is absolutely zero chance of it happening again."

Schroeder held up her hand, cutting off any other excuse Andy might come up with. For the first time, Jake noticed a holstered sidearm on her hip. DNR officials spent the day checking fishing licenses and making sure people cleaned invasive weeds off their boat trailers before they left. He'd never seen one with a gun before.

"This is the Troe place, right?" she asked.

The mention of his grandparents' last name straightened Jake's spine. His parents would kill him if they found out about last night, but for some reason imagining Grandpa Charlie knowing was worse.

"You boys up here alone?"

Jake nodded.

"That's what I figured." Her boat had drifted close enough that it bumped up against the pontoon, making a hollow thud with every wave that passed underneath. "Is it just the four of you through the weekend? Nobody else coming up?"

"We're staying till Sunday," Jake said. "I think my aunt and uncle are coming up that afternoon, but we'll be gone by then."

Schroeder kept the stern look she seemed to put on with her uniform, but flashed a crooked front tooth as a smile cracked through the tough veneer. Like she was enjoying this. Talking tough with a group of teenagers was probably the highlight of her day.

"Okay, here's the deal—and I'm going to be crystal clear this time so there are no misunderstandings," she said. "You guys are going to keep things low key over here, all right? And I'm going to be keeping an eye on you boys, too, just to make sure you do. I don't want any more calls from this side of the lake. If there are, I'll be making a few calls myself, understand?"

Jake opened his mouth to answer, but Andy jumped in again.

"Not a problem, ma'am. Again, we're sorry about all that, but rest assured it will not happen again. You won't have any problems with us, that's for sure."

Officer Schroeder reached over and grabbed the rail of their pontoon boat. Using just one hand, she pushed away. Jake could see the muscles stretch in her forearm. It was impressive, although not surprising for someone who made her living outdoors.

Still standing, she reached down and hit the ignition. Her motor roared to life, and the water started to churn behind them.

"I'd keep that boat tied up right there the rest of your stay." Without waiting for an acknowledgment, she threw her boat in reverse and backed away from the dock. "And go to bed early tonight."

"Absolutely. No problem at all," Andy said.

Jake looked over at Andy standing at the end of the dock and was surprised to realize he wanted him to shut up. For some reason it no longer felt right that Andy was talking with the DNR lady, as if he hadn't always been the one to appoint himself the spokesman of the group when dealing with adults. And, really, he probably was the best to do it, because Andy's ability to sweet-talk older folks had been a useful skill for them in the past. But that nagging feeling that something was a bit off had burrowed deep into Jake's brain that morning and wasn't going anywhere.

Was he jealous because Andy was pulling away the controls that should be in Jake's hands since it was *his* family's cabin? Or was he anxious because he could barely remember anything from the previous night?

Jake shielded his eyes from the sun and watched as Schroeder turned her little gray boat back into the lake and gunned the engine. He shook the paranoia out of his head and let out a nervous breath as soon as she was out of earshot. "Okay then."

"I guess that's it for the boat," Seth said.

"Whatever," Ryan said. "I didn't really want to go out again anyway. I'm totally fine chilling here."

Jake watched the DNR boat head along the shore toward the Dew Drop. They had a lift over there where they kept their patrol boat. Lake traffic was starting to pick up—people getting an early jump on the weekend—so she was probably not docking anytime soon.

But as long as they didn't do anything stupid, they shouldn't have to deal with her anymore.

Hopefully not, anyway.

"Not to change the subject, but we're out of worms," Andy said. "I know she said not to use the boat, but is it cool if I take the Jet Ski over to the Dew Drop and get some?"

Jake took his eyes off the lake and looked back at the empty container by Andy's feet.

"Can you wait a little?" Jake figured it was probably a good idea to let Schroeder get something else in her mind before she saw one of them ripping across the lake on a Jet Ski.

Chapter Seventeen

The trepidation Krista should have felt from the minute she decided to pay a visit to Jake Nelson didn't appear until she turned onto the long rural driveway in the nowhere section of southern Minnesota. It was a quarter mile of gravel that cut down to sharp eight-foot ditches on each side. Broken, overgrown fields that looked like they hadn't been planted in years bracketed the driveway.

Her last-minute decision to join the travel party hadn't raised any suspicion with their executive assistant, Tom, although he'd repeatedly warned her she'd be getting a back-row middle seat.

Harry never asked her why she was coming with, which meant he knew enough not to. Krista wouldn't tell him specifically what she was doing anyway, preferring to keep a wall of deniability between the two in the event things went badly.

Getting away for the afternoon was easy. There were a million things a congressional chief of staff might need to do in their home district, so she picked the first excuse that came to mind and was off.

Her rental car kicked up a squirrel tail of dust as she sped toward the old farmhouse and served as a beacon announcing that company was coming. A dilapidated barn loomed on the west side of the property. As Krista approached, she could see the back half had collapsed on itself long ago, the roof sagging down over a jagged pile of rotted wood.

The driveway emptied out between the remains of the barn and the house, although it was hard to see where the gravel ended and the yard began. What grass was there was beaten down and brown, randomly sprouting up from the hard-packed dirt like spots of acne.

The only difference between the house and the barn was that the house hadn't collapsed—but it looked like that was simply a matter of time. There was more exposed wood than paint on the outside, and the shingles remaining on the roof looked like they were held down with chewing gum and duct tape.

Krista pulled up next to an old green Ford pickup that was losing a war against rust and put her white Nissan Altima into park. She killed the ignition and sat for a second, breathing in whatever pungent chemical Enterprise used to spray down their cars between renters.

She looked over at the collapsed barn. A few boards stuck up around the fallen roof, making it look a bit like a twisted alligator with an underbite.

Krista shook the nerves out of her head and popped the door open. She'd barely pulled herself from behind the wheel when a voice cut across the yard.

"Can I help you?"

Krista startled. She looked across the roof of her rental at a short man standing with his hand on the aluminum screen door. He had one foot on the ground and the other back on an improvised step made from cinder blocks and a scrap of wood.

"Hi . . . yes . . . Jake Nelson?"

The silence of the countryside hung between them for a second before he answered.

"Who's asking?"

She paused before answering, taking in how alone she was and giving common sense one last chance to convince her to get back in her car and drive away. She'd debated how to approach this since she'd hung up with Seth Meloy two days earlier. If Jake was the guy sending the letters, he probably wouldn't appreciate a visit from one of Harry's staff.

But if it was him, he'd already written to a newspaper. That said he was willing to talk—to a reporter at least.

"My name is Krista, and I'm working on something about Harrison Leonard." It was all true, technically. "You grew up with him, right?"

The bang of the screen door snapping shut answered her question. She stood behind her rental car, waiting to see if he'd return.

After a minute of silence, Krista shut the door and walked around the hood of her car to the house. Her forearm picked up a swath of dust from the car, and she brushed it off, along with any concerns of what could happen to a woman alone with a strange man in the middle of nowhere.

She noticed a pair of holes in the screen big enough for a bird to fly through as she knocked on the metal frame. A small Formica table piled with days' worth of used dishes sat across the room, while the rest of the week's supply was piled in the sink.

Jake reappeared from the back of the house and made his way across the kitchen to the door. The look on his face said he wasn't interested in talking through the screen, just closing the wooden interior door in her face.

"I only have a few questions, and I'd really like to hear what you have to say," she said. "May I come in?"

Jake met her eyes through the screen and blinked rapidly. With his thinning hair and weathered skin, Krista never would have guessed he'd graduated in the same class as Harry.

The cold sweat of worry was still on her back as Jake stepped forward and pushed the screen door open. He beckoned her into his house with a silent nod.

———

Krista sat on the edge of a ratty couch in Jake's living room, amazed that a place could be so empty, yet so messy at the same time. Jake Nelson was in a recliner across the room. An upside-down cardboard box served as an end table next to it, holding an ashtray and a half dozen empty beer cans. A large picture window loomed behind him. It was coated in a dingy film built up from years of discount cigarette smoke. It gave the sunlight that filtered through an odd yellow tint.

Krista studied the short, unkempt man across the room. He hadn't said anything since ushering her into the house. Everything about the situation should have set off alarm bells. If one of Krista's friends told her she was planning on visiting a potentially unstable stranger in his run-down house alone in the middle of nowhere under false pretenses, she'd have tied them down to prevent it.

But despite all logic, Krista didn't get a dangerous vibe from Jake Nelson.

She pulled a digital recorder from her pocket—the same type reporters favored.

"You mind if I record this?"

He shook his head and squeezed his eyes shut briefly. She checked that the little red light was on and placed it on the arm of the couch, microphone pointed at Jake.

"How do you know Harrison Leonard?"

"He was Andy back then. Moved to Ranford in fourth grade. I don't remember how he started hanging out with us. It was like he just . . . belonged. He completed the group." Jake took a hesitant breath before continuing. "We did everything together. Me, Andy, Ryan, and Seth. Baseball, basketball, track—it was a small school, so you didn't have to try out or anything. Debate . . . Andy somehow talked us into doing debate."

Krista put out a genial chuckle. "He talk you guys into a lot of stuff back then?"

A half smile tugged the left side of Jake's mouth, but it didn't reach his eyes.

"He could charm anyone, get you to do anything."

Jake talked about his past for a while, slinging random stories about their group of friends. Most of it was inconsequential, but Krista let him go. Either he worked his way to something legitimately significant or he would ramble for twenty minutes and prove he was nothing but a disgruntled guy nursing a heavy grudge against his past.

It wasn't until he started telling stories about Harry's father being a drunk that she perked up.

"I didn't realize his father was that much of a drinker."

Jake gave her the smug, know-it-all look favored by teachers and three-year-olds. "That's because he didn't want you to know. It would change the way people looked at him, and Andy cared about that more than anything. We knew, of course, but we never mentioned it. His dad was constantly fucked up. Andy stayed away from home as much as he could because of it. He was always at my house or Seth's or Ryan's. Course the rest of us were always there, too, so whatever."

The possibility that there was something she didn't know about Harry was disconcerting. The fact that his parents had died in a Christmas house fire was public knowledge, but not something their campaign dwelled on. Harry didn't talk about them much, and Krista didn't want to seem like she was exploiting his tragedy for sympathy. At this point in his career, they were nothing more than characters in a story about a *lower-middle-class family of limited means* from which Harrison Leonard emerged.

"Was he abusive with the congressman?"

"Can't say I ever saw him hit him or anything, but he was damn nasty," Jake said. "One of those guys that could make the pope hate him, you know? We all knew enough to stay out of his way."

She couldn't believe Harry never would have mentioned a history of abuse—alcohol or otherwise. But that's assuming there actually *was* one and Jake Nelson wasn't just pulling delusions from the past.

"But boy, Andy hated him." Jake leaned back in his chair. "Never talked about it, but you could tell. I always figured that's why he was so obsessed with getting away from Ranford. Ended up at college all the way out East and all. I never thought I'd see him again, to be honest, and that was damn fine with me. Then there he is on the news."

"You hadn't heard he'd been elected?"

"I don't pay any attention to the mainstream media, 'cause that shit's all lies anyway. And even if I did, he ain't even going by his real name anymore, so what's *that* tell ya about him? Huh?" Jake stared at Krista long enough she thought he expected an answer before plowing ahead. "Anyway, one day I see him shaking hands with some people, and everyone is taking pictures of it and all like he's some big hero. All these great things he's doing for everyone . . . it's everything he always wanted. He gets to do what he wants the way he wants it. He's the boss, and everyone loves him for it."

Krista wasn't sure Jake Nelson understood how Congress worked, but she wasn't about to contradict him on how much power a freshman representative had—even a fast-rising political star like Harry.

"You seem to have a problem with that."

Jake let out a clipped laugh as his eyes quickly blinked twice, then one more time. Krista had noticed him blinking enough to realize it wasn't the dusty room, but probably a nervous tic. He leaned forward, propped his elbows on his knees, and sent a steely glare across the room.

"I *know* what he is. He's the nicest guy in the room. He's your best friend, as long as he gets what he wants. As long as things go according to *his* plan. But I've seen what's behind all that charm—what comes out when nobody's watching. What he'll do to get what he thinks he deserves. He'll leave you behind without thinking twice."

Krista held his gaze, considering her next move. It was obvious from the stories Jake told that he and Harry had been close friends once, but some of the stuff he was saying didn't fit with the Harry she had dedicated her career to at all. Jake was probably annoyed, and perhaps jealous, at the success of a guy who had been able to break free of their small-town orbit, but that didn't make him dangerous.

It also didn't mean he was sending threatening postcards. If she wanted to get answers, she needed to be more direct.

"What can you tell me about Cedar Lake?"

Chapter Eighteen

Jake lay on the narrow mattress of his twin bed, staring at the weird pattern of moonlight filtering through the blinds. It's amazing how quiet a lake house can be at 1:37 in the morning. An all-encompassing silence, almost a noise unto itself.

Ryan and Seth slept in the bunk beds across the room, while Andy was once again down the hall in Grandma and Grandpa's room. Jake still couldn't put a finger on why it bothered him so much, but it felt wrong.

With what he put his body through the night before, Jake should have been asleep long ago. Yet there he was, staring at the shadowed shapes on the ceiling and listening to the overwhelming nothingness of the lake.

The silence took him back to the island. The darkness of that tower, the shadows somehow able to make regular household chemicals seem menacing. It'd been at least thirty-six hours since they'd left it behind, but Jake couldn't get out of that abandoned house. He just couldn't shake the paranoia they'd be found out. The guys were right, it wasn't like they'd left any way to identify themselves—but logic took a back seat in the middle of the night.

Jake rolled onto his side and looked at the little red numbers glowing out from atop the dresser.

1:38 a.m.

He took a deep breath, pushed his covers off, and sat up on the side of the bed. There was no sense in lying here for hours, obsessing about every little bump in the night.

The wooden floor was cold on his feet as he stood up and quietly padded across the room, careful not to disturb Ryan and Seth. The latch on the old door made a metallic snap as he pulled it up, and the hinges squeaked when they opened.

Neither of his friends stirred.

It was brighter outside the bedroom. The large front windows in the living room below were uncovered, letting in a good amount of moonlight. Between that and the fact that Jake's eyes had adjusted from staring around a dark room for the past few hours, he could see just fine.

He walked down the hallway, stopping briefly to listen in at the door to his grandparents' room.

Nothing beyond Andy's light snoring.

He descended the stairs, familiar creaks bouncing around the vaulted ceiling above the open living room. At the base of the steps, a menacing figure loomed in the shadows near the front door.

Jake froze, his bare foot hovering between steps as his hand clamped down on the railing.

It took his brain a few seconds to realize it was just the coatrack.

He examined it as he stepped off the last step, amazed at how his imagination could turn two hoodies and a windbreaker hanging on a wooden pole into a masked serial killer. Logic didn't prevent him from taking the head off the serial killer by pulling one of the hoodies off the coatrack and tossing it over the handrail behind him.

Jake reached out and tested the knob on his way by the front door, even though he remembered locking it before heading up to bed. A flash of light caught his eye from across the room. The lure dangling from the toothy maw of his grandpa's northern practically glowed in the moonlight coming through the front window.

He stared at the fish from across the room. Its sharp fangs were intimidating enough, but what had always disturbed Jake more were the rows of needlelike teeth that lined the top of its mouth, currently hidden in the shadows. Hundreds of little daggers, all pointing inward. Any unsuspecting fish who found themselves in those jaws had no chance. Northern pike had evolved as a perfect hunter—the apex predator of Cedar Lake.

Jake shook the thought from his head and crossed the edge of the living room and into the kitchen, hoping a glass of juice might help reset his system so he could make another try at some sleep.

He considered flipping the light on as he entered the kitchen, but the moon was bright enough he didn't bother. Probably for the best, as a huge fluorescent bulb would certainly wake him even more.

The four glasses they'd been using that day sat on the island countertop where Andy had served as bartender the night before—just the thought brought back ghosts of the hangover he'd spent all day getting rid of—but Jake had no idea which was his and opted for a fresh one out of the cupboard. The curtains on the window over the sink were open, and Jake stared blankly out the side of the cabin as he reached for his glass. A flurry of motion in the trees to the right caught his eye. He leaned over the sink to get a better angle and was instantly paralyzed by what he saw. It wasn't a coatrack this time, as much as he wanted it to be.

Two men had stepped out of the trees and were approaching the cabin.

Jake crouched down over the sink but kept his eyes close to the window. Although dressed in dark clothes with black stocking caps, the men were easy to see. The moonlight flashed briefly on the guns in their hands as they crept across the yard and rounded the corner toward the screened-in porch in back.

Jake pushed away from the sink and kept low. Around the corner of the island countertop was a door to the porch, its top half made of glass. Between that and the long window to its right, he could see almost the entire porch from the kitchen.

Which meant anyone out there could see in.

The two men reemerged near the porch's screen door. Jake watched from behind the counter as one pulled out a box cutter, sliced open the screen near the handle, and reached in to flip the little hook that served as a very ineffective lock.

They were coming in.

Jake backed along the countertop, still crouching, trying to stay as invisible as possible. He saw the top of the screen door swing out and knew they'd gotten into the porch.

But they couldn't get in the cabin, right? The door onto the porch was easy to cut through, but the one leading to the kitchen was made of wood and glass.

They won't break the glass and risk waking everyone up. No way. They can't get through, and they'll have to go away go away go away—dear God make them go away . . .

These thoughts bolted through Jake's head as he peered around the counter. It was dark, but he could see the reflection of the brass bolt that sat unlocked above the door handle.

The one they'd forgotten to secure before going to bed.

Jake had to move. Dark or not, they were going to notice an eighteen-year-old boy rolled up in a ball behind the counter. He had to warn the guys.

Or maybe that would be worse. Maybe if he stayed quiet and the guys slept through it, the men would just take the TV and DVD player and be on their way.

But these guys aren't burglars.

Even if half his brain was in denial, Jake knew what these guys were and where they were from.

They couldn't be anyone else.

He had to do something, and time was rapidly running out. The two guys had crossed the porch and were standing outside the kitchen door. It would be a matter of seconds before they realized it was unlocked.

Crawling on all fours, Jake bolted from behind the counter and headed back toward the living room. He heard the doorknob twist behind him and realized it was too late to get upstairs. With no other options, he dove into the downstairs bathroom between the kitchen and living room. He briefly considered getting into the tub but realized pulling the shower curtain aside would make enough noise to alert the intruders. He stood up and slid behind the open door.

Jake's field of vision was limited to the small crack where the hinges opened. He didn't dare get too close and risk being seen, so his view was nothing more than the short hall outside and a sliver of the living room.

Soft footsteps shuffled across the kitchen as Jake desperately fought to control his breathing.

A muffled whisper broke the quiet.

"Over there."

The steps faded a bit before the sound of a door opening creaked through the dark—then quiet. It lasted longer than Jake could have imagined, but in reality was nothing more than a few seconds.

"Nothing."

It was the downstairs bedroom that Jake wished Andy had slept in.

They're looking for us.

"Upstairs."

As the footsteps got closer, Jake clamped his eyes shut and pushed his back into the wall, trying to disappear so they couldn't find him. Sweat beaded up on his forehead as he refused to breathe. He opened his eyes in time to see two shapes pass by his little window. The first guy glanced into the bathroom on the way past, and Jake saw the black face of a nightmare. Dark lines ran up and down his whole head, with white circling his eyes.

The second guy walked by with an identical face. The black caps he'd seen them wearing outside must have been snowmobile masks, which they'd pulled down to obscure their faces.

The two left Jake's narrow field of vision and continued into the living room. A few seconds later Jake heard the familiar squeak of the wooden stairs.

They were going after the guys.

I'm too late.

There was no way to warn his friends, but he had to do something. Jake listened to the footsteps climb the stairs as he mentally ran through every rescue scenario he could think of. There were no guns in the house, aside from a BB gun, and the odds of faking anyone out with that old Red Ryder were slim. Even if there were weapons available, the cocktail of fear and adrenaline coursing through his veins gave Jake a new appreciation of the unrealistic nature of every action movie he'd ever seen. As surreal as it seemed, this was real life, and he barely trusted himself to stand silently, let alone pick off a pair of intruders.

An image invaded his head of Seth hanging half-off the top bunk, his blood dripping down onto Ryan, who lay below with a quarter-size hole between his eyes.

He had to get help. Call the cops.

The phone was just around the corner in the kitchen. It was a relic, mustard yellow with a ten-foot cord and a rotary dial. But it worked.

They'll hear you.

With the silence of night filling the house, there was no way to make a call without the two guys upstairs hearing the whole thing.

And then they'll come get you.

But he had to do something. If he was quick, maybe he could get through the woods to the neighbors' house.

Assuming they're even there.

Even if they weren't, maybe he could get in and use their phone. And if that didn't work, he could go to the next cabin or the one after that. Hell, he'd go all the way down to the Dew Drop if he had to.

He had to get help.

Footsteps trod across the ceiling above him, and Jake knew if he wanted to get out, now was the time. He took a deep breath and slid out from his hiding place. He slipped out of the bathroom and padded across the kitchen to where the door to the screened-in porch was still open. The squeak of a bedroom door came from above as Jake ducked out onto the porch. He forced himself to leave it behind and quickly crossed the old wooden boards, pushed the unlocked screen door open, and stepped out into the night.

The air was still and unnaturally quiet, as if even the crickets and loons were tucked away in bed. No other sounds came from the bedroom windows above him, which was a good sign.

Jake looked at the thicket of trees that separated the cabin from its nearest neighbor. All those fallen branches and pine needles would extract a heavy toll on his bare feet if he tried to run through there. He could avoid it, however, if he went down to the water and followed the shore to their dock, then took the stairs up.

It'd be much easier, and probably quicker.

He bounded down the stairs, balancing quickness with quiet despite the fact there was no chance anyone upstairs would hear him all the way down here.

Jake reached the bottom of the steps and hopped down to the shoreline. A small stretch of large rocks kept the soil on the bank from washing away. When the water was high, the waves lapped up against them, but there hadn't been much rain that summer, and a thin strip of sand ran along the shore. Lake water squished up between Jake's toes, then ran over them as a small wave rolled in.

He was barely a step away from the dock when he noticed a set of lights out on the lake.

A boat.

The lake gently lashed at Jake's ankles as he stared at the glowing spots slowly gliding along in the distance. One shone both red and green, the other white. Both were on a slow trajectory in his direction.

Neighboring cabin forgotten, Jake jumped back on the dock and ran to the end, waving his arms in the darkness. The moon hung high overhead, casting a decent amount of light on the lake, but he had no idea if the boater could see him. Jake was dying to shout but was terrified whoever was back in the cabin would hear.

He continued waving, jumping up and down in a desperate attempt to catch the boater's eye as the vessel kept slowly gliding across the lake.

Jake looked over his shoulder at the cabin. The upstairs windows were still dark, but no shouts—*or gunshots*—had rung out yet.

"Help," Jake said. Not a shout. Nothing more than normal conversational volume. Sound traveled well across the water. Just the other night he and the boys had been marveling at how they could hear an entire conversation between a pair of boaters taking a cruise under the stars.

Of course, if they had heard the boaters from the screened-in porch, whoever was upstairs would be able to hear him now.

"Please, help." Louder this time, but still nothing approaching a yell. He tried to make up for his lack of volume with extensive waving and jumping up and down. Whoever was on that boat might not hear him over the engine, but they *had* to notice him frantically waving them in.

The lights crept closer, and Jake realized he had to do something quick if he was going to catch this guy's attention. He opened his mouth to give a quick shout, but was cut off by the sound of the boat's motor roaring to life. The lights changed course and made a beeline for the dock.

Jake jumped up and down even higher, frantically waving his arms above his head even though the boat had obviously seen him. He glanced at the dark cabin again, then back to the rapidly approaching boat. As it got closer, Jake could make out the shape of a small speedboat. The red and green lights were on the tip of the bow, while the white one was atop a pole sticking up from the back. Between the two was the harsh silhouette of a woman with a familiar-looking ponytail. He recognized Officer Schroeder at the same time her boat got close enough to make out the unmarked hull.

Relief flooded his veins as she skimmed over the water toward him. Jake couldn't believe his luck that the DNR boat just happened to be out this late, right in front of their cabin.

But it wasn't luck, of course. Schroeder said she would be keeping an eye on them after the ruckus they'd kicked up the night before, and there she was.

Who said nothing good comes from underage drinking?

Officer Schroeder killed her engine and expertly glided her boat alongside the dock.

The euphoria of seeing her kicked even more adrenaline into Jake's system, causing his words to come out in a rapid-fire whisper the woman had no hope of understanding.

She tossed a rope over to Jake, who fumbled it off his chest and flailed as it fell to his feet.

"What the hell's going on?" she asked as Jake snatched the rope off the dock and slung it over the nearest pole. He looped the rope around three times and again attempted to relay the situation.

"Calm down," Schroeder said, knocking Jake's offered hand aside and stepping over the side rail of her boat onto the dock. "What's wrong?"

Jake tried to take a calming breath, but the words bubbled up too fast to hold back.

"Two guys upstairs. They've got guns and masks, and my friends are still up there, and you gotta help them. Please, hurry. Please."

Schroeder's expression didn't change as she looked up toward the cabin. She exuded a concerned calm that helped Jake get himself in order. She might not have been a cop, but that didn't matter. She was authority.

"They still in the house?"

"Yeah," Jake said. "I mean, I think so. They were upstairs when I got out and came down here."

"How did you get down here?" she asked.

"I was down in the kitchen getting a drink," Jake pleaded, suddenly worried that she thought this was some stupid prank. "Saw them in the yard. They cut a hole in the screen. I hid in the bathroom when they came in and ran out the back when they went upstairs. Seriously, my friends are still in there. You've *GOT* to help them." His voice was getting louder. He wasn't as worried about being heard anymore. Help had arrived.

"Show me." Officer Schroeder stepped past Jake and made her way down the dock. He noticed as he followed that she wasn't wearing her patrol uniform, but her gun was still holstered on her hip, which gave Jake a lot of comfort.

"They've got guns," Jake whispered after her. She raised her right hand in acknowledgment but kept her sidearm holstered.

Jake jogged down the dock to catch up —scared to go back up the stairs but more afraid to be left alone. This woman was safety, and he wanted to stay under her umbrella.

She didn't seem afraid, striding up the stairs with purpose. Her confident presence was comforting, but also slightly disconcerting. Jake worried he hadn't accurately relayed the danger of the situation to her— or that she didn't believe him.

Jake wondered if she should have called for backup before approaching the cabin. She certainly had the look and temperament of someone who could handle herself—but she was still just a conservation officer. Her job was checking fishing licenses and patrolling the water. Gunfights and potential hostage situations were not the domain of the Minnesota Department of Natural Resources.

But she had an aura of authority and a gun on her hip, which was enough for Jake.

Most important, she was *here now.*

Halfway up the steps, Jake noticed a few cracks of light seeping out from between the blinds of the far window. It was the room he'd left Ryan and Seth in, and the light was on.

He reached ahead and tugged on the officer's shirt. She looked back with a scowl, and Jake pointed up at the window.

"That's where they are," he whispered, again afraid of drawing any attention from the cabin. "They were asleep when I left."

The officer's eyes squinted as she looked up to the window.

"How many?"

"Two of us were in there after I left . . . Andy was sleeping down the hall, but I thought I heard them opening the door when I was going out." Jake pointed up at the window on the near side. "But his window is still dark, so maybe they took him down the hall? I don't know."

Jake hoped they'd taken Andy down the hall to Seth and Ryan's room. Then he'd still be okay. He didn't want to think about the alternative.

They resumed their climb. Jake expected another stop at the porch door, a few more questions, and a final plan. Maybe a call into the police or a radio into DNR headquarters for some backup. At the very least, a deep breath as she drew her gun and a strict directive—*Stay here. Don't move. If I'm not back in this amount of time, do this and call these people, and whatever you do, don't do this.*

Instead, she climbed the last few steps, opened the screen door, and walked into the porch like she was coming home from a day on the lake. Jake jumped ahead and made a grab for the screen door as it swung closed. He got his fingers on the doorjamb as it snapped shut, preventing a loud bang but sending a jolt of pain up his arm.

Jake stifled a yelp and used his other hand to yank the door open. He pulled his throbbing fingers back into his midsection and elbowed his way through the door, trying to squeeze the pain out of his hand while not letting the screen door snap shut behind him with a revealing crack.

Schroeder was already through the open kitchen door and into the cabin when Jake hustled up behind her. She'd stopped in the middle of the kitchen, head cocked toward the ceiling.

Jake couldn't hear anything above them, and the quiet was disconcerting.

"Stairs are over there," Jake said in an almost inaudible whisper. He pointed through the kitchen into the living room, where the stairs were. She followed his direction. Unsure what to do and unwilling to stand alone in the dark cabin, Jake trailed her. It wasn't until they'd reached the bottom of the staircase that he realized he should probably hang back. Who knew what was going to happen upstairs? Jake thought she'd bust in with her gun drawn and keep it on them until the real cops came, and they'd all live happily ever after.

But what if she doesn't surprise them?

What if they start shooting?

What if they kill my friends in the chaos?

What if a stray bullet finds a home right between my eyes?

Those questions nailed Jake's feet to the floor as Schroeder started up the steps. She'd only climbed four when she turned around and faced him. There was just enough light in the room to make out her motion to follow.

Jake hesitated, torn between his fear of what was upstairs and the unease he would certainly feel standing in the dark living room while God-knows-what happened upstairs. In the end, obedience to authority won out, and he warily climbed onto the first step.

A familiar creak from the second step echoed through the room and gave him temporary pause. Schroeder nodded above him, imploring him onward. Jake resumed his climb, treading as lightly as possible to avoid the inevitable squeals of the old wood.

She waited atop the stairs for Jake to join her. The door to Andy's—*Grandma and Grandpa's*—room was open in front of them. Schroeder took a quick look inside before pulling back and shaking her head.

A strip of light outlined the bottom of the bedroom door at the end of the hall, and a few vertical streaks peeked out between the boards. Jake motioned to it and mouthed the words *in there*, even though it was too dark for lipreading and she wasn't looking at him anyway.

A burst of muffled speech drifted through the door and down the hall, barely loud enough for Jake to hear over his pounding heart.

"What the hell is going on in there?" The shock of Schroeder's voice in the silent dark sent a jolt of fear through Jake. She started down the hall, reaching back for enough of Jake's T-shirt to drag him along beside her. Panic made him grab at the railing, but a hard tug pushed him in front of the officer as she walked down the hallway.

"What are you doing?" Jake's voice remained strangled, despite their cover having been obviously blown. The only answer was more prodding.

Jake stared at the glowing streaks of light as they closed in on the door. She hadn't believed him after all, and now they were all going to pay. He couldn't help but wonder what it felt like to be shot. Books always described it as a hot poker tearing through your flesh, and that didn't seem like anything he was anxious to confirm.

A pair of feet made two dark breaks in the line of light under the door. Jake pushed back into the extended arm of the woman he'd hoped would save them all but was now herding him to his death.

"I'm opening the door," Schroeder announced. "Don't do anything stupid."

The snap of the door latch was louder this time—like a gunshot—and caused Jake to wince. He braced for responding shots to explode through the wood in a hail of splinters and lead. Schroeder pushed the door open, and light spilled out onto them and into the hallway, courtesy of the small bedside lamp on the dresser. Jake squinted and tried to take in the scene in front of him.

Seth, Ryan, and Andy sat on the bed Jake had abandoned just minutes before, all in the shorts-and-T-shirt combos they had worn to bed.

The intruders stood in front of them with guns leveled. Both still wore the dark snowmobile masks he'd seen from behind the bathroom door. In the light, he could see they were navy blue, not black, and their black clothes looked worn and faded. The nearest guy wore a tattered hoodie that draped loosely over his skinny frame. The other was the same height but at least a hundred pounds heavier. A long-sleeved black shirt stretched tight over his generous belly.

"What the fuck is going on here?" Schroeder's voice was amazingly calm for a conservation officer who'd just walked in on a pair of armed intruders holding three teenagers hostage. Like she would be able to scold the two guys into throwing down their guns and walking out with their sincerest apologies.

The guy in the hoodie wore a mask with a single large hole for the top half of his face instead of individual eyeholes, so his expression was easier to read than the other's. His gray eyes showed concern, but not the level of fear one would expect when busted by a law officer.

"I found this kid down on the fucking dock." Schroeder shoved Jake into the middle of the room. He stumbled toward his friends, fighting to keep his feet and not crash into the barrel of a gun. Jake's fear was preventing him from processing the reality of the situation.

He still thought the officer was help.

Chapter Nineteen

Krista listened from her perch on the edge of Jake's threadbare couch as he bounced back and forth in a befuddling and rambling rehash of the four boys' postgraduation trip to his family cabin.

It could have even been entertaining had it not been so disturbing.

She sat, playing the role of an objective journalist, as Jake blinked through tales of drug labs, masked intruders, and teenagers being held at gunpoint. She often wanted to interject for clarification, but before she could ask anything, Jake had moved on to something even more unthinkable. It was all impossible to believe, and Krista's head was buzzing with thousands of questions. Unfortunately, she had no confidence in any answers she might get.

Jake stopped his story and eyed Krista from across the room, where she fought to keep a neutral expression.

"You don't believe me, do you?"

Krista honestly didn't know what she thought—whether Jake was inventing crazy stories to hurt Harry's career or if he was truly delusional.

And she didn't know which was worse.

"Okay, here's my issue. You can't get elected without people going through your past with a fine-tooth comb. Representative Leonard's past has been vetted countless times, and nothing like this came up." Krista glanced down at the tiny red light on the little digital recorder between them and remembered she was supposed to be a journalist, not

Harry's chief of staff. "But I looked into this before I came out here, and there *was* a big drug bust on Cedar Lake, but nothing mentioned rogue DNR officials running drug cartels or anything like that. Even if you guys never said anything, the cops certainly would've figured out who was running things out there, and it would've been all over the news, right?"

He looked at her with the mix of disappointment and condescension that conspiracy theorists have perfected over the years.

"The DNR covered it all up."

Krista couldn't keep the doubt from her voice.

"The *Department of Natural Resources* covered it up?" She thought back to her elementary school days, when an old guy in a khaki shirt would come to their class once a year to teach them about water conservation or how to dissect owl pellets. His name was Roger or Rick or some other name that paired with *Ranger*, and he always had a bushy mustache that made him look like a walrus.

The DNR was many things, but an organization capable of operating and covering up a drug ring was not one of them.

Jake's eyes narrowed, and he leaned forward. Krista could smell the beer on his breath.

"This shit happens all the time. These fucking cops, politicians, guys like Andy . . . fucking evil. They don't ever want anyone to know what they're really up to, so they cover it all up. Kennedy, 9/11, that thing with the pizza shop . . ." He jabbed a shaky finger at her. "You're gonna tell me the kind of people who do that shit can't cover up a little drug lab in Minnesota? Don't be naive."

Krista slowly looked around the room, now convinced she would see a tinfoil hat in the corner. This guy was obviously disconnected from reality, which would work for her. A conspiracy theorist would be easy to discredit if she couldn't convince him to stay quiet.

"Okay, so even if the DNR covered up their"—Krista had a hard time keeping the skepticism out of her voice but couldn't allow Jake to think she was dismissing him—"involvement with the drug lab . . .

you said two men broke into your family's cabin and held you and your friends at gunpoint. Did you not call the police after they left? Tell your parents? Even if you didn't, I don't see how a story like that stays hidden, especially when one of those kids ends up in—"

Jake held up his hand. Krista assumed he was cutting her off, but realized he was showing her his palm. She peered across the room and saw a thin white line among the natural creases.

"What is that?"

"Andy's idea," Jake said. "He made us take a blood oath, to never say a word. Stupid kid stuff, right? But it worked, because nobody ever said a word."

Jake trailed off for a second, and the silence filled the room. Krista glanced down at the little red light on her recorder.

"All I ever wanted was to forget about the whole thing, but every time I wash my hands, it all comes flooding back," he said. "I've done everything I could to erase the memory of that trip, but I can't because of this fucking scar. Because of *him*."

Krista leaned forward and stared at the scar on Jake's hand. It cut straight across the center of his palm, ending in a jagged spot across from his thumb. Or maybe that's where he'd started the cut—hesitating after initially going too deep—before quickly drawing it across his palm. Krista thought of a teenage boy doing that to himself and felt like a drop of ice water was sliding down her spine.

Or he's full of shit and sliced himself opening a package from Amazon.

Krista had worked alongside Andrew Harrison Leonard for years. She'd sat with him and crafted his official bio, listened as he gave countless interviews, and had hours of deep conversations driving rental cars across Minnesota. If there was anything Krista was confident about, it was the fact that she knew every minute detail of her boss's past. There was no way he could have hidden this from her.

But Harry never said his dad was an alcoholic.

If he was an alcoholic, and with the stories Jake was peddling, that's a big *if.*

Krista didn't realize she was staring until Jake spoke again.

"You still don't believe me."

She tried to flush the skepticism from her face and keep a neutral tone. The last thing she wanted to do was provoke a delusional guy with a grudge.

"It's not that, but why would the congressman not want to report it to the police?"

Chapter Twenty

"He wasn't here when we came in," the guy in the hoodie said. His voice was muffled by the mask, but his eyes shone through the one long hole up top. "It was just these three."

"That's what we were asking them," the other said, absentmindedly sweeping his gun past the bed as he spoke. "'Cause you said there was supposed to be four."

"You're goddamn lucky I was out there." Schroeder's anger was palpable as she stepped into the room and pushed Jake onto the bed. "Sit down."

Jake half fell onto the edge of the mattress next to Ryan, whose confused look was transitioning back to fear.

"They didn't—"

"Shut up," Schroeder said. Unlike her underlings, she wasn't dressed in dark colors but a pair of faded jeans and a blue T-shirt. The scuffed leather belt she wore for work was pulled around her waist, the black handle of her gun jutting from the holster on her hip. A pair of handcuffs and a small canister of pepper spray were attached to the opposite side. Her dark, piercing eyes gave the boys the same stare she had leveled on them the day before, down on the dock.

"They give it up yet?"

"Nope. We didn't know if we should look for the money or the other kid first."

The woman Jake had hoped would be his savior turned back on them and pulled out her gun. She held it nonchalantly in front of her, the way their biology teacher would absentmindedly carry a ruler when he addressed the class. She gestured with the gun as she spoke.

"We're going to ask you some questions, and I want you to answer me quickly and, most importantly, truthfully. Understand?"

The boys stared at her blankly. Every bit of paranoia Jake had felt about their trip to the island flooded back into his head like a terrifying *I Told You So*. His mouth was so dry he couldn't have answered even if his brain had been able to form a coherent thought amid all the fear.

Schroeder raised her hand and pressed the muzzle of her gun against Ryan's forehead.

"Where's my money?"

Jake was shocked to feel his hand wanting to reach up and knock the gun away. He clamped down on that reaction before it turned into anything more than a flinch.

Schroeder pulled the gun back. It left a small circle indented between Ryan's terrified eyes. She wasn't a tall woman but still loomed over the boys lined up on the edge of the mattress. Her two henchmen had fallen in behind her to make an intimidating wall, backlit by the tiny lamp.

"I swear to fucking Christ we didn't know it was yours." The words burst from Seth like water from a busted dike, his voice on the verge of a full-fledged freak-out. "It was stupid, and we're so, so sorry."

Schroeder stepped over to Seth, gun at her side but seemingly itching to plant a bullet between his eyes.

"Where is it?"

She gave Seth a second to answer, but he chose to look at Andy first. Schroeder rolled her eyes and nodded back at the big guy. With surprising quickness, he lunged past her and grabbed Seth by the neck. The boy squealed as he pulled him off the end of the bed with the same ease Andy had pulled crappies from under the dock only a few hours earlier. The big guy slammed Seth back into the wall, sending a family picture clattering to the floor.

Seth's eyes bulged with fear as his face rapidly reddened and his feet fought to stay on the ground.

"Where is it?"

A wet cough was all he could manage.

Before his brain could stop him, Jake's legs pushed him up off the bed. He wasn't even fully to his feet when Schroeder planted a stiff left arm in his sternum, sending him back onto the mattress. She was on top of him before his chest registered the pain—right knee on the mattress between his legs, left hand full of his hair, and the barrel of her gun pressed into his right eye so hard that purple flashes swirled on the backs of his eyelids.

Jake could feel Ryan frozen on the bed next to him, while Seth gagged a few feet away.

"Apparently we weren't clear." Schroeder's voice had lost the eerie calm and picked up an edge that could cut through a tin can. "There will be no more fucking around."

She ground her gun into Jake's eye socket, coaxing a pained groan from between his clenched teeth, and looked over at Ryan.

"You have one minute to bring me the money you took." She didn't say what would happen if he didn't comply, but she didn't need to. The point had been made.

Ryan stood up without breaking eye contact or making any movements that could be misconstrued as a threat. He paused on his feet to put his hands up in front of him when Andy's voice interjected from behind.

"It's right—" He was cut off with a yelp when the skinny guy's gun slammed against his temple. Schroeder kept her own pressed into Jake's eye as her glare jerked over to Andy.

"I'm not talking to you. Believe me, you'll know when I want to hear from you. Until then, if I hear your voice again, I will put a bullet between your eyes. Understand?" She didn't wait for a response before returning her attention to Ryan. "That wasted about twenty seconds, so I would suggest hurrying."

Ryan nodded at the dresser on the far wall. "Top drawer."

Schroeder didn't move from atop Jake but looked over at the skinny guy in the hoodie. "Check."

He stepped around his partner and went to the dresser. The big guy still had Seth by the throat, but loosened his grip enough that some of the purple drained from his face.

Skinny Guy pulled the top drawer open with his gun hand and reached in. He dug around for a second before pulling out a folded wad of cash. The rubber band was gone, probably downstairs on the kitchen counter. He took a quick look at the bills, then rustled through the drawer some more.

"Well?" Schroeder asked.

He rifled through one last time, then turned to hand the cash to Schroeder. The pressure on Jake's eye let up as she reached across for the money. She threw it down on the bed next to Jake's head.

"What the fuck is this?" She ground her knee down farther, increasing the pressure between Jake's legs.

Ryan kept his hands up, but now it looked more like a pleading gesture than a surrender. "That's the money. Just take it, it's fine. Take it. We won't say a word."

Schroeder stared with a look that bordered on confusion.

Pissed-off confusion but confusion nonetheless.

"Where's the rest of it?"

"We spent a little," Ryan conceded. "I mean, we got some pizza . . . and a bottle of rum. But we'll pay you back, I swear to God."

Schroeder stood up from the bed, leaving Jake on his back. "Don't give me that shit. Where's my money?"

"That's it, I swear!" Ryan looked down at Jake for assurance. Andy remained silently plastered to the mattress behind him. "We had to pay the guy twenty bucks or something to buy the rum, but I promise we'll pay it back."

Schroeder stepped over to Ryan, while the big guy pulled Seth off the wall and threw him back onto the bed like he was an oversize stuffed animal.

"I swear—" Ryan's voice was cut off by the sight of Schroeder's gun rising toward his face.

"He's telling the truth." Jake pushed himself up while trying to keep his hands in a nonthreatening position. Something about Schroeder's reaction didn't seem right. They were only short sixty dollars at the most, but it probably wasn't the money but the idea that a bunch of kids had stolen from her.

"We took one of those rolls, and there was $440 in there. We bought two pizzas and cheese bread and a bottle of rum, so there should be like $380 right there."

Schroeder still looked pissed. Jake couldn't believe he'd allowed Andy to convince him they could get away with it.

"And we'll get you the rest," Ryan reiterated. "Swear to fucking God. I've got money right over there in my wallet you can have right now. Hell, take it all."

Schroeder's face was set in stone, but Jake noticed a look of confusion on the skinny guy's face. The silence of the night hung in the room as everyone waited for Schroeder's reaction.

A barking dog broke the silence. The neighbors had a golden retriever. A hunting dog. Jake had seen them tossing a rubber training dummy into the lake for it to bring back plenty of times. It was a well-trained dog.

It was also a reminder that they weren't alone, and it changed the tenor of the room.

"What do you want to do?" Skinny Guy asked. The big guy stood behind him in what looked like his natural state of waiting for instruction. Probably brought along for his muscle, not insight.

He got no response.

"What should—"

"Shut the fuck up and let me think."

Skinny Guy backed off as Schroeder stood silent. Her gun was still pointed at the middle of Ryan's face, but her expression had changed. Jake could practically see the scenarios bouncing around behind her eyes as she considered and discarded them.

The dog barked again.

"You need to get your boat off the dock," Skinny Guy said. "If somebody—"

"I know," she snapped.

Schroeder turned to the big guy, who'd faded into the back of the room. "Find that money, and be careful nobody sees you in here, you understand? You find it, you bring it straight back to the lab."

His double chin waggled under the ski mask as he nodded.

"Not to interrupt," Skinny Guy said. "But I've got to get back out there pretty soon if you want any product for next month. I can't stay here and babysit."

Schroeder looked back at her cook.

"You're right." She looked down the line of still-terrified boys along the bed. "We'll take them with."

━━━━

The back side of the cabin was as dark as it had been when Jake snuck out earlier, leaving two armed intruders behind to roust his three best friends. As quiet as when he'd made the decision to forgo help from the neighbors—whose barking dog had confirmed that they were indeed available—and go flag down the boat he saw out on the water.

Now, here he was, heading down the steps to the lake again. Only this time, his friends were with him, and they had guns at their backs.

Probably should've just gone to the neighbors, eh?

Jake could see the DNR boat gently bobbing in the water at the end of the dock as he descended the stairs. Some high, wispy clouds passed in front of the moon, playing havoc with the dim shadows around the lake.

"Keep moving." The gun Jake had been so desperate for Schroeder to take out only ten minutes ago dug into his back. He stepped out onto the dock, leading a parade of the damned. He knew where they were headed in that boat and was terrified they wouldn't be coming back.

Jake wanted to plead with them, explain they'd never tell anyone about what they'd seen out on the island. That they'd pay back the money they'd spent. That they'd do whatever they wanted if they could just go back to bed and forget everything.

Instead, he kept walking.

Schroeder pushed Jake to the end of the dock, her gun never more than a few inches from his spine.

"Get in."

Jake's bare foot stepped across the twelve-inch gulf and into the boat he'd always assumed was used for nothing more than handing out fishing citations. Schroeder held a fistful of his shirt the whole time and used his shoulder for balance as she followed him in.

"Sit down."

She pushed him into the front of the boat. He stumbled past the captain's chair into the bow area. There were no seats or benches in the front of the small craft, nothing but a flat, open space covered in scratchy marine-grade carpet. It felt like a scrubbing pad against his legs. Seth and Ryan were pulled down and squeezed in next to Jake. They looked cold and terrified.

Andy stepped into the boat with the skinny guy's gun right behind him, but instead of herding him to the front, Schroeder pushed him back by the large outboard motor.

"Ma'am, you don't want to do this." Andy's voice was far from panicked. It sounded like a lawyer making his closing argument. "Let us go and we won't say anything. Heck, nobody would believe us even if we did. We're just a bunch of dumb kids up at the lake. But if we disappear, the cops are not going to let that slide. And *that* will mess up your operation for sure."

The moonlight almost glowed off his sun-bleached Scandinavian hair.

"But it doesn't have to be this way. We can go back up to the cabin, get our stuff, drive away right now, and never come back. You'll never see us again."

Schroeder stood at the steering wheel but didn't start the engine.

"Put your gun right in his fat mouth," she said, motioning to Andy. Skinny Guy nodded and pulled off his ski mask. He shook his familiar stringy hair, and in the dark it took Jake a second to recognize him.

"I told you not to go over there." Blake Bourdeau gave Jake the same nasty smirk a cat gives a songbird. He grabbed a fistful of hair and jammed the barrel of his gun between Andy's lips.

Schroeder turned toward the other three boys, who went white at the sound of Andy gagging on Blake's handgun.

"Understand this. If any of you do anything stupid—anything that even remotely concerns me—he's going to pull that trigger and toss your friend over the side without even slowing down." Her eyes bored through the darkness and into the souls of the boys in front. "Do you understand?"

Ryan and Seth nodded. Jake wanted to, but his fear made him incapable of movement at the time. He just stared as Crazy Larry's grandson—a guy he'd bought minnows and candy bars and pop from—held a gun in his friend's mouth.

Schroeder reached down, and the engine sprang to life. Against the quiet of the lake, even idling the engine sounded like a roar. Blake pulled the rope off the pole and pushed away from the dock. The boat motored off in a slow arc, away from the barking dog and sleeping neighbors. Jake could see the muted glow coming from the bedroom window of the cabin, where the fat guy was probably tearing the place apart looking for money that wasn't there. Instead of cutting across the lake toward the back bay, Schroeder kept them circling south around the big island. It was a longer route, but there were significantly fewer cabins along the shore that way.

Jake scanned the wooded shoreline for any sign of activity. Anyone who might notice a boat in the middle of the night and think it was a little suspicious.

There was nothing but dark trees.

Once they hit the back side of the lake, the boat flew through the cove to Pike Island. Facing the rear, Jake couldn't see the approach but got a good view of Andy and the gun still pressed into his mouth. His eyes pleaded for help, but Jake had nothing to give him.

The engine slowed, and Jake felt the boat start to turn. The island slid past in the dark. The trees loomed over the water, blocking out the moon as they closed in on the shore.

Schroeder brought the boat around to the far side and headed to the same spot the boys had tied up on their own, much more voluntary, trip. Instead of killing the engine, she pulled past the tree they had tied onto and swung around behind it before drifting in.

They floated right up to the shore, tucked behind the tree and completely shielded from the rest of the bay.

"Stay on him," Schroeder said as she cut the engine, grabbed the docking rope, and glanced at the guys in front. "Remember not to do anything stupid."

She tied the boat up and herded the guys onto the island without incident. The moonlight that lit up the lake was almost nonexistent under the canopy of trees. The path below them was cold and rough on Jake's bare feet.

Schroeder produced a penlight from her belt and prodded them up the path.

"Go."

The walk to the house was a constant battle for balance. The underbrush grabbed at Jake's ankles, but he was scared to lose his balance and take a bullet in the back of the head because Schroeder thought he was making a run for it.

They eventually broke through the trees into the clearing at the center of the island. Backlit by the small amount of moonlight that filtered through the clearing, the house looked like something plucked from Jake's darkest nightmares. A push in his back prodded Jake across the yard and up the front steps. Schroeder reached past him and pushed the door open.

"Welcome back."

Chapter Twenty-One

Every time Krista felt Jake was ready to wrap up his story, he turned down an even crazier path. Listening to it was almost discombobulating. His telling was so detailed, but the more unbelievable it was, the more convincing his delivery became. He twitched but didn't fidget as he spoke. He'd stare straight ahead, then hold eye contact as he recounted vivid details. She bounced back and forth between being convinced he was making the whole thing up and being absolutely sure he believed every word.

And she didn't know which frightened her more.

It was Jake's tale of being herded into an abandoned house at gunpoint that reminded Krista exactly how isolated she was right then. He lived a good ten miles from town, and she'd seen precious few neighboring farmhouses on the drive out.

Certainly none within screaming distance.

Her rapidly clearing mind asked how she'd thought showing up unannounced and alone to a stranger's house in the middle of nowhere would be a good idea. Sticking around was reckless—borderline stupid.

So why was she still there?

Jake paused, and Krista seized the opportunity to let her good judgment take the wheel.

"Well, Mr. Nelson, thank you for talking with me, but I don't want to take up any more of your time." It wasn't as subtle as she'd hoped.

"What do you mean?" Jake's eyes squeezed tight for a second, and he tilted his head as if that was the only way he could unlock them. "I wasn't finished, and you need to hear this."

Krista took an exaggerated look at her watch and got up from the couch. She was practically a mime at this point, but the tension building in her chest hampered her acting ability. "I'd love to hear more, but I have a meeting I'm already late for, so we may have to finish up another time."

Jake popped out of his recliner and bumped his makeshift table, sending a dozen empty beer cans scattering across the floor. He looked at her with a nervous energy that reinforced her idea that getting out of that house was a top priority.

"But you need to know." His voice was quick. His face looked manic. "The truth needs to get out."

The realization that Jake could cut off her escape with a single step to his left trumped all pretense of politeness. Krista scooped up her recorder and stepped past him.

"No, wait." Jake reached out and grabbed her arm as she turned toward the kitchen. The feeling of his hand on her elbow sent a jolt into the panic section of her brain. "You've got to help me stop him because this is just going to keep happening until somebody stops him. I'm not going to end up like his parents. Like Ryan."

She jerked her arm away, but Jake's grip tightened and caught around Krista's wrist. Instinct and nine years of youth karate classes kicked in as she whirled around and drove the heel of her right palm hard into Jake's sternum. He dropped her wrist and staggered back, gasping for breath. Krista sprinted back into the kitchen. She bumped into an old chair next to the table, then turned and ran toward the screen door.

"Wait . . . ," Krista heard from behind as she banged through the door and hopped over the makeshift steps outside. She dug the key to her rental out of her front pocket, fumbling it to the ground and accidentally kicking it ahead of her as she sprinted across the yard.

Jake appeared in the doorway as Krista scooped up the key. She tore around the front bumper and threw herself behind the wheel as he shouted from the house.

"HE'S A KILLER, YOU KNOW! A FUCKING KILLER!"

She cranked the ignition and looked back, but Jake remained behind the screen door. His delusional shouting was replaced by the crunch of gravel as Krista peeled out.

She roared down the rural ribbon of gravel and squeezed the steering wheel to keep her hands from shaking. Her breathing gradually slowed as she left Jake Nelson's home behind and the adrenaline seeped from her veins.

———

The sound of Krista's knuckles on the door resonated down the empty hall. She'd barely seen anyone around the hotel who wasn't working or part of their little travel party, but capacity for small-town lodging was probably low during the middle of the week.

She knew Harry was in his room because she'd heard their entire crew come back from dinner twenty minutes ago. Krista hadn't joined them as she'd initially planned, instead choosing to lie on her bed and contemplate what the hell they were going to do about Jake Nelson.

Her hand went to knock again when the door opened.

"We've got to talk," Krista said, entering Harry's room. It was a mirror image of her own, which was a few doors down on the opposite side of the hall. His suitcase lay open on one queen bed, while the bedspread of the other was rumpled where he'd been sitting. She crossed in front of the dark TV and pulled out a rolling chair from under the countertop desk.

"I met Jake Nelson today."

Harry stilled for what could have been a myriad of reasons, then closed his laptop and pushed it out of the way as he sat back on his bed. "Jesus, I figured you were up to something, but . . . Jake Nelson? Why?"

"Because he's almost certainly the guy who sent those postcards."

"Wait, what?" Harry said. "He wouldn't have any political connections, so why would he care?"

Krista leaned back and propped her feet up on the bed in front of her. "Let's just say he's not a fan. He talked a lot about you being fake. How your charm is nothing more than an act to manipulate people. About what you'd do to get what you thought you deserved."

"What the hell?" Harry swept his fingers back through his light hair and held his hands behind his head. "I mean . . . what did I ever do to him to deserve this? Succeed? I mean, I get small-town resentment for people who leave and make something of themselves, but that can't be what this is all about, can it?"

"I don't know, but you can tell he isn't well. He lives alone in the middle of nowhere in a house that is practically tumbling down around him. And between the ranting, the conspiracy theories, and the tics, I'd guess there are some serious paranoia issues going on too. I wouldn't be looking for a whole lot of logic." Krista paused a second before continuing. It was probably pointless, but she felt compelled to ask. "There isn't anything you haven't told me about what happened out there, is there?"

"No, why?" Harry said.

"Because he said all kinds of crazy things." Krista thought back to sitting in Jake Nelson's living room, the earnest look on his face as he told his stories of what had happened out on that island. "He kept jumping around, trailing off, so it was kind of hard to follow sometimes. He said you guys found the drug lab out on that island, but that the DNR was running it as part of a drug ring. Then they somehow found out you knew about it and broke into the cabin you were staying at and held you at gunpoint."

Harry swung his legs off the bed and leaned forward, an incredulous look on his face. "What the hell . . ."

"Oh, that's not all," Krista said. "Amid the '9/11 was an inside job' and the 'Illuminati runs the world' ranting, he implied you were responsible for Ryan Kelter's *and* your parents' deaths. Well, he didn't say that so much as scream '*HE'S A KILLER*' at me as I was running to my car."

"What? The last time I saw Ryan Kelter was when we were in college." Harry looked up at her with distress. "And my parents—wait. Why were you running?"

The thought of her escape released a small shot of adrenaline into her bloodstream.

"When I tried to leave, he freaked out." Krista chose not to mention that she'd had to fight him off.

"*Jesus*, Krista. You shouldn't have been out there by yourself. I mean, who knows what a guy like that can do?" Harry dropped his head into his hands, elbows propped on his knees almost as if he were in prayer. He mumbled something into his palms, but Krista heard only a garbled mess.

"What?"

Harry lifted his head and looked across the room at her. His eyes had the glassy facade of a man who'd gone one scotch and soda past his recommended daily allowance, and it took Krista aback. "This is all my fault."

"What do you mean?"

"I mean I can't have anyone else get hurt because of me, okay?"

Krista's jaw dropped. She tried to say something but couldn't. It was as if somebody had pulled the plug on her brain and she had to wait for the system to reboot.

"The other guys . . . Jake in particular . . . just wanted to go home and forget it. He didn't want to get involved, so that's what we agreed on." Harry stood up and wandered around the end of his bed. "But I couldn't do *nothing*—they were ruining lives with that junk. I saw a pay phone when we stopped at a gas station on the way home. On the side of it was a sticker for the DNR TIP line—you know, Turn In Poachers—and I figured I could call that line anonymously and not have to worry about them tracing the call or anything. Then they'd contact the sheriff's office, and it would get taken care of without anyone knowing about us."

Harry stood in front of the window, staring out into the dark parking lot as he spoke.

"Jake came around to use the bathroom right as I was hanging up the phone. God, he was pissed. Kept saying how I broke my promise and betrayed them. I argued that it was our responsibility to do something, that nobody would ever know, but he wasn't having it. He was completely paranoid they'd find out we were out there. That we took the money. I figured it would blow over eventually . . . then I saw the news a few days later."

Krista stared at him, having not moved since he started talking.

"So you knew what happened when it got busted."

"We actually saw that DNR officer who died while we were up there. I'll never forget it. Her name was Kim Schroeder. She got after us for being too loud. You know, dumb kid stuff. Last thing Jake said to me was *She died because of you.* I'm not going to take the blame for Ryan's addiction or whatever, but I was the one who called the DNR, so I guess he was right about that."

The quiet of the room swallowed his words. Krista could understand his guilt, however misplaced it might be, but no levelheaded person could put the blame on his shoulders.

"You did the right thing," she said. "The people who started a drug lab in an abandoned house are the ones responsible. It's not your fault something went bad."

"I know, but that doesn't make me feel any better."

Harry sat on the end of the bed and didn't speak for a while. Krista watched him process his perceived guilt, but didn't try to be a fixer. Emotions were often illogical and couldn't be fixed by someone else, no matter how good their intentions.

After a few minutes of silence, she could see Harry click back into practical-politician mode.

"So, if he's the guy, what do we do about it?"

"Same thing we always do; prepare for whatever may come," Krista said. "Unfortunately, with as unhinged as Jake is, there's probably nothing I can do to keep him quiet if he's determined to warn the world about you."

Harry closed his eyes and sighed, probably imagining the sight of Jake Nelson on cable news.

"But the good news is even if he talks, nobody's going to take him seriously," Krista said.

Harry looked over at her with a glimmer of hope on his face. "He's that far gone?"

"Fucking bonkers. Anybody who hears it will think he's completely delusional," Krista said. "And his house was littered with empty beer cans, so it's obvious he's also got a drinking problem. Sad, but it'll work for us. Any truth about the money will get muddled up with the crazy rantings of the town drunk who's always talking about conspiracy theories. Hell, Maggie Wander already thinks he's a loon, and that's without hearing his psychotic ramblings in person."

Harry's brow furrowed.

"Hold on, Wander knows about him?"

"She got a letter a few days ago, same as the ones we got. Unsigned. Told her to look into Cedar Lake. She called me about it. I convinced her it was a stalker we already had on our radar. I asked her to keep it quiet for security reasons, and she agreed."

"Is that how she had the 'rumor' that I was being looked at for a future VP spot?" Harry asked.

"I had to give her something to write about if I wanted her to ignore the letter, didn't I?"

The hint of a smirk flashed on Harry's lips. "I thought you were dead set against the whole VP thing. Now you're leaking it to the press?"

"I *am* dead set against it, because it's a horrible idea, but that doesn't mean I won't use whatever I have to solve the problem at hand." Krista flexed her wrist as she spoke. It was still a little sore from earlier.

But it gave her an idea.

"Speaking of, I need you to squeeze my wrist." She held her hand out to Harry. "Hard."

Harry stared like she was speaking a foreign language.

"Trust me." Krista pointed to the spot Jake had seized when she tried to get out of his living room. "Squeeze right here as hard as you can."

Harry carefully wrapped his hand around her wrist and looked to her for an explanation. Krista clamped her other hand over his and pressed.

"Harder." She felt his grip tighten and took a sharp inhale. "Good. Now twist some."

Harry twisted her flesh and brought a fresh sting of pain, like the "snake bites" her brother would give her when they were kids. Krista closed her eyes and let Harry work as the pain crept up her forearm.

"Okay, that's good." She looked down at her wrist, where the slight red mark Jake's grip had left was evolving into an angry red bruise. She pulled out her phone and took a few pictures of the damage.

"What the hell is that for?" Harry said.

Krista examined the pictures, then moved her arm toward the desktop lamp behind her and took one more shot.

"He made a grab for me when I tried to leave. This is evidence of that."

Harry sat back onto his bed with a loud sigh. "Jesus. That's a little extreme, isn't it?"

"You want to discredit a guy, bruises on a woman are pretty damn effective," Krista said. "In that vein, I think Seth Meloy could help us out, should we need some sort of character witness. He said Jake was drunk at Ryan's funeral and always seemed bitter that he got stuck back home while you guys all moved on. He was also at Cedar Lake with you and could directly counter any wild accusations coming from Jake."

"You talked to Seth too?"

"Over the phone." Krista shifted in her chair, and the cheap plastic squeaked. "He's down in Kansas City. Wife. Family. Seems pretty stable."

Harry looked dubious. "Maybe. But I haven't really talked with him in years."

"Yeah, but you should've heard his voice perk up when I said I worked with you. Seemed like the kind of guy who would do about anything for the ability to brag to the guy in the cubicle next door that he's friends with a congressman. A call from you would mean a lot to him."

Harry dropped back onto the bed with a groan and put his forearm over his eyes. "Fine. I'll do it when we get back."

Krista smiled at him. "We're going to get through this."

For the first time since she'd run out of Jake Nelson's house, she truly believed it. Now that they knew what they were up against, they could get their ducks in a row and be ready to counter whatever came at them. Krista had made her career as a problem solver, and she'd yet to come across something she couldn't handle. The work Harry would do was too important to let a whack job like Jake Nelson derail them.

Krista got up from her chair, crossed to the end of Harry's bed, and smacked his foot as she passed. As is often the case in most nonluxury hotel rooms, the only light was coming from a large lamp perched on the table between the two beds. It kept things relatively dark, with a weird yellow hue from the lampshade, and if Harry's hand hadn't been lying across his forehead at the perfect angle when Krista left the room, she never would have spotted the scar across his palm.

———

By all common sense, Jake Nelson was a delusional nut peddling trumped-up stories meant to damage an old friend who had left him behind. Harry himself had confirmed that the tales of DNR-run drug labs and kidnappings were nothing more than the rantings of an unbalanced man.

But that scar on Harry's hand whispered to Krista as she lay on her cheap hotel bed.

The laptop was getting hot on her legs. She'd been digging through the internet for anything she could find on Jake Nelson, the drug bust at Cedar Lake—anything that would shine some light on a situation that was still riddled with shadows.

She thumped her head on the wall behind her, hoping to shake some epiphany loose.

Nothing.

Krista scrolled fruitlessly, clicked "More Results," then scrolled some more.

Even twenty-five pages deep into Harrison Leonard's search results, at least a third of them were links to the viral video that had launched the two of them into the stratosphere.

She clicked on one.

Krista had seen that video countless times, and each time it gave her the same hope it did the first time. The Supreme Court's decision had dropped like an anvil from the sky about forty-five minutes before their event. They'd huddled up to figure out what to say about it, since there was no way Harry could ignore the most consequential judicial decision of their lifetimes. Their picnic-in-the-park events were always light, more a chance to let Harry schmooze with constituents than make heavy policy speeches. They were also in Waseca, which, while not a deep-red enclave, had a lot of conservative-leaning voters they hoped to woo.

They went back and forth for a while, but at some point Krista trusted her gut and told Harry to trust his.

Let it rip.

And he did.

This is the culmination of a decades-long assault on women, and if you think it's going to stop here, you're delusional.

She watched Harry address the group without a microphone—the event was small enough none was needed—not knowing his message would be heard by millions over the coming days.

I want every woman out there to know I stand with you. Every gay person who just wants to keep the same rights as your straight brothers and sisters, I stand with you. Every trans person who just wants to FUCKING EXIST . . . I see you, and I stand with you.

The words brought her back to that day. Standing off to the side, barely out of frame, watching Harry with his sleeves rolled up, skin glowing in the midday sun and light hair blowing in the breeze as if they were on a movie set, feeling everything come together with every word of support he said.

Hey, I'm a cis white male, and as much as I empathize, there's no way I can feel the pain of women today. I can't feel the fear of LGBTQ+ people, knowing that the hard-fought victories they've won over the years can—and if we don't do something, WILL—be ripped away by an activist, illegitimate court that is willing to put their own biases ahead of the Constitution of the United States. But I promise you this . . . I will use every bit of my cis white male privilege to fight for every person out there whose rights have been trampled today.

No matter how many times she heard it, those words gave her chills.

Krista knew what it was like to be afraid to tell people—including those who loved you—who you were. She thought back to the months of inner debate before she came out to her parents, and the months after, when she was terrified she'd wrecked their relationship forever. She thought about the family members who treated her as well as they always had, then voted for candidates who wanted to treat her like a second-class citizen. Members of Congress who said the vilest things to rile up their base, then had the audacity to smile at her when they sat next to her on the tram.

So to those of you celebrating today, know that you won't win. We'll never stop fighting for equal rights for everyone. And to those five so-called judges on the Supreme Court who bowed to their puppet masters today . . . no matter what you do for the rest of your lives, you'll never get the stink of this betrayal of justice off your bought-and-paid-for hides. Fuck you forever.

She'd known Harry was an ally, but to see it laid out that way, so raw . . . that was the moment she knew he could be truly transformational. A real ally, not just someone paying lip service who would slink to the back when the chips were down. Someone who could be counted on to fight for everything they believed in. To be a bulkhead against the rising tide who wanted to marginalize people like her.

And that she'd do whatever she could to put him in a position to help.

Chapter
Twenty-Two

Schroeder and Blake pushed them into the dining room, where the house's strange odor assaulted their senses again. Only this time they knew it wasn't time and grime, but common household chemicals cooked together upstairs to make a potent drug.

And this time the smell was much stronger.

There was almost no light coming through the dirt-encrusted front windows, so Schroeder's penlight provided the only illumination. Jake felt a leg sneak in front of his foot as she pushed him forward and sent him sprawling across the dusty floor.

"Have a seat." Her voice still had that eerie, calm quality that was more unnerving than if she were ranting like a lunatic.

Jake pushed himself up into a sitting position as his friends joined him on the floor. Schroeder stood over them, waving her little flashlight back and forth. The repetitive bursts of light in Jake's face kept his vision from finding any foothold in the darkness. He couldn't see his friends, but he could feel the fear radiating off them. His mind was racing to figure out a way to get out of there alive.

"Let's pick up where we left off, shall we?" Schroeder said. "I'm hoping the little ride over gave you time to think. Where's my money?"

Jake looked down the row of his friends, but with the light in his eyes, he couldn't see anything more than pulses of purple and faceless shapes.

"We gave it to you," he said carefully. "Like we said, we'll get you the rest, I pro—"

The light dropped from his face as Schroeder let out an exasperated breath. She gave a slight nod to Blake, who lashed out with a savage kick. Sneaker met ribs, and Andy shrieked in pain beside him.

"See, this is why we had to bring you guys out here," Schroeder said. "You didn't seem like you were in a cooperating mood, and the only way I know how to get you to talk is a little . . . loud. We wouldn't want to wake the neighbors."

Andy curled on the floor in the fetal position, hands tucked around his side, breathing nothing but a series of moans.

"You didn't spend almost $100,000 on fucking pizza," she said. Jake's stomach dropped. He was confused, scared, and not exactly thinking straight. Why did she think they'd taken more than that roll? "So, I'm going to ask you one more time . . ."

The cheap digital watch on Blake's wrist beeped, interrupting Schroeder's threat.

"I've got to get upstairs," he said.

"Fine. Go." Schroeder's voice betrayed her impatience, but Blake didn't leave. "What?"

"Well, Jeffery's still back at their cabin, and I need another set of hands up there." Blake spoke with trepidation. "Just for a couple minutes, but it's kind of important."

Andy's shallow gasps continued from a few feet away, but Jake kept his eyes on Schroeder, who eventually gave her cook an agitated nod.

"What about them?" He spoke as if the boys weren't there; the indifference to their presence was chilling.

"Put 'em in the basement," Schroeder said. "It'll give them a little quiet time to reflect on honesty and how much they enjoy breathing. Because when we're done upstairs, we'll continue our talk."

She shifted her gaze back to the boys and seemed to grow a foot taller with her words.

"And I'm going to start shooting until one of you decides to tell me what I want to hear."

The first floor of the abandoned house was dark, but it was a sunroom in July compared to the cellar. With no windows and a solid floor above, there was nowhere for even the smallest crack of light to creep through.

Jake's tics were coming faster now, but it was so dark there was no difference whether his eyes were open or closed. The darkness was overwhelming.

The four guys stood at the foot of the stairs, unwilling to wander around the darkness with no idea what they might run into.

Even though Jake couldn't tell in the dark, the cellar felt small—much smaller than the footprint of the house above. Maybe it was claustrophobia brought on by the absence of light and the heavy smells filtering down from above. Or maybe it was the rising feeling of dread that was threatening to overwhelm him. His sense of confusion and disbelief had kept things in check so far, but as the realization of how dangerous the situation had become settled, Jake could feel it roiling in the depths of his gut. If he wasn't careful, it would boil over into a full-fledged freak-out.

They stewed for an inordinate amount of time before Ryan broke the silence with a whisper. "What the hell was she talking about . . . $100,000?"

"Yeah, what the fuck was that?" Seth said. "She doesn't think we took that much, right?"

The thought turned up the heat on Jake's bonfire of anxiety, but he took a deep breath and did all he could to push it down. "She can't. Andy only took that one roll. Whatever she's missing, she's gonna find it up there and know we didn't take it, and it's all going to be fine."

"What the fuck are you talking about?" Seth's tone left little room for unrealistic optimism. "Even if they do find it, you think they're just going to say *Oops, our bad* and let us go? Jesus Christ, we're in the basement of a fucking meth lab. They've got guns, man. We've got to find a way out of here before they get back."

Jake couldn't acknowledge Seth's logic. Because if what he said was true, they were in serious trouble, and Jake wasn't ready to handle that.

"No. She's gonna find it somewhere and—"

"She's not going to find any money up there." Andy's voice cut through the dark and sliced right through Jake's hope. His knees weakened to the point he thought he was going to collapse onto the dirt floor. A panicked sweat broke out on his skin.

"What do you mean?"

"I mean nobody just misplaces $100,000. Besides, you saw yourself that it was locked up in that steel cabinet when we left." Andy's voice disappeared in the dark for a beat. "If she says it's missing, then somebody took it."

"Fuck." Ryan's voice filtered quietly through the dark.

"Who could've taken it?" Seth asked. "I mean, you're right. It didn't just disappear from that cabinet. You think it was a rival gang or something?"

"No, it's got to be someone with access to that cabinet," Andy said. "Someone with a key."

"You think it was one of those guys?" Seth asked.

"Probably, but I don't think it really matters who took it. Like you said, no matter what happens, it's not like she's going to let us go. We've seen too much," Andy said. "We're going to have to find a way out of here."

A faint thump came from above them, driving home the reality of their situation.

"What do we do?" Seth asked.

"I don't know, but we've got to figure it out quick," Andy said. "Either we find a way to sneak out, or we find something down here we can use to fight them off."

Jake swung his head around instinctively, trying to find something hidden in the pitch black of the cellar. It was pointless.

"Maybe there's a window or something?" Ryan said.

"Spread out and look," Andy said. "A window or something we can use as a weapon."

Jake turned away from the base of the steps and slowly edged out into the darkness. He put his hands out in front of him, feeling for anything that might spring up in his path. Grit and dirt ground under his bare feet as he slowly shuffled forward like a blind man without a cane.

Every step taken into the unknown of the darkness shifted Jake's anxiety from what the two people upstairs would do to them to what hidden horrors he might discover in the black of an abandoned cellar.

A jolt of pain shot down the middle finger on his left hand as its tip ran into something. He swallowed a yelp and pulled it back, squeezing his finger against his chest. He tried to flex the throb out, opening and closing his fist while he reached ahead of him with his other hand.

Whatever had jumped out and jammed his finger had seemingly retreated into the dark.

When he pulled his hand back, it brushed against a smooth surface hanging a few feet in front of him. Jake warily slid his hand around, then put his other alongside it.

It felt like wood.

He raised his right hand until it bumped into a similar surface a foot or so above, then pushed his left hand forward until he brushed against the rough stone behind the wood.

"Found some shelves," Jake whispered across the room. "Up against the wall over here."

"Anything on them we can use?" Andy's reply floated in from the dark.

Jake swept his hands carefully across the shelf, but it was bare.

"Nothing I can feel."

"Follow the wall around, and see if there are any windows at the top." Ryan's voice came from his left. Not that far away.

Jake felt along the wall in that direction, peering up through the dark for any signs of light. The stone walls didn't feel like they'd have a pane of glass stuck in them, but Jake felt for one anyway.

The shelves ended after a few steps. Jake put his hand on the wall and used it as a guide to get him around the room. His fingers picked up cobwebs as he dragged them across the stone, and he forced any thought of the spiders that spun them out of his head.

About five careful paces past the shelves, the stone disappeared from under his fingertips. He stopped short and reached back, finding the corner where the wall disappeared to the right. Jake swept his right foot around the corner, and his toes crunched into something. He lifted his foot and grabbed his big toe in an attempt to rub the pain out.

Jake braced himself on the corner and gently put his foot back down, only to feel the edge of something about six inches off the ground.

It felt like a step. He quickly moved his foot forward and felt the second one just beyond.

Jake looked up and made out a faint blue line in the darkness above.

Relief flooded through Jake's veins. It was an old-fashioned storm cellar door, covering a small set of stairs from the basement to the backyard.

"*Guys.*" Jake's voice was still an attempted whisper, but it echoed through the empty cellar. His excitement at getting out overpowered his fear of being heard by the guns above. "Get over here."

The cellar was still too dark to see anything, but he felt the air change behind him right before he felt Ryan's hand.

"What is it?"

"There's a door up there," Jake said. His arm fumbled back behind him and ran into Ryan's stomach. He felt around his friend's side and pulled him in closer. Jake felt Ryan's hand find his biceps and hold on. It was comforting, like an anchor.

"What?" Seth's voice came from the other side of the steps.

"Careful," Jake said, mostly out of habit. He reached in front of him, trying to find Seth, but felt nothing but air. "Where's Andy?"

"Right here."

Jake jumped a bit at the sound of his friend's voice, having assumed he was clear across the cellar. He reached out to where Andy's voice had materialized. His fingers brushed up against a shoulder. He took a gentle hold of Andy's shirt and pulled it slowly toward him.

"It's a storm cellar," he said. "There's steps right over here, and I can see a door at the top. Look." Jake slid his hand around the back of Andy's neck and did his best to tilt it up the stairs to the faint crack of light above.

"I see it," Andy said.

Jake felt Ryan's hand tighten around his arm at Andy's confirmation. "Let's go," he said.

Jake looked back over his shoulder, still not used to the fact that there was nothing to be seen in the dark of the cellar.

"Yeah." He cocked his ear to the ceiling, listening for any sounds above.

There were none.

"Okay . . . Seth?"

Seth's voice came from the dark, a few feet ahead of Jake. "Yeah?"

"Just checking," Jake said. "The steps are over here—like two feet in front of me. Let's go up together."

Jake slid his hand from Andy's neck down his shoulder and onto his arm. He pulled it behind him and bumped it into Ryan.

"Grab a hold," Jake said. "I'll go first. Ryan, you got me?"

"Uh-huh." The nerves were evident in his voice.

"I've got Seth," Andy said. Jake felt his friend pass behind him to the back of their awkward conga line.

Jake listened one last time for anything above.

"Okay, let's go. Slow now." Jake shifted his foot forward and found the edge of the first step. Ryan's hand moved up to the back of his shoulder as he stepped up with one hand on the wall and one stretched out in front.

"First step is right here."

Jake started up slowly, allowing the guys behind him to feel their way onto the staircase. They whispered directions to each other as they started the ascent. Just a few steps after hearing Seth confirm he was on the stairs, Jake was within an arm's length of the door.

"Okay," Jake said, standing a few steps down from the tiny strip of gray light that promised their escape. He reached out and felt along it, searching for a handle or latch, but found only rough wood.

"Let's go." Seth's panicky voice crept up the staircase, its volume higher than someone still attempting to hide his actions.

"There's no handle." Jake ran his fingers over and across the cellar door above him, ignoring the small splinters of wood sticking out at random intervals.

"Just push it," Andy said.

Jake felt Ryan's hand fall away from his back as he climbed two more stairs and braced his shoulder against the door. He pushed up against the reinforced wood, and the door raised about two inches before stopping with a metallic clatter.

He pushed again, harder, only to hear the jangling of chain links on the other side. A fresh wave of panic flowed through Jake.

"It's locked."

Chapter
Twenty-Three

It wasn't hard for Krista to beg off the trip to Mankato the next morning. The only person she had to answer to was Harry, and she made sure to tell him in front of the rest of the staff. She could tell Harry didn't like the idea of her going off on her own again, but knew he couldn't mention anything about Jake Nelson in front of the rest of their party.

From her time on the campaign trail, Krista knew the Rice County Sheriff's Office was in Faribault, less than an hour from their hotel. Whatever reports there were on the drug bust at Cedar Lake would be there, available as public record to any interested party via Minnesota Statute 13.82, and should be enough to snuff out the tiny ember of doubt glowing in the back of her head.

She didn't get into details when she requested the file from the sheriff's secretary, a friendly old woman named Lorna who looked like she'd been there long enough to remember not only the incident on Cedar Lake, but every crime committed since the Nixon administration. Krista instead commented on the multitude of grandkid pictures that plastered Lorna's work area and let the stories flow while she filled out the required form.

Not wanting to pause the story of her granddaughter's heroic exploits on the hockey rink at local prep school Shattuck-St. Mary's (*she's gonna end up with more goals than anybody they ever had there—boys too*), Lorna invited Krista back to the storage room while she dug up the file.

"Here you go, sweetie." Krista hadn't let anyone call her sweetie in a long time, but found it surprisingly endearing coming from Lorna. The old lady handed over a thin manila envelope before ushering her back to the front. "Now, you can't take it with you, but you can read it here and make a copy if you want. We're supposed to charge twenty-five cents a page, but the boss ain't here, so you just ask, and I'll copy you whatever you want."

"Thank you so much." Krista felt the folder and couldn't imagine more than a single sheet of paper inside. She had no experience with police reports but was expecting a lot more for something involving the deaths of three people.

"I've got to get another pot of coffee on before the boys come back, so you just sit right there at my desk," Lorna said. "If you need anything, give me a holler. And if the phone rings, just grab it and say 'Rice County Sheriff's Office.'"

Before Krista could protest, Lorna disappeared into the back again.

Krista chuckled and sat down among the sea of pictures surrounding Lorna's chair. Most were of kids of various sizes in full hockey gear. More than one had a ponytail flowing out the back of her helmet, and Krista assumed the biggest one was Lorna's Olympic hopeful.

Krista opened the folder. A handful of sheets were there, held together with a paper clip. The top one was an incident form, filled out with a typewriter.

She read through the report and learned little she hadn't found in the *Faribault Daily News* articles she had dug up back in DC. Details were sparse, with most of the form consisting of checked boxes and single-word answers.

The bottom half of the page was reserved for comments. Like the rest of the report, there was surprisingly little detail for such a major incident.

Response to reports of drug activity on Cedar Lake island. Fire from drug making operation active in abandoned house upon arrival. Island location prevented extinguishment. Fire damage total. Remains of equipment consistent with manufacture of meth-amphetamines found. Body of BLAKE BOURDEAU found inside, identified following forensic exam. Cause of death smoke inhalation. Body of JEFFERY GONSALVES found inside, identified following forensic exam. Cause of death smoke inhalation. Body of KIM SCHROEDER (MINNESOTA DNR) found deceased inside, identified at scene and confirmed by forensic exam. Cause of death smoke inhalation.

Krista turned the page over. It was blank. She shuffled through the papers clipped to it, but only found a list of evidence taken from the scene—mostly damaged drug-making equipment. The final page was a handwritten statement from Deputy Sheriff Charles Larssen, who was apparently one of the first on the scene from the sheriff's office.

I responded to reports of smoke on the back island of Cedar Lake. When I arrived, Kim Schroeder (MN DNR) was already on site. Deputy Ron Kellington radioed that he and Sheriff Dean Schroeder were en route. Kim entered the house to search for victims while I returned to the water so I could direct the sheriff to the scene. When we returned the fire was out of control and the roof had collapsed. We were unable to approach the house due to the fire, but used fire extinguishers from our boats to put out fires around the yard and keep it from spreading to the woods until Faribault FD arrived.

"Terrible thing, that." Krista hadn't heard Lorna return from the back and jumped at the sound of her voice. "Oh, sorry to give you a fright, sweetie."

Krista reshuffled the papers in front of her and smiled back at the gray-haired secretary. The woman had so much grandma in her that Krista was surprised she wasn't holding a plate of fresh-made brownies.

"Not a problem." Krista closed the folder and stood up. "Here, let me give your desk back."

"Oh no, you sit," Lorna said. "All I do in that chair is work."

Krista picked the folder up and walked to the other side of the desk. "I'm done, actually. Not much to read in there. Kinda surprising, really, considering what happened."

A cloud of genuine sadness rolled across Lorna's face.

"Such a shame. Kim was such a good girl."

"Did you know her well?"

"Of course. She was Sheriff Dean's daughter."

Krista nodded. "I suppose he took it pretty hard."

"Yeah. She was his only girl. Not sure if he ever got over it, really. I remember typing up that report. Usually they're much longer, like you say, but that was all he gave me to type. Probably hurt too much to think about, you know? I'm just glad the bastards that did it burned up in that fire too." Lorna snapped back from her grim story and put a smile on her face. "Sorry, I shouldn't say that."

"Not a problem." Krista gave a reassuring smile, but it hid a kernel of apprehension in the back of her mind. Everything seemed to have been dropped after the fire. She thought back to the minuscule report. Was there really no follow-up investigation?

"Did they ever find anyone else involved that wasn't out there when it exploded?"

"No." The wrinkles in Lorna's face bunched up in a scowl. "But I tell you, that Blake Bourdeau was a bad seed. Between you, me, and the lamppost, the whole family was no good. They used to own the resort out on Cedar Lake, and I heard talk back then he'd been selling that junk from right behind the bar."

"But they never looked for accomplices or anything?" Krista asked. "Maybe friends or family members?"

"Sheriff said the case was closed." Lorna didn't sound like someone comfortable questioning her boss. "Even if there was, can't really blame a man for not wanting to drag things out when it was his own daughter who got killed."

That thought process didn't sit right with Krista. She would have expected a law enforcement officer to not rest until anyone remotely connected to his daughter's death was punished. Jake's conspiratorial ranting pinged through her head, but Krista batted those thoughts away. She'd expected the official report to contradict Jake's story, and it certainly did. But there were enough holes that it still gnawed at the back of Krista's brain.

"Is the sheriff still around?"

A melancholy smile crossed Lorna's lips. "No, sweetie, Sheriff Dean passed on going on five years ago. Why do you ask?"

"I'm curious if he ever had any suspicions. Maybe somebody he thought was involved but didn't have the proof to do anything about it?"

Lorna gave her a knowing look.

"Charlie used to always talk about how Blake was too stupid to run an operation like that all by himself—and I'm not gonna argue that— but the sheriff didn't want to hear it. He'd got the guy who killed his girl, and he was okay with that. They got into it a little bit every now and then, I remember, but they never got along about anything after Charlie ran against him that one time."

It took a second for Krista to realize who Lorna was talking about; then she remembered the handwritten statement stapled to the back of the report.

"Deputy Charles Larssen?"

"That's him," Lorna said. "Sheriff never forgave him for coming for his job. Ugh, that was an ugly time. Longest month of my life, trying to pretend that they weren't running against each other. They both said they buried the hatchet after the election, but it was never the same as before. Charlie eventually left and went to work at the lumberyard."

"Is he still around?"

A surprised look hijacked Lorna's face. "Charlie? Sure, he's down at St. John's. Not in the nursing home part, but assisted living. Got a nice apartment and his own car and everything. We still meet to play cards every blue moon or so."

Krista thanked Lorna again and made her exit with at least five recommendations for lunch and one for a "great little weekend vacation."

Out on the street, Krista pulled out her phone and punched in *St. John's Assisted Living*. The gnawing feeling that there was more to this story wouldn't go away.

Chapter Twenty-Four

"No."

Jake had barely heard the word when he felt Andy push past him and slam his shoulder into the cellar door above. The chain outside flew up and slammed back down on the wooden door with a sharp bang.

"Don't, they'll hear," Jake said, pulling down on Andy's arm.

"Fuck that. We've gotta get out of here." He took another step toward the top and crouched down under the door to get leverage from both legs.

His efforts only made more noise.

"Come on, everybody get up here and help," Andy said, springing up against the door a third time.

Jake couldn't hear anything from the house, but there was no way Schroeder and her minion could've missed the banging on the door. They were most likely on their way down right now.

And if that was the case, noise didn't matter anymore.

Jake lurched up and wedged himself alongside Andy beneath the door. The tiny amount of light that streamed down between the doors was enough to see Ryan's face in front of him, arms braced against the wood above them as Andy counted them off.

"One . . . two . . . *three.*"

The four of them—Jake assumed Seth had joined them and was helping in the darkness—vaulted into the door with a crash.

"It moved," Andy said. "I think the screws are coming out."

Jake couldn't tell if it had gone any higher than in his previous solo efforts, but it didn't matter at this point.

"Again," Andy said. "One . . . two . . . *three*."

That time Jake felt it open a bit more. Something was giving somewhere. If they kept at it, they might be able to get out. He thought back to their first consequential visit here. The backyard wasn't very big, so if they got into the trees before they were grabbed—*or shot*—they could hopefully disappear into the woods.

No. Schroeder wouldn't simply let them fade into the night and vanish. They had to get off the island because she would eventually hunt them down if they tried to hide out.

The only advantage they had was numbers. Schroeder and Bourdeau couldn't chase down all four boys if they were smart about it. They could split up. Scatter as soon as they got out. Find a way off the island. At worst, only two of them could be followed, which meant a clearer path for the others.

But the two who are followed . . .

Jake shook that from his head. If just one of them got away, they could get help like he was supposed to do earlier. And if they got help, everything would be okay.

Footsteps pounded across the ceiling right before the door above the stairway flew open. Jake looked back and saw the bright beam of a flashlight dance across the floor below them.

"They're coming." He gave the door above another push on his own. The fear and adrenaline brought on by the thought of Schroeder and her gun flying down the cellar steps gave his muscles a swell of strength.

"One more," Andy said. "One . . . two—"

The crack of a gunshot blasted into Jake's eardrum, and a hot chunk of stone bounced off the steps in front of him. One of them, it might have been Jake, let out the same yelp a cat does when its tail gets caught in the screen door. The scream bounced between the walls alongside the gunshot for a second before Schroeder's voice cut through the darkness.

"Don't fucking move." The spot of light steadied on the floor below, and the sound of Schroeder's boots taking the last few steps into the cellar shuffled over to them. "You guys really want to get yourselves killed, don't you?"

The glowing circle crept across the cellar floor to the base of the stairs. Jake stared into it, his pupils shrinking to adjust to the glare. He got his first view of the floor, which was nothing but packed dirt. The walls were made of the same rough stone he'd pictured as he ran his hand along them for guidance.

Seth was a backlit silhouette on the third step. Ryan had backed against the wall to his left, the light fully in his face, while Andy remained beside him under the still-locked door. His hand clamped down on Jake's forearm, tense like he was preparing to spring into action.

"Don't," Jake whispered. He didn't know what Andy was thinking, but Jake couldn't think of a single thing that wouldn't end in one or more of them taking a bullet to the face.

"Get back down here now . . . slowly," Schroeder said. They ignored the contradiction and started back down to the floor. Seth stepped into the perimeter of Schroeder's flashlight, hands up in front of him. Ryan started down, and Jake filled in behind him.

He was three steps from the floor when he realized Andy hadn't moved.

"Come on," Jake hissed over his shoulder.

"Let's *go*," Schroeder said. "Over here."

Her voice spurred Andy, who started down the steps behind.

Jake made his way to the floor and squinted across the room. The cone of light Schroeder's flashlight gave off washed out everything else and left a purple swirl in Jake's vision when he tried to look away.

"JEFFERY, GET DOWN HERE!" she yelled back through the floor above. A wide, dark shadow shuffled down the steps behind her. The sheer size of it told Jake that the big guy had abandoned his search of the cabin and joined them on the island.

"What's going on?" Jeffery held a light much brighter than Schroeder's. Maybe the lantern they'd borrowed their first time out here?

"We've got four boys here who want to do things the hard way." Schroeder's voice was saturated with venom, and it raised the anxiety in Jake's chest well past anything he'd ever experienced. His heart pounded on his ribs as if it were trying to burst out like that creature in *Alien*.

"We can still work this out," Andy said as he stepped toward Schroeder, hands held in a nonthreatening pose.

The words were a spark that lit the tinder of Jake's fear, and he felt the rage burn through him like an untamed wildfire. He wanted to hold Andy back. Tackle him. Pummel him into silence before he made the situation worse. Before his arrogance got them all killed.

"Goddammit, Andy—"

The flash from Schroeder's gun was brighter than anything Jake had seen—a supernova among distant stars—and Jake felt the bullet rip through the air near his head as the thunderclap exploded on his eardrums. The blast bounced off the stone walls and around the inside of Jake's head, more discombobulating than the dark.

"What do you want to do?" Jeffery's voice was barely audible through the gunshot still ringing in Jake's ears. He wanted to rub some functionality back into them, but he was too scared to move.

"We're going to have a talk with these two." The eye of light shifted between the four of them before settling on Jake and Andy. "They seem the chattiest."

"Okay, but Blake said to get right back up because he's gonna need another pair of hands soon."

"That's fine." Jake could hear the ideas forming in Schroeder's voice, and it was extremely disconcerting. "You stay down here and keep an eye on the other two. I'll go. We can talk upstairs."

Jeffery used an old extension cord to lash Seth and Ryan together at the base of the stairway. Schroeder pulled Jake past them, her gun pressed into his back.

She herded Jake and Andy up to the main floor, then pushed them up the ornate staircase. The open door glowed at the end of the upstairs hallway, light spilling down from the lab above. Jake wanted to resist Schroeder's push to the door, but the fight had been scared out of him.

Schroeder's grip tightened on his shirt as they approached the stairs to the lab.

"Up." Her gun dug into the soft hollow of Jake's lower back. He almost put his arm on the wall to steady himself as he stepped into the stairway, but was afraid his movement would be misconstrued as aggressive. He tried his hardest to keep his balance.

The padlock they should have never touched hung on the open latch screwed into the doorframe. He remembered advising against it, warning of dire consequences, but couldn't drum up any feelings of vindication while there was a gun in his back.

Jake emerged into the lab and squinted his still-sensitive eyes against the battery-powered shop lights glowing from behind the tables. Unlike the last time they'd been there, when the only light had been from the borrowed lantern, the whole tower was bathed in stark white and random shadows. A harsh chemical smell attacked Jake's sinuses and threatened to burrow through to his brain. He rubbed his eyes to keep the invisible mist out, but succeeded only in blurring his vision even more.

Still, he could make out a propane burner flickering on the table across the room, where it was obvious a cook was in full swing. A large metal pole held a pair of glass beakers above the flame, while tubes snaked down to a bucket on the floor beside a white propane tank. A metal canister about the size of a paint can was on the table, the inside covered in blue-green corrosion. It looked like the gunk Jake had found growing on a pair of ancient D batteries he pulled from an old Operation game last year during the family's annual spring cleaning.

Schroeder pushed him toward the center of the room, where Blake was measuring out some sort of powder. She reached back, grabbed Andy by the shoulder, and shoved him into Jake.

"What the fuck?" Blake's tone didn't challenge Schroeder, but it was obvious he wasn't happy with a pair of kids in the middle of his cook.

"Trying a new strategy." Schroeder leveled her gaze at Jake and Andy. The harsh light of the lab blanched out some of the wrinkles she'd earned working for years under the hot sun. "We still have some product from the last cook, right?"

"A little," Blake said. "Jeffery was supposed to take it out last week but never did. It's in the box."

Schroeder's expression was hard, a small grin exposing her crooked tooth in front.

"Get some."

Blake crossed the room to the large gray cabinet Jake wished they'd never opened. Its door hung open; the padlock dangled from its shackle the same way the one downstairs did.

Blake knocked the door to the side. He crouched down in front of the cabinet and dug through it. The handle of a gun stuck up from the back of his waistband. Jake noticed Andy looking down at it and prayed he wouldn't make a grab for it. The gun was only a few feet away, but there was no way Andy could grab it before Schroeder pulled her trigger. A bullet would be out the back of Andy's skull before he got his fingerprints on Blake's weapon.

Unless it tore through Jake instead.

"You're not gonna believe this, but Jeffery looked all over that cabin of yours, and he still couldn't find my money." Schroeder's gun moved slightly as she spoke, but never to a point where it would hit anything but flesh if fired. "And that makes me really upset, because I worked hard for that money, you see."

Blake stood up from the cabinet and swung the door shut behind him. It bounced off the latch the padlock hung from with a metallic gong and slowly drifted open again.

He held a small baggie up for Schroeder. It was full of pea-size white crystals.

"You have any hypos over there?" she asked.

"Yeah."

"Go load up two."

Blake's eyes had a confused look, but he was obviously used to taking orders and turned back to the table immediately.

"Use it all," Schroeder said. Blake didn't turn around but gave a barely perceptible shrug before dumping the remaining crystal out of the baggie. He crushed the rocks into a powder and reached over for a bottle of water.

Jake watched Blake work in the background, and a fresh wave of fear washed through him when he saw the first hypodermic needle. Blake held it up to the light, which shone through and made the solution inside almost glow. He set it down on the table and went to work on the second.

"I've been trying to figure out what to do with you." Schroeder's harsh voice ripped Jake's eyes away from what Blake was doing behind her. "You guys not only found my operation out here; you stole my money. That's a big problem for me, as you can probably imagine."

Blake turned away from the table; a flash of light bounced off the loaded needles as he held them out for Schroeder. She picked one out of his palm and looked at it in the light. The entire barrel of the syringe was filled with a cloudy solution.

"Like you were saying earlier, I can't really just shoot you," Schroeder said. "Murder is a real fucking hassle, you know? It raises a whole lot of questions. Cops find bodies, they usually want answers, and around here they don't have much else to occupy their time. But if I shoot you and bury you out here on this island where you'd never be found, well, that's almost worse, because missing kids . . . oh man . . ."

Jake never imagined someone explaining the reasons she *wouldn't* kill you could be so terrifying. Schroeder's voice was calm, but her eyes hid a fierce anger behind them. If she reached out toward a sleeping puppy, you wouldn't know if she'd stroke its forehead or snap its neck.

"So, the problem I have is, I've got four stupid fucking kids out there that not only took a whole lot of money from me but also know where I make my money. You can see the issue I'm having, right?"

"I swear to God we won't tell anybody." Andy's voice was so calm compared to the alarms that raged inside Jake.

"Now how am I to believe that when you guys have already lied to me about the money?" she asked. "You'll forgive me if I have trust issues."

But they didn't have the money. They had to think of something to convince her they were telling the truth, but Jake's mind couldn't gain any traction. He looked over at Andy and saw his eyes wide and focused into the distance. If they didn't tell them something soon, they'd never get out of there.

Jake was blinking so often he barely noticed it anymore.

"So, as I was saying," Schroeder said. "I can't shoot you, and I can't make you disappear. But I also can't let you go to the cops and tell them about our little operation out here."

She held up the syringe full of meth.

"Luckily, I think we've got a solution right here."

The back of Jake's throat started to burn as he sucked in panicked breaths.

"We've got a meth 'problem' in this county," Schroeder said, eliciting a chuckle from Blake. "Unfortunately, it's even made its way down to kids your age. Kids who don't know anything about moderation. Kids who don't have any self-control. And they like to party, sometimes loud enough that I get a telephone call."

She snatched Andy's wrist. Blake reached under the table and pulled out an empty five-gallon bucket. He flipped it upside down and slid it behind Andy. Schroeder slipped her gun into the holster on her right hip and pushed Andy down onto the bucket. Blake backed behind her, his gun pulled from his waistband and moving between the two boys.

Schroeder loomed over Andy. Her eyes drilled into his face, and her hand still held his arm. "You know what meth feels like, kid? I've seen a lot of tweakers out there who got a little too deep, and it isn't pretty. One guy had scratched half the skin off his face. He just couldn't stop. Can you imagine that? Scratching your cheek so much that you don't even stop when the blood starts flowing?

"But you won't have to worry about that." Schroeder lifted the syringe between their two faces. Andy's eyes were focused behind her, so she tapped the needle on his forehead and snapped his attention back. "You listening to me, kid? You aren't going to have to worry about insomnia or losing your teeth or anything like that, because there is enough ice in here to make your fucking heart explode. Just another kid who didn't know what he was doing and tried *way* too much. Four guys on a weekend alone at the cabin. Partying, drinking, lots of fun. But one of them decides they need to try something a little harder. It's a tragedy, but one we see all too often nowadays."

"Hold on before you do something we're all going to regret." Andy's face was a mask of calm, but Jake was surprised he was even capable of speech. "We had no idea what was out here when we came out the other day. We were just dumb kids exploring an old island. And when we opened that cabinet, we should have shut it and gotten the hell out of here like the guys said. But I grabbed a wad of bills. It was unbelievably stupid, but with all the cash that was in there, I honestly thought you would never notice."

Jake listened in awe as Andy kept his gaze confidently on Schroeder's face.

"But I swear to God that's all I took. We left, and we locked it back up. The rest of the money was still there, so if you're missing any more than that single roll . . . well, I don't know what to tell you. But it wasn't us."

A snort came from behind Schroeder. "Bullshit."

Andy never took his eyes off the woman in front of him. "You don't think we would have given it up the second you guys showed up with guns? Or when you locked us in the basement of a meth lab? Think about it. There has to be someone else who knows where you keep your money."

He let his eyes drift behind her to the cook.

"Maybe someone had a key and figured it would be easy to blame a group of kids for it."

Blake's face darkened, but Jake caught an edge of panic in his voice: "You know I wouldn't touch that money."

Schroeder waved away her cook's protests and met Andy's gaze. "My guys aren't stupid enough to steal from me."

"He doesn't look that smart to me."

Blake turned on Andy, and another jolt of fear swept through Jake as he braced for a gunshot, but Schroeder held her cook back.

"The kid's good." Schroeder chuckled. "Woulda made a hell of a politician giving speeches like that. I mean, I almost believed him, but . . ."

Schroeder straightened up and held her hand out to Blake.

"Give me your belt."

Blake took a step back and undid his tarnished metal buckle. He slid the worn leather strap from around his waist and handed it over.

"You sure you wanna do this here?" he asked.

"Yeah," Schroeder said, looking back at Andy. "There's no way we'd get them back without doing something stupid. It'll be dark for a few more hours."

Jake watched in horror as she pulled Andy's wrist forward and looped the belt around his biceps. Andy's face was blank, his eyes again focused on something behind Schroeder. As she spoke he'd bring his eyes back to her, then dart them behind her again in a pattern Jake had seen plenty of times.

He's fucking with her.

A shot of adrenaline mixed with the fear pumping through his veins as he realized what Andy was doing. All Jake could think about was the gun in Blake's hand, terrified it would open fire the second they tried anything.

To her credit, Schroeder didn't flinch and stayed right in Andy's face, prepared to inject a syringe full of poison into his arm. She was either too focused or too smart to fall for something stupid like that.

Unfortunately for her, Blake wasn't.

He spun his head around to check the shadows behind them. The gun drifted with him, briefly leaving it pointed at the six-foot gap between the boys.

Jake let his instincts take over before his brain could tell him he was crazy. He flew at Blake with a feral intensity and shoved his captor back onto his heels. Jake wasn't a big guy, but he outweighed the scrawny cook by at least twenty pounds and drove Blake back like an offensive lineman taking on an undersize linebacker.

The gun went off with a concussive blast, sending a bullet into the darkness behind them. Jake's ears rang as he continued to push Blake across the room, with no real plan except to push. It was enough to break Schroeder's unrelenting attention, and Andy was ready as if the two boys had coordinated it. The second her gaze left his face, Andy sprang up from the bucket like a cat dropped in a bathtub and hit the crooked DNR officer with a tight bear hug.

Jake and Blake flew back in a tangled embrace of their own until the cook stepped over the nothingness of the stairwell. His defensive grip on Jake disappeared as he teetered backward over the abyss, arms flailing at the handrail in a desperate attempt to stop his fall.

A wild hand found a fistful of Jake's shirt and pitched him forward. Jake slammed into the rickety banister and jarred to a painful stop before he could follow Blake down the steps. He heard the sleeve of his T-shirt rip as Blake fell backward down the dark stairwell, followed by the disturbing thud of his skull smacking against the fifth step from the top. Blake's legs cartwheeled back over his body as he continued, unconscious, down the stairwell.

Behind Jake, Andy tried desperately to hold on to Schroeder, who was a much more formidable opponent than her drug-addled assistant. Jake pushed away from the banister and ignored the pain screaming in his shoulder. Before he could take a step across the room, Schroeder pivoted and shoved Andy away. His hand caught on her belt for a second before he went flying into the worktable behind them. Glass jars and metal canisters went crashing to the floor and skittered into the shadows as Andy fought to right himself.

Schroeder's gun was back in her hand before Andy could push himself up from the table. Jake saw it rise, not in slow motion like the movies, but in a smooth arc he had no chance of stopping.

With Andy still bent backward over the table, Schroeder leveled her gun at Jake. The gap between them might as well have been a mile of open water. Even at full speed, Jake would get maybe three feet before his brains were plastered all over the stripped-to-the-studs wall behind him.

The look on her face said she knew it, too, and it stopped Jake in his tracks. Despite the chaos of the last few seconds, Schroeder still had the aura of someone in complete control.

Resignation crashed through Jake's system as he realized they'd taken their shot at escape and come up short. Any chance of getting away was gone. They'd played their final card and forced Schroeder's hand. The weight of defeat collapsed down on Jake as he waited for the end. Standing in the middle of the room, he braced himself as he wondered if she'd kill him or Andy first.

Would it be worth living an extra thirty seconds if he had to see his friend shot right in front of him?

A small smile crossed Schroeder's lips as she turned her eyes back to the table she'd pushed Andy into moments before. A hearty blast of liquid splashed across her face and brought forth a shriek that echoed around the top of the tower. Schroeder's hands, one still holding the gun, flew up to her face to shield her eyes.

Andy slowly strode toward Schroeder, his outstretched hand coating her face with a steady stream of the pepper spray he'd pulled off her belt when she pushed him away. She buried her face into her right elbow, forcing the gun she still held away from Andy and toward the ceiling, while her left hand waved out in front of her in a futile attempt to block the stream of chemical irritant.

Jake stood frozen, trying to comprehend how their situation had ping-ponged from hopeful to dire and back again in a few short seconds, then jolted back to the moment with the realization that they weren't off the island yet.

Andy circled to his right as the small canister of pepper spray sputtered, positioning their blinded adversary between the two of them. A series of coughs racked Schroeder's body as she desperately wiped her sleeve across her reddened eyes. The barrel of the gun flailed around, then flashed twice before Jake registered the blast and dove to the ground. The shots were wild and ended up buried in the wall behind them, but it was only a matter of time before Schroeder's vision cleared enough to aim.

Jake briefly caught Andy's eye before crawling over behind Schroeder.

Andy's juvenile prank had kicked this sequence off, so another of their old playground tricks might as well end it. With Schroeder turning to Andy, Jake set up on all fours behind her knees and Andy stepped around her blinded thrashing and gave her a hard two-handed shove to the chest. The DNR officer turned drug lord flipped back over Jake and landed flat on the wooden floorboards.

The back of her head cracked against the floor, and the impact knocked the peppered breath out of her, which brought on a seizure of coughing. Combined with the short circuit of her motor skills, she looked like a flipped snapping turtle floundering on the ground.

Jake quickly bent down and scooped up the gun that clattered to his feet. He'd never held a real handgun before, and it was lighter than he'd expected—not much different from a toy. He thought that something so deadly ought to have some heft to it as he leveled it on the writhing woman in front of him.

Andy saw Jake had secured the gun, then stepped forward and delivered a savage kick to Schroeder's ribs. She flopped forward into the fetal position and took her hands from her face for the first time, arms instinctively wrapping around her midsection. The entire upper half of her face was bright red. Her eyes clamped shut, but tears fought their way out along the sides. She coughed and coughed, randomly sending the snot that ran from her nose flying out like a party favor.

"Give me the gun," Andy said.

Jake circled around Schroeder as if she were a coiled snake, keeping well out of her bite radius. He wanted to wipe his eyes but didn't dare, so he blinked against the chemical haze that hung in the room. It burned his sinuses, so he couldn't imagine how Schroeder felt. Andy delivered another vicious kick to the upper part of her chest before he reached out to take the handgun. Jake was happy to get rid of it. There was something unnerving about the handgun. His hand fit into the grip like it had been designed for him, almost like *it* was holding *him*. It was a feeling he'd never gotten with any of his uncle's hunting rifles. It would be far too easy to pull the trigger. Like it *wanted* to be fired.

"Go check on the other guy."

Jake turned back to the stairs and peered down. Blake lay in a clump at the bottom of the stairs, not moving. The position of his limbs suggested he was unconscious. Nobody with a working brain could lie like that.

"He's out," Jake said. "I don't know if he's . . . you know . . ."

"Good," Andy said. As impossible as it had seemed a minute ago, the fight had been fully stripped from Schroeder. She remained curled up in a ball, retching and moaning as Andy trained her own gun on her from above. He pulled the belt Schroeder had strapped on his arm off and tossed it to Jake. "Get this around her feet."

Jake hesitated for a second, reluctant to step back into the room. Their escape path had somehow opened up, and his instinct screamed against going any direction that wasn't out, and out immediately.

"Come on," Andy said. "This stuff will wear off eventually. We've gotta be quick."

He delivered a third kick, stomping his heel into the meat of Schroeder's thigh, which worked to straighten her legs. Jake bent down and looped the belt around her feet as fast as he could, bracing for a series of defensive kicks that never came. He pulled the belt around her ankles and cinched it tight. Blake must have been using this belt for his own drug use, as Jake found multiple holes already punched along the short end. He pulled it as tight as he could and threaded the end through the buckle.

"Good," Andy said. "Now go see what's up with that guy down there."

From where Jake stood, the stairs were no longer an escape route but a cave descending into blackness. He could picture Blake Bourdeau lurking at the bottom, head lolled to the side where his broken neck was unable to sustain it, waiting for a vulnerable ankle to step past. The adrenaline that had surged through his veins only moments ago was dissolving into fear.

"I'll keep an eye on her." As scared as Jake was, there was no panic to be found in Andy's voice. He trained the gun on Schroeder's head, but remained just out of arm's reach in the event she was able to break through the fog of chemicals caked across her face. "Go on."

He tasted the residual pepper spray on his breath, or maybe it was the continued stink from the uncompleted cook behind him.

The thought brought a fresh worry to Jake's head. He had no idea what chemicals were bubbling behind them, or if they were rapidly becoming more dangerous as they were ignored. He'd heard meth labs were prone to explosion but had no idea why. Andy had knocked a whole line of glass bottles down when Schroeder threw him into the table, spilling God-knows-what all over the floor.

"Hey!" Andy reached back onto the table and grabbed a flashlight. He tossed it across the room to Jake, who fumbled it to the ground. By the time he got a grasp on it and stood up again, Andy was holding a small white mask over his face. It was the kind carpenters and painters used, covering only the nose and mouth and giving his voice the same muffle that Jake had heard from Blake and Jeffery when he was hiding in the cabin bathroom. "I need to know if that guy's out or dead or what."

Andy's voice left no room for debate, and Jake's underlying fear kept him out of argument mode. He pointed the flashlight down the stairs and saw Blake still crumpled at the bottom.

He braced his left hand on the narrow wall and gingerly stepped toward the unconscious heap, flashlight dancing around in the darkness.

Jake bent down slightly and put the light on Blake's face. A small pool of blood had formed on the last step under his head, but Jake couldn't tell if he was still breathing.

How long did people stay knocked out for? If he was still out, did that mean he had a serious head injury? Was he dead? Dying?

Does it matter?

Jake warily stepped past him, both worried the man was dead and terrified he was alive, lying in wait to lash out like a rattlesnake in the underbrush. His back foot brushed against Blake's hip, and Jake leaped down into the hallway with a jolt of panic.

The flashlight's beam was more potent at such close range, concentrating the light on the body below as Jake studied Blake's face for signs of life. It was impossible to tell if he was breathing, so Jake slowly extended his hand under Blake's nose. Before he could confirm an exhale, a flicker of motion came from behind the unconscious man's eyelids. Jake's hand flew back fast enough it smacked against the door behind him. He steadied the flashlight on Blake, but saw no other movement. He was alive, but unconscious.

"Andy . . . ," Jake whispered, afraid anything louder could rouse the guy behind him.

Andy's voice filtered down from the lab above.

"He still out?"

Jake opened his mouth to respond but was cut off by a voice from the dark at the far end of the hallway behind him.

"What the fuck?"

Chapter
Twenty-Five

St. John's was a massive building on the west side of town, and Krista parked on the wrong side. She went inside and quickly found herself wandering the halls of the long-term care unit. A woman in pink scrubs swiped her ID to open a door at the end of the hallway. Krista stepped up behind her and caught it before it closed.

The white, antiseptic feeling on the other side was more reminiscent of a 1950s asylum than a modern care facility. An elderly man sat in a wheelchair holding a ragged stuffed rabbit at the end of the hallway. He looked to be in a world of his own, mindlessly stroking a threadbare spot along the bunny's ear.

As Krista stared, a nurse who looked to be the same age as the man approached him and knelt down with a warm smile. The nurse spoke at length with him as one would an old friend. The old man offered little in terms of conversation, but his eyes brightened with the interaction.

The nurse noticed Krista at the end of the hallway and acknowledged her with a nod, but continued talking to the man. The kindness the nurse showed buoyed Krista's spirit, knowing that such people still existed in the world.

Eventually the nurse stood back up and gave the man a warm pat on the shoulder. He reached up from his rabbit and held her wrist for a second, giving her a squeeze before she left.

"Hello," she said. "Didn't mean to ignore you."

"Oh, of course not," Krista said. "I don't mean to pull you away or anything."

The nurse turned back down the hallway. The man hadn't moved, but the ghost of a smile remained on his face.

"He's having a good day, so that's good. I've known him since elementary school. It's not easy to see him go through this, but I am glad he's here and I'm able to help out."

Krista smiled. "I'm sure he's lucky to have you."

"Ronnie actually took me to prom," the nurse said. "We talk about that a lot. It's one of the few things he remembers on a fairly consistent basis, and I think that drives his wife a little crazy." The nurse wore a smile as she turned back to Krista. "How can I help you, hon? Looking for someone?"

Krista asked her about Charles Larssen, and the nurse walked her through the maze of hallways of the memory ward to the independent and assisted living wing. She scanned her ID to open the door and held it as Krista walked through.

"Room 124, down there on the left."

Entering the assisted living wing was like walking through a portal from the bleachy air of a hospital to the casual coziness of a midpriced hotel. Soft lights above illuminated the maroon-and-orange carpet of the hallway, and dark wooden doors lined the walls on each side. Krista found the brass plate that read 124 about halfway down. The door was unadorned, unlike that of Larssen's neighbor, which had an elaborate summer wreath of plastic grapevines around the peephole. She took a breath and gathered her thoughts before knocking. The murmur of a television turned up to top volume bled into the hallway and made her wonder if she'd been heard. She'd just raised her hand to knock again when a voice came from inside.

"Who is it?"

"Hi, Deputy Larssen, my name is Krista Walsh, and I was wondering if I could talk to you for a second."

There was a pause, and Krista waited for the door to open.

"What?"

She leaned in and did her best to direct her voice through the dark wood.

"My name is Krista Walsh, would it be okay if—"

"Quit talking through the door, and just come in."

Krista walked in to find an old man with his feet propped up in a well-worn recliner across the room. A rickety-looking wooden TV tray held a remote control and a folded-over newspaper. The acrid smell of burnt coffee was seemingly baked into the old carpet. A giant television seemed out of place hanging on the wall to the right of the doorway, but the home-repair show that was playing at least seven clicks above normal volume seemed appropriate.

"Who are you?" The old man didn't move from his chair, nor adjust the volume of his TV.

"My name is Krista Walsh. I work . . ." She paused, accustomed to using her position with the congressman to open doors but unsure how much she wanted to bring Harry's name into the conversation. "I'm doing research on an incident from back when you were with the sheriff's office and was hoping I could ask you a few questions."

Larssen gave a noncommittal nod to the couch beside him.

"Might as well sit down then. Don't have many pretty girls come to my door these days wantin' to talk to me, so probably ought to take advantage when it happens."

"Actually, I'm a woman, not a girl, but I'd like to talk to you nonetheless if that's still okay with you." She picked up an old off-white afghan and draped it over the back of the couch before sitting down.

"That you are. My apologies," Larssen said. "I'd offer you some coffee, but my daughter bought me one of those pod machines that only makes one cup at a time, so there's no pot up there. You can make one for yourself, I guess."

Krista offered a smile at his halfhearted attempt at hospitality.

"I'm fine, thanks."

Larssen shrugged, and his eyes drifted back to the television. The wrinkles he'd earned throughout his life stretched along the side of his face like tributaries. "So, what do you want to talk to an old codger like me about?"

"Do you remember an incident on Cedar Lake about twenty years ago? A drug lab burned down out on an island, and a DNR officer was killed?"

The old deputy didn't turn from his show, but glanced over from the side of his eyes.

"Yeah, that was a pretty big deal back then," he said, unconvincingly nonchalant. "What's got you asking about that after all these years?"

His tone told Krista her instincts were spot on.

"Well, I've been looking into what happened, and there are a few things that just don't add up for me. You say it was a big deal, and I'm sure it was, but the police report is barely three pages long."

Larssen kept his eyes on her. "Sheriff didn't like paperwork."

"But his daughter—the DNR officer—died out there. Wouldn't he want to exhaust every option to make sure everyone responsible for her death would be punished?"

Larssen reached over and plucked his coffee mug off the TV tray.

"Lorna send you over here?"

"She showed me the file, which had your statement in it. She said you disagreed with the sheriff on a few things, this being one of them." Krista waited a beat before continuing. "She said you always thought there were others involved."

Larssen laughed and took a sip from his mug.

"That whole file was bullshit, if you'll pardon my French."

"What do you mean, bullshit?"

Larssen's eyes kept cutting back and forth between her and his show. Krista wanted nothing more than to grab the remote and toss it into the forty-inch screen across the room, but she held it together.

"Made up," he said. "Not one damn word of it true, but the sheriff had me write it up anyway."

"Why?"

The question finally snagged Larssen's attention away from the pretty "girl" tearing up the master bathroom in a late-'60s-style ranch.

"Because he *knew* who else was involved in that operation, and she was laying right there in the wreckage."

The realization hit Krista like a bolt from a faulty extension cord.

"Wait—the DNR *was* involved with the drug lab?"

Larssen gave her a knowing look.

"Not all of 'em." His eyes drifted back toward the TV as he spoke. "We'd suspected Kim was into something for a little bit. I did, at least, but the sheriff wouldn't hear of it. When we found her in there, though . . . no denying it after that."

"But what about your statement?" Krista asked. "The report? If you suspected she was involved, why didn't you say that?"

"Sheriff made me write that out, saying that she was first on the scene and she went in while I stayed back. Bullshit. The thought that I would've let that girl—sorry, woman—run in a burning building while I stood outside doing nothing is downright offensive. Anybody who knows me at all will tell you that." Larssen took a deep breath and let his head fall back in his recliner. "Truth is, the first time I laid eyes on her was when they pulled her out of the ashes that afternoon. Couldn't hardly recognize a thing, she was burned up so bad, but her belt . . . that's what I noticed. Practically melted to her body, it was. She liked to wear the same sheriff-issue holster we did even though she spent her whole damn day checking fishing licenses. Sheriff gave it to her. And since we were all out at the scene and accounted for . . ."

Krista sat silently while Larssen continued.

"I knew right away he was gonna try to hush it up. But I didn't think he'd make me lie like that . . . officially. On the record. He said the guy responsible for this was dead and it didn't matter and there was no reason to drag his little girl through the mud over a bunch of rumors. Yeah, the person in charge of the lab was dead, but it sure as hell wasn't Blake Bourdeau. That boy didn't have two thoughts in his head to rub together, but Dean insisted he was some sort of drug mastermind and pinned the whole thing on him. So he tells me what to write, and I write it. Not a damn word of it true, but we filed it away and never mentioned it again. Sheriff says the case is closed, so it's closed, and the truth don't make a noise. Can't say I felt good about it, but he was the boss. He knew I needed that job."

"So you think Kim Schroeder was running the lab?"

"I think she had the Bourdeau boy running it for her. Don't know if it was her idea in the first place or what, but she was the one in charge. My guess is she found out about it somewhere along the way and figured there's more money to be had in taking it over than turning them in."

Krista found herself on the edge of the couch, the loud drone of the TV pushed to the background as her head swirled with competing narratives. What Larssen told her dovetailed with what she had dismissed as the fantastical stories of Jake Nelson. But the more she considered it, the more confused she got. Larssen still didn't say anything about kids and kidnapping. Were they ever actually out there? And if so, when?

"So, if the report is BS, what did you *really* see when you got out there?"

Larssen adjusted his position and drew a loud squeak from his old recliner.

"I was coming off a night shift—last one on my stretch before I went back to days, I remember. Anyways, I was headed back to the office when the call came in about someone seeing smoke out on that back island of Cedar Lake. Shift don't end till you punch out in the office, so I turned around and drove out there. And they were right. You could see the smoke all the way back from the road, and right then I could tell it wasn't no campfire like I'd thought when I got the call. I had my fishing boat docked out there, but by the time I get out to the island, it was already burning itself out and pretty much gone. Old house like that ain't nothing but a pile of tinder, and it probably went up quicker than you'd believe."

"Did you know there was a house out on that island?" Krista asked.

"Yeah, some rich guy from St. Paul built that back in the '40s. Rumor has it the guy was getting older and his gears were getting loose upstairs—like I should talk—but he was out there standing over the builder's shoulder the entire time they were putting it up. He'd decide he wants a whole new room over here. Or that he wants a tower. He did that, you know. There was a big tower on one side like some half-ass castle—pardon my French."

Krista let him ramble about the idiosyncrasies of the building.

"When it was finished, he moved all his stuff out there and then up and died of a heart attack. He either didn't have family or his family didn't have nothing to do with him, so it just sat."

"You ever go out there?" Krista asked. "I mean, besides that day?"

"I was probably out there a few times as a young man," Larssen said. "People made up all kinds of stories about it, how it was haunted or a family was killed there, so of course kids had to go see it. But reality was it was just a weird old house in the middle of nowhere. When I was in high school, kids used to take beer out there sometimes, but then one day the pastor's daughter goes out there with her boyfriend and pretty soon finds herself in a bit of a delicate condition. Well, when the good reverend found out about that, he instructed the mayor, the police, the teachers, and every parent in the congregation that that place was to be off limits. They cracked down hard, so us kids eventually found another place to go."

Larssen chuckled at the memory.

"After a while, people just kind of forgot about it. Now the weeds are so bad in that part of the lake you could hardly get your boat back there anyway."

"So the day of the fire, you were the only one out there? You didn't see anyone else?"

"Right away, yeah," Larssen said. "I looked around as best I could, but between the heat and the smell, you couldn't get near the house anyway. That smell was god awful—never smelled anything like it in my life or since. It burned my eyes, my throat, just breathing it. I felt sick for days after that. How anyone can put that shit in their bodies—pardon my French—is beyond me."

Krista shifted on the couch.

"So you're out there by yourself . . . What did you do?"

"Waited. I put out a few little fires with the extinguisher from my boat before they could spread into the woods, but it was early enough in the morning that things were still pretty wet and there wasn't much risk of that. We probably caught a break there. If it had been dry like it's been the last few years, the whole damn island could have gone up. About fifteen minutes later I got a call on my radio saying that Kellington and the sheriff are at the lake but don't have a boat, so I gotta go get 'em."

"Did you know his daughter was out there then?" Krista asked.

"Her boat was tied up on the back side of the island, so I didn't notice it right away," Larssen said. "But we saw it when I came back with the sheriff. That's when he starts saying Kim must have seen the smoke and come out herself. I looked at Kellington, but he never said a word of disagreement against the boss in his whole damn life. Gave me a bad feeling right then and there."

Larssen took another swig from his coffee mug and held it propped up on his leg.

"They didn't find the bodies till that afternoon. By that time the fire department was out there with their Floto-Pumps and axes, pulling the rubble apart and spraying down what was still smoldering. I knew as soon as I saw that belt, and it fell on me to go tell the sheriff. He didn't react to it—at least not how a normal person would. Maybe he knew, or at least expected something like this to happen, because he never even went over to see her himself. He just kept saying to anyone who would listen she got out here before any of us. Well, if she was out here before me, that means she was out there before the sun came up, while not on duty. I knew it was all bull, but I wasn't about to contradict a man who just found out his little girl was dead."

Larssen's eyes drifted back to the television, but he was paying no attention to the show.

"I was okay letting him go on like that because I figured once it was time to get down to brass tacks, he'd come round to the ugly truth. Regardless of whatever he thought of me, I get no joy out of exposing his family's dirty laundry. But when it comes down to official reports, we can't be fast and loose with the truth just because you're afraid of what the women at church will say."

"But you never talked to anyone about it?" Krista asked. "About what you think really happened?"

"I couldn't," Larssen said. "Once I signed that report, I was just as guilty as he was. Probably more so. Lying on an official report ain't jaywalking."

"Why tell me then?"

Larssen chuckled.

"What are they going to do to me now? Sheriff's dead five years, and I'm an old man sitting in the home. Hell, I'll waive the statute of limitations and let them arrest me just to have something to do with my day."

The former deputy drained his coffee cup and set it on the TV tray. He might've been living in the good end of an old folks' home and lost more hearing than he'd retained, but the gleam in his eye told Krista he was still sharp when he needed to be. "So you answer me a question. Why do you care about all this old stuff?"

It was a question Krista thought she'd managed to avoid, but Larssen dropped that card on the table like he was slow playing his hand. She respected the old man, and lying to him felt wrong.

"I've got a friend who used to vacation at Cedar Lake," Krista said. "He's told me some crazy stories, and I'm trying to figure out what is true and what isn't."

"Aren't we all."

A knock on the door interrupted the conversation. A middle-aged nurse with a Mickey Mouse scrub top popped her head in to say hi and make sure the old deputy had taken his pills. The banter between the two suggested it was a daily occurrence.

"I haven't taken my pills yet," Larssen said after Nurse Mickey had continued down the hall. He had the look of a five-year-old who had learned how to pull one over on his mom.

"Oh yeah?" Krista said.

"I like to take 'em with lunch, but if I tell her that, the Gestapo will be in here every morning at 7:00 a.m. to jam a funnel down my throat."

Krista laughed at Larssen's little rebellion. As someone used to having her hands on the levers, she could see herself pulling little power trips of her own against a nursing staff that was only trying to help.

"So, is your friend Harry Leonard?"

The question flew past Krista like a ninety-mile-per-hour fastball in a slow-pitch softball game.

"How did you know that?" The admission was out of her mouth before she realized what she was saying, and she kicked herself for letting her guard down and tipping her hand.

"It ain't no secret that Harry Leonard is back in the area giving speeches all over this weekend," Larssen said. "And right after I see in the paper some rumors he wants to be vice president or something, Lorna calls me and mentions some woman from the Democratic Party is asking questions about something that happened twenty years ago. Then you show up at my door. I may be old, but I haven't checked out yet. What I don't understand is why Harry Leonard cares about Cedar Lake."

Krista studied the old man she had obviously underestimated.

"We're doing some background research," she said. "Somebody is saying they sold him drugs while he was staying up there back in high school. He denies it, but we can't leave any stone unturned. I'm sure you understand."

The story was flimsy, but it was the best Krista could come up with on such short notice. She was disappointed in herself for not having a cover story ready to go, but she'd never expected the old man to put those pieces together.

"Politics is a dirty business," Larssen said. "Do you think our esteemed congressman is telling the truth?"

The question hit Krista hard. The more she dug into Cedar Lake, the less capable she was of answering that question.

"If I'm honest, I don't know."

Larssen gave a small nod and retracted the footrest on his recliner. Krista took it as a not-so-subtle indication that her time was up.

"But out of curiosity, did you ever figure out if anyone else was involved out there?" she asked with as much nonchalance as possible.

Larssen shook his head slowly. "Like I said, we never did any more looking."

"You don't sound convinced."

For the first time since Krista showed up, Larssen's unreserved, conversational nature seemed to slink away. "I can't say what happened out there for sure, but I was there when they pulled that Gonsalves boy out and—" He paused, then went on. "God as my witness that kid had a nickel-size hole in his forehead."

"You think he was *shot*?" Krista asked.

"Coroner's report says he died of smoke inhalation," Larssen said. "I asked Doc Charlson about that, and he said there was no evidence of violence out in that house. Just a tragic fire like the report said. Doc was also Sheriff's golfing buddy for a whole lotta years."

Krista's head swirled with the steady stream of new information. "You think Schroeder's daughter shot him?"

Larssen grabbed the remote off his tray table and shut the television off. The sudden disappearance of high-volume renovation was jarring.

"I don't, actually," Larssen said. "Like I said, that was an odd house. They had the lab set up in this big tower on one side—probably to keep it hidden just in case somebody remembered the old place was out there and decided to go exploring. The remains of the door had a padlock still on it. That's where Kim and Bourdeau's bodies were—right behind the door to the lab. Pretty much right on top of each other. Some of the fire department guys were making cracks about what they were doing like that before they realized who they were joking about. But that Gonsalves boy was found in the hallway, on the other side of the door."

Krista's ears rang in the quiet as she contemplated what the old cop was saying. "Maybe Schroeder and Blake were up in the lab when they heard this guy coming? They could have easily come down the steps and shot him in the hallway, right? What's so crazy about that?"

Larssen took a deep breath.

"First off, we found two guns out there, but both were fully loaded. Like I said, Kim was wearing that holster her daddy gave her—but it was empty. Her gun never turned up," Larssen said. "But what really gnawed at me was that the padlock we found was on the outside of the door. There's no way to lock it from the inside. So somebody else had to have locked 'em up there, but the only person we found that could have done it was already dead."

The old deputy's eyes hardened.

"That tells me somebody else was out there, and they probably have a lot of answers on how those three people died."

Chapter
Twenty-Six

Terror shut down Jake's nervous system as he stared at the gigantic shadow looming at the dark end of the hallway. The crumpled, unconscious body below was forgotten as the black shape moved slowly toward him.

A sheen of clammy sweat broke out on his palms, and Jake felt his eyes clamp shut for even longer than normal. Panic made him tighten his grip on the flashlight as the beam stretched down the hall.

"Jesus, what'd you do?" Jeffery's voice was menacing, but had more than a note of confusion. Jake's thoughts were jumbled enough he was about to apologize when Andy's voice popped up behind him.

"Don't move." He held Schroeder's flashlight alongside the gun in front of him like he was starring in his own action movie. He kept both trained on Jeffery and casually stepped over Blake's unconscious body into the hallway.

The big guy's momentum stopped at the sight of the gun, and his hands shot out in front of him. "Whoa, whoa, man. Take it easy."

The harsh glare of the flashlight stripped the aura of intimidation from Jeffery. It cast strange shadows around his face, and his eyes were huge despite the assault of light coming from Andy's hand.

"Keep your hands where I can see them." Andy's tone was steely and gave Jake goose bumps on the back of his neck.

"Careful with that, okay, man?" Jeffery seemed scraped clean of confidence and control. "Let's not get crazy here."

"Shut the fuck up," Andy said. He stepped past Jake and positioned himself between the two. "Where are Seth and Ryan?"

"The other guys? They're downstairs, right where you were. They're fine, okay? I didn't touch 'em."

Jake was still crouched over Blake, his own flashlight slick with sweat in his hand.

"Where's your gun?" Andy asked.

"In my jeans—right side." Jeffery kept his hands in full view as he spoke. "It's not a—"

"Show me."

Jeffery kept his eyes wide and locked on Andy as he slowly lifted his shirt. Around the far side of his generous belly, the handle of a pistol jutted out from the waistband of his jeans. Despite the situation, Jake found himself wondering how it fit in there.

"You can have it," Jeffery said. "Take it and go. I'm not looking for any problems here."

Andy took another step down the hall, Schroeder's gun still out in front of him.

"Pull it out very slowly, and put it on the ground."

Jeffery's cheeks jiggled as he nodded. He kept one hand in front of him and carefully reached down for his gun. It slipped away from his waist easily. Jake's anxiety ticked up a notch with the gun in full view, but Jeffery held it with just three fingers at the base of the grip. He bent down slowly and carefully and set it on the floor in front of him as if he were handling a bomb.

"There it is." Jeffery rose in full surrender. He kicked the gun into the shadows of the hallway and took a step back. "I don't want any trouble. This whole thing is *her* deal. Only reason I'm even here is because I bought some of their shit one time and now if I don't do what she says, she'll turn me in. I don't care about you, I don't care about the money, I don't care about whatever you did."

Andy's gun never wavered from the spot between Jeffery's eyes, raising the pitch and speed of the big guy's voice.

"You can leave. Your friends are fine. They're right downstairs. You can go get them and go. Just go, okay?"

A slight movement came from Blake's body and sent Jake flying up to his feet. He whipped his light down to the base of the stairs, but Blake was still unconscious. Maybe he was waking up, or maybe it was just gravity, but Jake kept the light on him as he backed toward Andy.

"Let's go, man." Jake's voice cracked with another wave of encroaching panic. "Come on, let's get out of here."

"We will," Andy said.

A massive flash filled the hallway with a bang, and Jake thought the house had exploded. The reverberation in his right ear discombobulated him enough he never heard Jeffery's body hit the floor, and it took a second to realize the house was still standing but the big guy was not.

Jake felt Andy's hand on his shoulder and watched his lips move without comprehension. A hand slid up his shoulder and grabbed the back of his neck. "You understand me?"

Understand? Understand what?

"Go down and get the guys," Andy said. "Seth and Ryan are in the basement, and you've got to let them out so we can go. Can you do that? We're getting out of here."

Jake blinked himself back to coherence and nodded.

"All right," Andy said. "Quickly, now. I'll meet you guys out front."

Jake followed the shaky circle of light from his flashlight past Jeffery's body, his brain not registering the hole between the man's eyes. His mind was still running a step behind, but his motor skills returned as he descended the stairs to the first floor. By the time he opened the cellar door, he'd pushed everything out of his head besides escape.

Ryan and Seth were seated back to back at the bottom of the stairs, their hands lashed to the railing behind them. They both instinctively looked up, squinting into the light Jake was casting down on them.

"Guys . . ."

Both started pulling at their restraints at the sound of Jake's voice. Ryan slid his hands up the post and tried to get his legs under him as Jake flew down the steps.

"What's going on?" Ryan's voice was still a tepid whisper.

"We need to get outta here." Jake tucked the flashlight under his arm to free up both hands so he could work on the extension cord threaded around their wrists. "Scoot forward."

The two guys maneuvered apart to give Jake as much room as they could.

"Where's Andy?" Seth asked. His voice was slightly louder than Ryan's but held the same fear. Jake ignored the question and kept pulling behind them. Andy didn't matter. They had to get out. The cord was cinched tight, the rubber coating holding the knots together. He dug his fingers in and strained to untangle the cord. Jake's hand slipped, and the corner of his fingernail bent backward in a flash of pain.

"FUCK!"

Everything he'd suppressed was beating back the composure Jake desperately clung to.

"What happened up there?" Seth's voice lowered. "Are they coming?"

The flash Schroeder's gun had made in Andy's hand came back, but Jake tried to shake it away. He was able to work the plug end of the cord out, and the knot finally loosened. His hands struggled with eagerness as he tried to pull Ryan's hands free, ignoring Seth's questions and the visions they brought up. Ryan untangled his hands from the makeshift rope and spun around to face Jake.

"Dude." Ryan glanced up the stairs as he fought to keep his voice composed. He reached over and replaced Jake's fumbling hands working on the cord around Seth's wrist. "Where's the big guy?"

Seth cut him off before Jake could find an answer. "Hey, get me loose here."

"Sorry." Jake turned back and focused the light on the hands behind Seth's back. Ryan worked the knot, which came undone easier without a second person tied up in the way. Seth pulled his hands out, and the green electrical cord slumped to the ground. The two of them stood up alongside Jake, who was already on the first step headed up when Ryan grabbed his arm and pulled back.

"What the hell is going on?"

"We've got to go." It was the only set of words Jake could string together. He stood up and pointed the flashlight back up the empty stairs.

The three of them emerged on the first floor, and Jake swept the light around the front hallway before fixing it on the front door. Andy was still upstairs.

The memory of the gunshot flashed in his head again. It cleared enough mental fog that a question Jake had been too scared to ask emerged.

Why?

Schroeder and Blake had been taken care of. Jeffery had dropped his gun. He said they could leave, that he didn't care about the money. The path was clear; they'd done it.

And Andy shot him anyway. He'd killed an unarmed man.

The thought sent a chill through Jake as he glanced at the stairway.

"You guys go. I'll run up and get Andy."

Ryan reached out and tried to grab Jake's shirt as he turned up the steps. "Whoa, man, we're not separating."

"Just get out of here, okay." Jake wasn't going to let his friends delay their chance at escape.

And he couldn't let them see what had happened upstairs.

"I'll get him, and we'll be right behind you."

Chapter
Twenty-Seven

Larssen's words bounced around Krista's head like a mental game of *Pong* as she drove west on Highway 60.

Somebody else had to have locked 'em up there.

The former deputy had kicked around a few theories over the years—rival producers, maybe a disgruntled member of Schroeder's crew—but none was anything more than vague conjecture. They'd never been able to find anyone who knew about the lab's location, let alone place someone at the scene that night.

Krista, on the other hand . . .

HE'S A KILLER, YOU KNOW! A FUCKING KILLER!

There's no way, though. Jake Nelson was an unhinged man obviously nursing a multidecade grudge against Harry. An isolated drunk holed up in a shack held together with duct tape and cigarette smoke who'd come after her at the mention of Harry's name.

Just because he had known about Kim Schroeder didn't mean Harry was a liar. Or worse.

No, she'd been by Harry's side for years. There was no way he could hide something like this from her. If he was capable of something like what Jake was implying, she'd know.

Krista tried to rationalize the disparate threads as the flat country-side blurred by her, but nothing came together in a way that explained anything. Doubt had taken root. It burrowed deep into her brain and was releasing a steady stream of unwanted thoughts she couldn't shake.

Krista's head overflowed with questions she was no longer sure she wanted answers to.

It wasn't a conscious decision to drive past Mankato, where Harry still had a full afternoon of meetings and events at Minnesota State, but her Altima didn't slow down when the off-ramp flew past. She knew it was a terrible idea—reckless and dangerous—but that house was calling to her, so she kept her car pointed at the afternoon sun.

At some point she had to know, and Jake Nelson might be the only one who had answers. Part of her was hoping he was truly a raving lunatic. It would mean she was willingly returning to an extremely dangerous situation, but at least she wouldn't be working for a murderer.

Road signs got her back to Ranford, but Krista had to stop and pull out her phone if she expected to find Jake's run-down rural shack again.

The home screen showed thirty-two unread messages and twelve voicemails. She didn't have to look to know who they were from.

Parked on the side of the road was the perfect time for logic to step in and send her back to Mankato. As chief of staff, she belonged alongside her congressman, taking notes and helping guide him through the potential minefield that was political appearances.

That was her job, not tracking down ghosts and digging up dirt on her own candidate.

But instead, she put her car back into drive and wove through rural roads toward a man who had threatened a congressman and come after her the last time she'd seen him.

It wasn't ill advised; it was dangerous and stupid.

Krista looked down at her phone as she drove deeper into the countryside—the little blue dot that stood in for her car was no longer moving.

No service had replaced the row of bars at the top of her screen.

The back tires of her Altima hit a patch of loose gravel and fishtailed ever so slightly, jolting her eyes back to the road and clamping her hands around the steering wheel. She straightened the car out and eased her foot off the accelerator. The car coasted to a stop in the middle of the rural ribbon of gravel.

Krista sat there, just breathing, as a few beads of sweat bubbled up on the back of her neck. It took another couple of minutes before she realized she was effectively parked in the middle of the road, yet not a single car had passed her from either direction, emphasizing how isolated this section of southwest Minnesota was.

Lush, green cornfields dominated the landscape—the leafy seven-foot stalks bracketing the road like the walls of a canyon. The late-afternoon sun hung low in the distance, allowing creepy shadows to crop up all over.

Undeterred, Krista thought back to her trip out to Jake's homestead the day before. She remembered a little bridge before making a turn and thought if she could find that road, her memory would take her the rest of the way.

She pulled her foot off the brake and crept forward. The car drifted toward the middle of the road and didn't break twenty-five miles per hour, but no other drivers were around to complain. The bridge spanned a little creek about a mile up the road, and Krista's turn was right where she expected.

Her memory navigated as she'd hoped, and within five minutes she saw the little clump of trees surrounding Jake's house in the distance. Krista slowed but didn't stop as she turned down the long driveway cutting through the soybean fields that buffered his place from the road.

The fear returned when she saw the house. What the hell was she doing?

Krista pulled her car into the same spot she'd torn away from the day before and killed the ignition. The ruins of the old barn to her left loomed even more ominous in the fading light of day.

She couldn't help but marvel at the dichotomy of the broken structure. From the road it looked like any other old farm building. It needed some paint and a few shingles, but was no different from any other. It wasn't until halfway down the driveway that the rotted and collapsed back half revealed itself.

The engine ticked as it cooled before giving way to an almost unnatural silence. She stared at the front door and expected Jake to appear behind the old screen door again. As if he'd stood sentry since the day before.

But there was no sign of him. Both the screen and inner doors stood shut.

She waited another ten seconds in the hopes good judgment would intervene, then popped the driver's side door and stepped out. The silence from inside the car followed her out and settled over the yard like a blanket—as if even the birds and crickets had better sense than to come out here.

Bits of gravel dug into the soles of Krista's shoes as she walked around the front of her car and crossed the yard toward the house.

Krista punched the doorbell and heard an echo from inside. She didn't bother taking a deep breath before rapping her knuckles on the aluminum frame of the screen door. The sharp, metallic sound reverberated back through the kitchen and into the living room.

Instead of reconsidering, she knocked again, but the run-down house remained silent.

Before the idea that Jake wasn't home could spur her back to the car, Krista caught a flicker of motion to her left and saw Jake's head duck back around the corner.

"Jake!" Krista backed off the improvised cinder-block-and-wood step in front of the door. She briefly considered going after him, but instead took a few more steps away from the door, keeping her eyes on the corner of the house as she backed up over the dying grass.

Krista opened her mouth to call out again when Jake appeared, a rusty shovel in his hands. The patchy stubble from the other day had thickened around his face, and his thinning hair had devolved into a greasy nest.

"What the hell are you doing here?" His bloodshot eyes were full of what she hoped was only agitation.

"I just want to talk." Krista continued a slow side step with both hands out in front in a reassuring stance, but one that could quickly become defensive if needed. Out of habit, she closed her profile to keep her dominant hand back and ready.

"You bring the cops?"

The question surprised Krista, until she realized that Jake was the one who was scared. That made sense, if what he'd said about Harry was true.

"No," Krista said. "But I was at the sheriff's office this morning. I saw the case file about what happened on Cedar Lake."

Jake eyed her skeptically and kept both hands on the shovel.

"Kim Schroeder—the DNR officer who died out there—was the sheriff's daughter," Krista said. "They'd suspected she was involved in something like that for a while, but never had any proof until they found her out there. But the sheriff had them write up a fake report and made up some BS about her discovering the place on her own. He wanted to protect his girl."

Krista stared at Jake as the information clicked for him. It was a puzzle that had sat uncompleted for twenty years, and someone had fished that final missing piece out from under the couch at last. The validation of all those years of paranoia and conspiracy was evident on Jake's face. He set the tip of the shovel down on the ground and rested his arm on the top of the handle. He stared at the dying grass in front of him and shook his head slowly.

She took a cautious step closer, and Jake jolted. His grip on the handle of the shovel tightened to the point his knuckles whitened. It stopped Krista in her tracks.

"I didn't tell you who I was the last time I was out here." She struggled to keep her voice as calm and soothing as possible. Even though he seemed relieved that she'd confirmed what he'd been saying, Jake remained volatile. "I'm not a reporter, but you probably know that by now. My name is Krista, and I am Harrison Leonard's chief of staff."

She put her hands up in reassurance and took a nonthreatening stance. She'd kill for Harry's people skills right then. Hell, he was probably good enough to talk Jake down no matter what their shared history was.

"You sent those postcards, right? You sent that map," Krista said. "You said *justice is coming*."

"People need to know about him," Jake said. "About what he did. About what he's capable of."

"Whatever your reasons, it wasn't something we could just let go. You had to know somebody would be looking into it." Krista took a half step closer to Jake. "Well, I looked into it . . . and I still don't know what I've found. But I do know this: Everything you told me last time I was here sounded crazy. Honestly, I still don't know if you're telling me the truth or not, but I think there is a hell of a lot more to what happened out there than what I've been told."

A crow cawed off in the distance, breaking the eerie silence that had settled on the farm. The sun had dipped below the trees, casting long shadows across the yard.

"You could say that," Jake said. His voice had that same distance it did when he first recounted his fantastical stories the day before in his living room.

A chill went through Krista's body, and not from the sudden lack of sunlight.

"Tell me."

Chapter
Twenty-Eight

Blake appeared in the flashlight's beam at the far end of the hallway, where Jake purposely kept his eyes as he raced past Jeffery's dead body. The cook was still crumpled at the bottom of the stairs in what Jake thought was the same position. He paused for a second, then braced his hands on the sides of the stairwell and vaulted over the unconscious form. The stairs creaked as Jake bounded up to the lab.

The remnants of the pepper spray and the interrupted cook combined to give the air a harsh chemical taste that burned the inside of Jake's nose.

Schroeder remained on the floor. The belt Andy had made Jake loop around her ankles was still tight, and now he had her hands lashed behind her as well. Her eyes were swollen shut, and her entire face had taken on the angry red of a sunburn. A fresh gash ran along her hairline. The blood mixed with the mucus flowing from her nose to make a disgusting, frothy pink paste.

Andy was over by the shelves on the left side of the lab, his back turned.

It took Jake a second to find his voice, and he had to clear his throat before it would work. "The guys are downstairs. Let's go."

"Just a sec." Andy rummaged through the stuff on the shelf.

"Come on." Jake hurried across the room, ignoring the DNR officer slowly pulling against her restraints to the left. The fact they were going to get out of this house alive was a miracle, and Jake kept his thoughts on that fact. He couldn't comprehend how his friend could be thinking about anything but escape at this point. "The guys are outside waiting. We've gotta go now."

"I know, I know." Andy turned back toward Jake and hastily scanned the area around him. After a second of deliberation, he reached back for one of the camp stove cans lined up below the shelves. Jake also noticed Schroeder's gun stuffed in the waistband of Andy's shorts.

"What the fuck are you doing?" Jake's voice had gained an impatient edge.

"We've got to make sure nobody knows we were out here." Andy's smooth voice was gone.

The fear that made Jake meek was now fueling his aggression.

"We have to get the hell out of here right now and call the fucking cops," Jake shouted.

Andy's eyes narrowed, and he scanned the table for something, not bothering to look at Jake as he spoke. "We can't call the cops."

"What are you talking about?" Jake couldn't fathom why Andy was fighting him on this. It wasn't like they could just walk away and leave Schroeder out there to track them down. The situation had gone well past simply forgetting it ever happened.

Andy turned back to Jake. "You think cops aren't going to ask about the money?"

Jake was about to argue that the cops wouldn't give a shit about the $440 they took when Schroeder's and Jeffery's voices echoed in his head.

My guys aren't stupid enough to steal from me.

I don't care about you, I don't care about the money.

You didn't spend almost $100,000 on fucking pizza.

Jake went cold. "You didn't . . ."

Andy's lack of an answer hung in the air between them, but Jake didn't need it. He'd seen the look on Andy's face when they saw the money. He should have known he wouldn't let it go.

"No, you put it back . . . I *saw* you put it back." Jake said it more out of obligation than belief, because he knew it wasn't true. Of course it wasn't. Had he really expected Andy Leonard to do what he'd asked? "This is all your fault. All of this. How the fuck could you do this to us?"

All the fear that had coursed through Jake turned to rage. He shot his hand out and grabbed a handful of Andy's T-shirt.

"I fucking told you to put it back." He shook Andy as much as his muscles allowed. "Why didn't you just put it back?"

Andy's hand flew up to knock Jake's away, but the grip was too tight.

"I did." Andy's voice had no trace of remorse. "Then I came back out on the Jet Ski last night when you guys were passed out."

Jake thought back to all the drinks Andy had made for them the night before. Always making sure everyone had a full one. Andy saying he was going to bed, followed by the sound of the porch door banging slipped through his hazy memory.

"You almost got us fucking killed." Jake shook his friend. "Why?"

"Because I had to," Andy said, his voice indignant as he struggled with Jake's grip.

"The hell you did." Jake pushed him back into the shelves, sending a cascade of ingredients to the floor. "We could've just walked out of there, and none of this would have ever happened, you greedy motherfucker."

"Greedy? Fuck you. You've got no clue." Andy kicked a bottle of camp fuel into the dark room. "None of you do. Money doesn't mean a thing to you because you fucking have it."

"What are you talking about?" Jake asked.

"I *need* that money. That money gets me into college. Gives me a future. Without that, I've got nothing."

Jake couldn't grasp what his friend was saying, and the fumes building up in the lab were probably not helping.

"What about the money from your grandma?" Jake said. "You said she left enough money for school, any school in the goddamn country."

There was a pause where the only sound was breathing.

"It's gone." Andy's voice had quieted considerably, and the defiance had drained from his face. "Dad had to go to a . . . facility. Up by Brainerd. It cost a shitload, and we don't have insurance, so Mom said we had to use the money Grandma left me. Every goddamn cent of it. She said they'll pay it back, but maybe I'll have to wait a year . . . but fuck, you know . . ."

A series of hacks from Schroeder snapped the boys back to the reality of their situation.

"I fucked up and I'm sorry, but there isn't shit I can do about it now," Andy said.

"But we can't just leave and pretend this never happened." Jake looked over the table full of drug-making supplies and settled on Schroeder. Her face was still red, but it looked like her eyes were clearing. His voice lowered to a whisper. "You . . . you killed that guy."

Andy stepped in front of Jake and peered into his eyes. "I had to, because nobody can know we were here. You want the cops asking how that other guy ended up dead at the bottom of the steps? Even if he's alive, *YOU* pushed him down the steps and broke his neck." Andy's voice was soft but full of accusation.

Panic flowed back into Jake's head. "But—"

"Don't listen to him, kid." Schroeder's voice came up from the floor and shocked Jake into silence. She sounded like a lifelong smoker climbing five flights of stairs. She hacked again before continuing. "Trust me, he'll turn on you the second—"

Andy smacked the butt of Schroeder's gun across her temple and cut her off midwarning. He stared down at her crumpled form before turning back to Jake.

"Don't listen to her." Andy's voice had lost all aggression and was as close to soothing as the situation would allow. But his eyes told the truth. They were hard. "Like I was saying, we have to make sure there's no way they can know we were here. There could be fingerprints or whatever else all over, and none of us want the cops asking questions, right?"

Andy picked up the camp fuel he'd grabbed earlier. He twisted off the top and flipped it on its side, sending a cascade of fuel onto the floor. Jake jumped back from the splash. The petroleum odor beat out the other chemical smells to briefly fill his nose before retreating to the background. The pool spread across the floor as Andy swung the can in an arc, saturating the old floorboards with the flammable liquid.

"What about them?" Jake stood frozen, barely able to comprehend what his friend was doing.

Andy flipped the empty can upside down and tossed it under the table, where it clanged against a white propane tank. He wiped his hands down his shorts and reached over for a box of wooden kitchen matches.

Andy nodded at the stairs as he slid the box open and pulled out a match. Jake thought he saw the match tremble slightly in Andy's hand. "You see it on the news—these places burn down all the time."

He pulled the red tip across the side of the box, and Jake flinched, terrified the spark would ignite the entire room. It didn't catch and made nothing but a dull scratching sound.

Andy looked up into Jake's petrified face and stepped over to him, unlit match in hand. "Where are Seth and Ryan?"

Jake's mouth was dry. He had to swallow a couple of times before he could talk.

"Outside. I told them to go and we'd catch up with them."

Andy attempted a smile.

"Good plan," he said. "Go find them. I'll be right behind you."

He waited a beat before turning back to the fuel he'd sloshed across the floor.

"Nobody's going to know we were here. We can just leave it behind and forget about it. It's going to be fine." The last part came out like Andy was speaking to himself.

Another series of hoarse coughs snapped Jake out of his nervous haze as Schroeder stirred. She rolled onto her side, now barely three feet from a whole row of combustibles.

Jake stepped across the room and reached down toward her restraints. His fingers shook as he fumbled with the belt around her ankles. "We've gotta get—"

The second the belt loosened, Schroeder's foot lashed out with a blind kick. Jake felt the air move as her boot missed his nose by less than an inch. He scrambled back as Schroeder's legs bucked out repeatedly.

"What the fuck are you doing?" Andy rushed over and yanked Jake to his feet. Schroeder kicked a few more times, then used her feet to inchworm herself across the floor toward the back wall.

"I thought . . . I mean, we can't leave her tied up here."

"You need to go. Now!" Andy's voice was full of command and authority. "Go find the guys. I said I'll take care of this."

Jake's mind whirled in a fog, and he didn't know if it was fear or the chemical haze he'd been breathing in since Schroeder brought them up there, but his thinking was muddled.

"Go find the guys."

Jake nodded but didn't turn to go. Schroeder, whose hands were still behind her, had used her newly unbound legs to scoot away from the pool of fuel. The snap of Andy's match against the rough strip rousted Jake into action. He turned down the steps as Andy tossed the lit match across the room. The whoosh of ignition burned away any trepidation Jake had about Blake Bourdeau coming to at the bottom of the stairs, and he leaped over the still body without a thought. Jake didn't need stories of meth labs exploding for motivation. The number of fuel canisters he'd seen was enough to press his overdrive button.

He was almost to Jeffery's body when he heard Andy land off the stairs behind him. A quick glance back showed Andy's silhouette framed in the doorway where Blake lay.

"Come on!" Jake's voice echoed down the hallway.

"Just go," Andy said.

Jake ran back toward Andy's shadow. All the thoughts and fears in his head had morphed into a clock. Glowing red numbers counting down from an unknown number, each tick bringing them closer to disaster.

He skidded to a halt and almost tripped over Andy, who'd knelt over Blake's crumpled form. A moan escaped the man's lips as Andy dug his hands behind his shoulders. If Blake was alive, they could probably drag him out before the fire got too out of control. And Schroeder's feet were loose, so she could conceivably work her way free and find her way out.

After we are long gone.

Before the fire consumes the house.

"Quick, gimme a hand," Andy said.

Jake shook the creeping fears to the far corners of his head and lifted Blake by his narrow shoulders.

Thank God it wasn't the fat guy.

It was a random thought for their situation, but accurate. There was no way they could've lifted Jeffery, but Blake's DNA and drug history left him plenty movable.

Blake's eyes fluttered open as Jake got him off the ground. Andy stood up and grabbed the door.

"Good." He swung the door shut until it hit Blake's back and knocked Jake aside. Andy put a shoulder into it and pushed, shoving Blake back onto the lab's staircase.

Jake looked up from the ground in disbelief as Andy propped his foot against the door and lifted the padlock off its ring. He flipped the latch with one hand and closed the padlock over it.

"Come on." Andy held his hand down for Jake. A dull crackle kicked up from the other side of the door. Jake stared at Andy as the red numbers in his head ticked down. "Dude, we gotta go. Now."

Andy reached down and grabbed Jake's forearm, trying to spur him into motion. "Come on."

His brain didn't register the pain in his arm as Andy's fingers dug in, trying to lift him up. It didn't register the sting when Andy slapped him across the face.

"We gotta go now, man!"

Survival instinct eventually kicked in and took the wheel, pulling Jake off the ground and toward the door. Andy kept a hold on his forearm the entire trip down the stairs and out of the house.

Seth and Ryan were standing along the tree line in the front yard. They sprinted over as soon as Andy dragged Jake onto the porch.

"What the—"

A concussive blast from the tower cut him off. The blackened windows blew out in a shower of painted glass. Orange flames stretched out from them like devil horns.

"GO!" Andy shouted, dragging Jake behind him with one hand, Schroeder's gun stuffed in the back of his shorts. If Seth or Ryan noticed it, they didn't say anything as a second explosion sent the guys sprinting through the woods.

Chapter
Twenty-Nine

Listening to Jake tell his story left Krista numb. He had the same frantic tone and far-fetched tales as before, only this time she believed him. Not because of what she'd learned at the sheriff's office or what Deputy Larssen had told her, but because of the way Jake told the story; blinking eyes full of fear and regret, but without a trace of malice.

She tried to rationalize Harry's actions on that island, but couldn't pull her mind up that mountain. A lot could be justified from that night, including Jake's pushing Blake down the stairs, but as soon as Jeffery dropped that gun, any arguments of self-defense went up in smoke. Their path to safety was clear, but Harry shot him anyway. Then he locked the door to make certain the other two never had a chance to get out.

All so nobody would know he'd taken the money. Not the beer money he'd claimed, but a whole lot more. Enough to pay his way through college and start a political career.

A career she had helped build.

"There was a fishing boat tied up next to Schroeder's—I figure that's how the big guy got out there—but Andy wouldn't let us take it. Said the cops would know somebody else was out there. He made us swim to the shore." Jake blinked. "Those fucking weeds . . . grabbing at you from below. The whole way across I was terrified some big fucking pike was gonna blast out of those weeds and sink its teeth into my leg. Haven't set foot in a lake since."

The words hung in the heavy evening air before Krista found her voice. "How did you get back to the cabin?"

"Walked," Jake said. "Barefoot. My feet hurt so bad. I don't think anyone said a word the whole way around the lake. It was like we were a platoon of soldiers returning from something awful. I guess we were."

Sunlight was retreating fast, but Krista noticed a tear running down Jake's face as he blinked it away.

"When we got back, the cabin was trashed. Jeffery had turned the place upside down before heading out to the island, and it took forever to get the place together again." Jake trailed off for a minute. "He broke one of the drawers in the living room by the TV. Man, my parents were pissed when they saw that. But what do you say? Couldn't tell 'em the truth."

An image of four shell-shocked teenage boys putting together a ransacked house in silence stirred up a fresh load of emotions in Krista. She looked at Jake Nelson's beaten-down face and couldn't imagine someone so young going through that, then hiding it away all these years.

"But he didn't find the money?"

Jake lifted his gaze at the mention of money.

"Wasn't in the cabin." Jake took an agitated breath. "I was down on the dock getting the boat put away when Andy came down. We had an old paddleboat down there on the shore. Nobody ever used it because it had a leak, so it was just kinda shoved back halfway into the trees. He reached underneath, and there was the money. He'd cleaned out the whole cabinet. I don't think he knew I was there when he came down, but he saw me after he pulled out the bag. He yanked out a wad of bills and tried to hand it to me. Said he was sorry and it was for the cabin."

"What did you do?"

"I told him to fuck off. Just seeing that bag made me so angry. I could've killed him right there. I said if I ever saw that money again, I'd call the cops. Tell them everything that happened out there."

Krista could hear some of that anger returning to Jake's voice.

"He said he was sorry." Jake started moving his shovel back and forth, grinding the pointed scoop into the dry, packed dirt below. *"I'm sorry."*

She still couldn't conceive of the Harry she knew pulling that trigger, but Krista could absolutely see Harry convincing his friend to go along with what he was doing. Not only helping him but getting him to bury that secret for years.

"Is there any proof of this? What happened out there?"

Jake looked up from his shovel.

"I never threw away the gun."

"Wait . . ." Krista's mind spun as the crickets started to sing in the fading daylight. "Which gun?"

"The DNR woman's gun. The one Andy shot that guy with. I wanted to get rid of it so bad—bury it at the bottom of the lake. And I was going to. But . . . maybe I knew I would need it someday, if I was ever brave enough to tell. So I stashed it under the paddleboat. Same place Andy hid his money."

A small breeze kicked up a swirl of dust on the gravel driveway.

"How did you end up with it?"

Jake ignored the question. "We had an old shed where we'd keep all the water and yard stuff. Life jackets and floaties and fishing poles. The lawn mower, gas cans, that kind of stuff. Before we left I took it in there, found a loose floorboard in the back, and stuffed it under there."

Krista stepped forward, getting within arm's length of Jake for the first time. She put her hand on his shoulder and drew his gaze to her. "Jake, is the gun he used still there?"

"I tried to forget about it, but I couldn't get it out of my mind. It would call to me when I slept. Like that freaking "Tell-Tale Heart" thing we had to read in high school. I thought going off to college would help, but it didn't. I couldn't get away from it. The farther I got, the worse it seemed to get. So, one time during freshman year, I drove down by myself and got it." Jake's hand tightened on the shovel's handle, and

Krista could see his knuckles whiten again. Blood flowed back when he released. "Something about having it quiets things down for me."

That last sentence gave Krista a shot of worry. She'd read a lot about suicide earlier in the year when a large bill involving Veterans Affairs was moving through Congress.

"Does holding it make you feel better?" she asked.

Jake shook his head.

"I've never even actually touched it," he said. "It's still in the same Wonder Bread bag I stashed it in all those years ago. I think it's become like . . . I dunno, a talisman or something. If it's around, I still have it. I control it. It's proof I didn't just dream all that stuff up. No matter what the hell Andy Leonard says."

"Where is it now?" Krista asked.

Jake nodded across the yard to the dilapidated barn.

"It's been in there since the day I moved out here."

Krista took a moment and then made a decision in the fading light. "Show me."

She had no doubt that Harry Leonard was a murderer, just like Jake had said. That old handgun could potentially prove it.

Chapter Thirty

The cabin wasn't in pristine shape, but no worse than would be expected after being occupied by four teenage boys for the week.

Nobody would suspect what had happened.

The boys had worked in relative quiet, the shock of their experience weighing on them like a heavy fog.

It wasn't until they started packing up Ryan's car that the dam of silence finally broke.

"Wait . . . we've gotta talk about this. What the hell happened out there? Aren't we going to call the police?" Seth jabbed his finger at the gun still in Andy's waistband. "And what the fuck are you doing with *that*?"

"We won't have to call the police," Andy said, ignoring Seth's question about the weapon. "Somebody will see the smoke for sure. Heck, they're probably on the way or maybe even out there already. They'll see all the drug stuff, and that will be it."

"What happened with Schroeder and that bartender guy?" Ryan asked. "How did you guys get away?"

"Jake did it," Andy answered, even though the question was clearly directed at Jake. "He knocked the guy down the steps, and I was able to grab the pepper spray off Schroeder's belt when she was distracted. I sprayed her with it and grabbed her gun. But it was Jake that started it all. He did it, man. Fucking hero."

The image of Blake's crumpled body flickered through Jake's mind. The way his eyes moved beneath their lids, showing he was still alive.

"What about the big guy who was watching us?" Seth asked.

"I don't know, man. Never saw him. We came down and he was gone." The words flowed from Andy's mouth with no hesitation. Jake stared at him, amazed at how natural he sounded. Effortless. "I bet he was the one who stole the money in the first place and took off with it."

"So why do you still have the gun?" Ryan asked.

That loud bang echoed from that dark hallway into Jake's head again.

Andy shrugged. "I don't know. I wasn't thinking about it, really. I guess I was afraid that guy may come back here or something."

Jake looked at Seth and Ryan, trying to read their faces. Maybe the confusion and trauma of the last few hours had scrambled their thinking enough that they weren't ready to ask a few easy questions and connect the dots. People had a way of protecting themselves, and sometimes ignorance was bliss.

"All that said, we can call the police if you want, but after that we've got to keep quiet about this," Andy said. His voice had hardened, and his eyes passed between the guys with an edge of gravity. "Nobody can ever know we were out there. Just forget this whole thing happened. Never talk about it again . . . even among us."

Andy reached into his pocket and pulled out a small pocketknife. It was something they'd done only once before, but all four guys knew what it meant.

Standing behind Ryan's light-blue Buick LeSabre, Andy unfolded the knife and pulled it across his palm, a thin red line appearing in its wake. He handed the knife over to Seth, who hesitated for a second before doing the same.

Jake did it without thinking, no passion or promise behind it. By the time the small bubbles of blood had welled up on his hand, Andy had Seth's and Ryan's hands in his grasp. Words were said that satisfied the group. But instead of a weight lifted, Jake felt pressure setting in on his shoulders.

"All right," Andy said. Ryan ducked into the front seat of his car to grab something to cover their new wounds.

"What do we do with the gun?" Ryan handed Seth a white paper napkin that might or might not have been used on the trip up.

"We throw it in the lake." Jake's voice left no room for debate, but Andy tried anyway.

"Well, maybe I—"

Jake held his hand out. "Give it to me."

He could have easily reached over and pulled it from his waistband, but he wanted Andy to hand it to him. To know that he wasn't the only one in charge. This wasn't *his* situation—it was theirs—and for what he was asking, Andy had to give up something too.

It apparently wasn't a battle Andy wanted to fight, so he pulled out Schroeder's pistol. Jake wondered if the grip put the same feeling in Andy's hand as it had in his. He imagined Andy squeezing off three shots, destroying the quiet of the lake to ensure their silence, hopping into Ryan's car and driving off into the horizon with his bag of drug money.

He eventually handed the gun to Jake. "Good idea."

With his right hand covered with a bloody fast-food napkin, Jake took the gun in his left and carried it off toward the back of the cabin.

"What are you doing?" Seth called after him.

"I told you, I'm throwing this in the goddamn lake."

Andy moved to go after him, but Ryan put a hand on his shoulder. "He'll handle it."

———

Jake stood at the end of the dock, boat back in the lift and waves gently rolling in from the far side of the lake. He held the gun and felt the same pull, that warmth from the grip, that he had out on the island. He turned it over in his hands and saw a dark smear of blood across the handle from when Andy had handed it to him. In the distance, a thick tendril of black smoke snaked into the morning sky.

Jake watched it for a moment, then turned back toward the shore.

Chapter
Thirty-One

The old barn loomed across the yard, a broken-down blight that fit in perfectly with the aesthetics of Jake Nelson's dilapidated homestead. A large door stood out near the southeast corner—the side that was still standing—its faded gray slightly contrasting against the faded red of the barn.

Jake motioned toward the collapsed end of the barn. "A huge storm came through last summer and took down that end. Don't know if it was a real tornado or just straight-line winds, but it made a hell of a lot of noise."

"Is it safe in there?" Krista thought the upright end looked solid enough, but the roof took a sharp turn down about two-thirds of the way along, where it had collapsed.

"Probably," Jake said. "I don't come out here much."

The rusty brown handle resisted the turn before acquiescing with a crunchy snap. The screech of the hinges told Krista that Jake hadn't lied about not coming out here. The door sounded like it hadn't been opened in years.

She followed Jake, gingerly stepping through the doorway into the dusty gloom of the old barn. The last remnants of dusk filtered down from the holes torn in the collapsed roof on the far side. It was enough to illuminate the dust they'd kicked up, turning it into tiny glowing snowflakes hanging in the air around them.

The inside of the barn was littered with old farm equipment, much of it in the same shape as the barn itself. Two old lawn mowers sat beside a piece of antique field gear that apparently harvested corn by stabbing it with giant spikes.

Everything around them was rusty, dusty, and old. In the shadows, it looked like the headquarters of a pioneer serial killer. The thought that Jake had lured her to the barn in order to kill her popped into Krista's head. She casually slipped her hand into her pocket and made a fist around her rental's key fob. The key stuck out between her knuckles, where it would add a significant punch if she needed to hit him again. She slowly pulled it out and slid it behind her hip.

"It's back there," Jake said, motioning toward the area where the roof had come down in a pile of rubble. He started his way around the equipment scattered about the intact half of the barn.

Krista's eyes strained to adjust to the rapidly growing darkness, but she couldn't make out anything beyond a pile of broken boards and buried junk. She pulled out her phone and switched on the flashlight app, splitting her attention between the ruins around her and Jake. Her other hand was still tight around her weaponized key.

Half of an old workbench stuck out from the pile of rubble against the near wall. It was littered with debris from the roof and tools that looked like they were from the 1890s.

"Be careful not to step on anything," Jake said. "There's probably nails all over round here."

The statement calmed Krista a little, since she assumed someone looking to kill her wouldn't worry about tetanus.

Jake worked his way to the end of the bench that was under the wreckage. A large slab of shingles lay atop it, forming a splintery lean-to. Jake peered underneath it and motioned Krista over.

"Under here," Jake said. He grabbed the edge of the boards and lifted. He got it up a couple of inches before a shingle and the piece of rotten wood it was nailed to came off in his hand. The wood slapped back onto the bench in a cloud of dust.

Jake buried his face in the crook of his elbow and hacked out as much old barn dust as he could. Krista blinked against the onslaught of grime and looked up toward the damaged ceiling. There were plenty of holes torn where the roof had splintered, but the light streaming through them was getting more and more sparse.

"Come here," Jake said, motioning toward the boards that had just broken off in his hands. "Hold this up for me."

Krista kicked away the rubble in front of her and sidled up behind Jake.

"Grab here," Jake said, indicating a solid-looking piece a little farther back. "I just need a little room."

She stuffed the phone in her back pocket and threaded her middle finger through her key ring so she could grab the wood without putting her key away. An old splinter dug into Krista's palm as she lifted, getting the chunk of roof about six inches off the bench. It was enough for Jake to duck underneath and come out with an old wooden box.

Jake stood and slid the box onto the workbench, pushing the debris aside while Krista dropped the section of roof she was holding. She peered down at her hand and pulled a quarter-inch piece of wood from the pad under her thumb.

Krista got out her phone and fixed the light on the box. It was worn but sturdy looking, and the coat of blue paint appeared newer than the tarnished brass accessories that held it together. It looked right at home in an old barn like this. Krista wouldn't have been surprised if Jake had found the box out here when he first moved in.

It was held shut by an old combination lock. He reached down and spun the black plastic dial on the front of the lock with precision. When he stopped at the third and final number, Jake gave a tug, and the shackle popped from the silver case. He pulled it off with a twist of his wrist and lifted the cover.

Krista peered over Jake's shoulder and immediately recognized the rainbow polka dots of an old Wonder Bread bag. Jake reached down carefully, as if dipping his hand into a beehive, and pulled it out. His fingers undid the blue twist tie and warily pulled back the plastic.

The silver barrel of the handgun shot back the light from her phone and almost glowed. Krista looked over at Jake and could tell it still held him.

"Can I see it?"

Jake's expression didn't change as he transferred it between hands, pulling back the plastic but keeping it around the handle.

Krista adjusted her light and saw a dark stain along the grip.

"What's that?"

"Blood," Jake said. "From that fucking oath he made us take."

"Yours?"

Jake shook his head. "His."

The scar on Harry's palm flashed through her mind. Krista reached her hand toward it and jumped when Jake pulled it back.

"Sorry," he said, dropping his eyes from her like a puppy caught chewing on the couch. "I just . . ."

"It's okay," Krista said. "It's got to be hard to share this with someone after all these years. I mean, telling the story is one thing, but this—"

Jake's head snapped up and startled the words out of Krista's mouth.

"What?" she asked.

"Shhh!" His eyes were wide enough she could see every bloodshot thread tangled across them, and his ear was cocked toward the holes in the wall above them.

Krista stepped back from the table and spun around, looking for whatever had snapped Jake to attention like that. The barn behind her was much darker than when they'd entered; the only things she could see were the faded blue strips of light that seeped through the boards. Her heartbeat roared through her ears, so it was a few extra seconds until she heard what had rattled Jake.

The faint sound of tires on gravel crept in from the driveway.

Krista whirled back toward Jake, who was creeping up onto the workbench. The barn had no windows, but a jagged hole sat a few feet above the bench. Jake raised himself up on his knees and peered out into his front yard.

"What is it?"

He didn't shush her again, just held a single finger down toward her without taking his eyes away from the hole.

The crunching gravel got louder and was accompanied by the gentle purr of a motor. Krista stepped around the workbench Jake knelt on and found a small seam between the boards of the wall. The splinters jutting from the old wood pricked her hands as she pressed toward the little slit of light coming from the yard.

A dark-gray Chevrolet Malibu crawled into the tiny sliver of outside Krista could see. It was too dark to see the driver, but Krista didn't need to. She'd been standing right beside him when he rented the car at the airport.

It rolled up behind her own rental car and stopped. The engine shut off, returning the suffocating silence that had unnerved her earlier. She heard a sharp intake of breath from beside her as the driver's side door opened and Harry Leonard stepped out.

A crush of emotions sloshed through Krista's head at the sight of her boss. Part of her wanted to call out to him, while another section of her brain told her it was best to stay hidden. She had no idea how he knew she was here, or how he'd found his way.

Harry walked alongside Krista's rental car, crouching down to peer in the windows. He stood back up and studied Jake's house. The windows were open but dark, and Harry slowly crept around her car and over toward the house.

"What is he—"

"*Quiet!*" Jake's harsh whisper cut her off immediately. "Shut that goddamn light off."

Krista fumbled with her phone and stuffed it in her back pocket once again. As confused as she was, Jake was obviously more frightened. He climbed down from the workbench and hurried around to her side.

"He's here for me." Jake pushed his face up against the gap between the boards. "Ever since I heard about Ryan, I knew it was just a matter of time before he came for me."

Krista grabbed his shoulder and pulled him away from the barn's wall. "Don't get crazy. He's probably looking for me, that's all."

"If that was the case, he'd have called you," Jake said, taking another look out between the boards.

Krista wanted to knock back Jake's paranoia, but realized she was no longer sure about anything. She had the sudden urge to look out the crack between the boards, to know where Harry was. Had he gone in the house? Returned to his car? There was nothing moving in the barn and no sound from outside. Was he headed over here to the barn? And why did that suddenly scare her?

"He's gone," Jake hissed.

"He left?"

Jake pushed himself away from the wall and slipped past her toward the other end of the barn.

"No, his car's still there. But I don't see him."

Krista stood there, still straining to get her thoughts together while Jake was halfway across the barn. One thing she knew was that she didn't want to be alone in the dark, so she hurried after him.

She caught up to him just inside the door. "Wait, what are you doing?"

He opened the door slightly, giving them a decent view of the yard. Her car sat by the house, with Harry's right behind, but he was nowhere to be seen. Jake ducked back inside and pulled the door back as slowly as possible in a relatively successful attempt at keeping the rusty old hinges from screaming.

"Okay, he's probably gone around back . . . maybe inside," Jake whispered. "You have your keys?"

"Yeah." She held the fob up for him to see, and a last stream of light bounced off the metal that jutted out from her fist. Her fear of Jake had subsided, yet she was surprised to find she still gripped the key like a weapon.

"Good," he said. "Get over there as quickly and quietly as you can. I'll follow."

The idea that she'd be in a hurry to get away from Jake's house again had certainly occurred to her. She just never thought he'd be in the passenger seat when she did.

"Hold on a second." Krista's head swirled with a cocktail of confusion and fear. Was she suddenly afraid of the man she'd spent her entire career working with—the man with whom she'd done so much good? And based on what, the word of an unstable stranger? "Let me go talk to him. I'm sure we can work out whatever we need to."

"Are you crazy?" Jake grabbed her by the shoulder and spun her back toward him. "He's not here to talk."

For the first time she was close enough to smell alcohol on his breath.

"Whatever he did when he was a kid, he's a congressman now." Krista shook Jake's hand from her arm. "He didn't come out here to kill you or anything. Let me go talk to him."

There was just enough light leaking through the cracked barn door to show a paranoid glint in Jake's eyes. He was blinking almost constantly now, sometimes squeezing his eyes shut for a full second as if he was trying to dislodge a rogue eyelash. "Seth didn't want to face the truth either. He said I was nuts, but I know Andy couldn't let things lie. He's got to be stopped."

From the first time they'd met, she'd tried to figure out if Jake was telling the truth or suffering from severe mental delusions.

She'd never considered it could be both.

The thoughts swirled through her head. The Harry she'd known all these years wasn't a murderer. He wouldn't hurt her, right? Krista stared at the twitching man in front of her and realized she had to stop this situation from spiraling out of control. At the very least, she needed to get Jake away from Harry.

"You're right," she said. "I'll drive you wherever you want to go. We can even go to the police."

Jake looked at her skeptically in the silence of the barn. She could see the debate raging behind his eyes when he pushed the door open again, the hinges screeching across the empty yard.

"All right, let's go."

He didn't wait for an answer before stepping out of the barn. Krista followed as close as she could without getting their feet tangled up.

With the sun below the horizon, the shadows that had stretched across the lawn earlier had been swallowed up by the night. The broken light fixture above Jake's kitchen door was giving no help, but the darkness of the barn had opened her pupils enough that she could see decently. Her rental was boxed in from behind, so she'd have to whip around in the yard to get out.

Harry was still nowhere to be seen as they jogged quietly across the yard. The crunch of rocks when they hit the end of the driveway sounded like boulders in an avalanche to Krista, but they didn't draw him out from wherever he'd gone.

Jake went around the hood of her car as Krista reached for the driver's side door handle. She pulled it open while Jake continued toward his house.

"What are you doing?" she whispered. "Let's go."

He shook his head while his eyes scanned the yard.

Krista straightened up and stepped around the open door. The dome light had come on and spilled out through the windshield, providing just enough light for her to notice Schroeder's gun had come out of the bread bag and was now in Jake's hand. The back of her neck broke out in a cosmic array of tingles at the sight of the weapon.

Jake saw the look on her face and gestured toward the car.

"Go on now." He spoke as if he were directing a stray dog that had wandered onto his property.

"Hold on—"

"Go." Jake nodded toward the car again. His voice was low but audible. "I've got to end this. Get out of here."

"How? You can't just shoot him."

Jake stepped back toward Krista and used a volume that was much higher than that of someone looking to keep a low profile. Either he couldn't control it, or he didn't care anymore.

"You know what he is. I've told you, and now you've seen it for yourself. Guys like that . . . they're the most dangerous. They put on a good face, show the whole world what good guys they are. They may even do good things, helping people and all that. But that's *not* who they are. Deep down, they don't give a shit about other people. They're nothing but a means to an end. If helping people gets them what they want, they help. If fucking someone over gets them what they want, then they fuck them over. And if someone gets in the way, if they know too much, if they might prevent them from getting a hold of the power they feel is owed them, then they *SHOOT THEM IN THE FUCKING HEAD!*"

The outburst echoed across the rural property, bouncing down the gravel driveway and resonating out toward the woods in back. Even in the dark, Krista could see the manic fear and anger that dominated Jake's face. Years of repressed memories were bubbling to the surface and threatening to take him over completely.

If Krista didn't find a way to pull him back from this abyss, the situation would go somewhere they couldn't come back from. She stepped away from the driver's side door and caught an apprehensive look as Jake eyed her. Krista put her hands out in what she hoped was a reassuring manner and stopped, not wanting to set him off. The gun was still at his side, but she could see his hand tensing around the grip.

She took a deep breath, put on her most nonthreatening face, and took another step toward Jake. "I know what you're saying, but you know—"

"Krista?"

The sound of Harry's voice shattered the quiet more than Jake's outburst had. Krista briefly closed her eyes in resignation, almost embarrassed that she'd somehow believed Jake's eruption could have gone unheard.

Harry stepped around the corner of the house he'd disappeared behind just a few minutes before, a concerned look partially obscured by the shadows. She barely had time to react before the gun Jake held at his side jumped toward Harry. The blur of movement ripped Harry's attention away from Krista and brought him to a sudden stop.

"WHOA, WHOA, HOLD ON!" Krista's hands went into the air as if she were imploring an oncoming train to pull the brakes. Harry's expression showed a level of fear Krista had never seen from him. Throughout his entire career, Harry had shown an uncanny ability to remain, outwardly at least, unflappable.

Staring down the barrel of a gun blew that right out the window.

"Jake, Jake . . ." Krista kept her hands up, but slowly stepped toward him. "You don't want to do this, Jake. Listen to me. You don't want to do this."

Jake's eyes kept squeezing shut, but his hand held the gun aimed steadily into the middle of Harry's face. The congressman remained a step past the corner, probably too far out for him to retreat for cover before one of Schroeder's old bullets exploded between his eyes. His hands were held in front of him, fingers splayed out in surrender.

"You don't know what the fuck I want," Jake said.

"Yes, I do," Krista said. "And this isn't going to get it for you."

She gently slid to her right, trying to ease into Jake's field of vision without jarring him into pulling the trigger. The gun wavered slightly as Jake's grip on the handle tightened.

"You want him to pay for what he did. To be held accountable. You want people to know what he is."

Harry's voice came up from the corner of the house, the same soothing tone he'd used throughout his career to win over countless people.

"Jake, buddy, let me—"

"Shut the fuck up, Harry," Krista said, never taking her eyes off Jake. She understood why he thought he could talk his way out of this. He always did. But with what she'd heard from Jake—and what she'd uncovered herself—in the last two days, she didn't see a way smooth talk was going to work. Jake didn't see him as an opposing politician, but as a monster who had to be put in his place.

And he might be right.

"I know what you want." Krista kept slowly sliding to her right, trying to put herself between Jake and Harry. "And I honestly couldn't agree with you more. Our system, our whole society, is messed up, and it's all because of guys like this. Guys who say the right things, who *do* the right things, who appear to be helping, but deep inside don't give a damn about anybody but themselves. Who never do anything without a selfish motive. Our system is rotting from the inside because the guys in it are rotten on the inside."

She let the words hang for a second, unable to judge their effect aside from the fact Jake hadn't pulled the trigger yet. Krista kept her focus on Jake, but could hear Harry's rattled breathing behind her.

"Guys like this make all the right moves, until something gets in their way. Then they bend the rules. Maybe it's no big deal, or maybe it ruins somebody's life. Either way, they don't care. They've got what they want, and they move on. I maybe never saw the extent of it that you did, but believe me, I've seen it too."

Jake's brow furrowed slightly, and Krista was briefly afraid he was going to shoot.

"That's why we have to do something," Jake said. "We have to stand up and say *No, you can't fucking do this*. We can't let them get away with it over and over and over."

"And we won't," Krista said. "But if you shoot him, how do you think that's going to play out? If the cops covered up for a drug-dealing DNR officer, what do you think they'd do for a sitting congressman? You're just a former friend who's fallen on hard times. Who drinks too much. Who sent threatening mail to his office and talked to reporters about murder conspiracies. You'll be some obsessed, tinfoil-hat-wearing whack job who snapped and shot a congressman, and everything you say will reinforce that, no matter how true it is."

Jake kept the gun leveled on Harry but looked at Krista. For the first time, she felt she was getting through to him.

"But we can turn him in." She'd purposely used *we* so Jake would feel he finally wasn't alone. That if he would just listen to her, she'd be with him every step of the way. "If he's killed, he's a martyr. But if we come forward and tell the truth . . . if we have proof"—Krista nodded at Schroeder's gun—"we can take him down and show the world that people can't get away with this stuff."

Krista let her words sink in and slowly stepped toward Jake. The barrel of the gun shook ever so slightly in front of him. She reached out for it, careful not to make a grab, but offering her hand.

"Everyone will see the real . . . *Andy* Leonard."

Krista kept her hand outstretched, silently pleading with him to hand it over. A tear slipped out of Jake's eye and rolled down his face.

"We can do this," she said. "Let's show them who he is."

Jake lowered the gun, and Krista gently caught his arm with one hand while putting another on his shoulder.

"You're very brave," she said. "We can do this."

Krista didn't take the gun from his hand, but kept a light hold of his wrist as she guided him over to the makeshift cinder block steps in front of the kitchen door. The board bowed slightly as Jake sat.

She looked over at Harry, who hadn't moved from the corner of the house. She motioned with her head to their cars. He slowly moved away from the house as Krista tenderly slid her hand down Jake's wrist and over the gun. Her fingers curled around the barrel in a way her late grandfather, who'd always stressed gun safety when he taught her how to shoot as a girl, would have scolded her for. Jake's grip instinctively tightened before allowing Krista to ease the gun away.

She glanced up at Harry and saw a look of relief on his face as he stood by the front grille of her car. There was surprisingly little conflict in her head as she considered what they would have to do. Harry had done, and could do, so many good things for so many people, but there was no way to sugarcoat what he'd done at Cedar Lake. It wasn't a scandal to be ridden out, but something that would end his career and quite possibly put him in prison for a long time.

The image of a sign her third-grade teacher had made in Print Shop popped into her head. She'd spent hours staring at the gray dot matrix words hung up prominently over the chalkboard.

Sometimes doing the right thing is hard, but we do it anyway.

With her hand still on Jake's shoulder, Krista felt the tension ease out of his body. She took a half step back and transferred Schroeder's old gun to her right hand before quickly pressing it against Jake's left temple and pulling the trigger.

The gunshot tore through the still of the night as violently as the bullet tore through Jake's skull. A splatter of blood and brain tissue fanned out across the dying grass below them, and a small chunk of skull stuck to the worn siding by the door.

Jake's lifeless body slumped off the step, and Krista jumped back out of the way. She turned to Harry, who wore a gray expression of absolute shock.

"You're fucking welcome."

Chapter
Thirty-Two

It took a good minute before Harry found his voice. Even then, he didn't muster any more than a mutter.

"Jesus . . ."

Krista ignored him and evaluated the scene in front of her. Jake's body was still half on the makeshift front step, which was good. She wanted to avoid moving it if possible. A poor, depressed man sitting on the front step of his run-down, pathetic house to shoot himself made sense. If he was found in the middle of the yard, that might raise questions, and it was imperative to raise as few questions as possible.

"Go get me something to wipe with." Krista could tell Harry's thoughts were still disjointed. The shock of the gunshot had kicked out the plug on his brain, and his mind was still rebooting. *"Hey!"*

Harry's eyes finally snapped back to the moment, and he looked over at her.

"I came here to—"

"I don't care. Go check the cars for something I can wipe this down with," she said, hefting the gun into his sight line. He turned back toward the car door without a word.

Krista pulled the phone out of her back pocket and pointed the light toward the ground. She circled around Jake's body, stepping to avoid the spray of blood that shone black from the ground under his head.

There was a lot more than she expected—it was amazing how much blood could flow from the head—and they'd have to be extremely careful not to disturb it.

"Here." Harry had returned with a T-shirt. It wasn't one of hers, so he must have pulled it out of his own rental. "What are we going to do?" The shock had left his voice, and he spoke with a practical tone.

Krista looked back at him and studied his face. His color was back, and he was in work mode. He might have been taken by surprise at seeing a man shot in front of him, but he'd put that away and was all business. If she had any doubt over what Jake said had happened in that lab, that confirmed his account. Harry had no problem with murder if it served a purpose.

"We clean the gun off, put it in his hand, and get the hell out of here."

"Is that enough? I mean, aren't you worried about forensics or ballistics or anything?"

Krista thought a second before answering.

"It'll be fine. The guy was a hermit, and there's nothing connecting either of us to him. Nobody's going to think of this as anything but an alcoholic loner committing suicide. Open and shut. And the body is outside. The longer it sits out here in the elements, the better. Honestly, I wouldn't be surprised if nobody finds him for at least a week."

She looked down at the gun in her hands.

"Did you notice a spigot anywhere along the house back there?"

Harry thought a second.

"I think there was a hose out back," he said. "Why?"

Krista held Schroeder's gun up to him and pointed out the old dark-brown smudge on the grip.

"I'm going to wash your blood off this gun before I put it in his hand . . . You recognize it?"

Harry stared at the silver handgun, and Krista could see the memories flickering behind his eyes as if they were an educational filmstrip he had to sit through in elementary school.

"Good God." The words seeped out of his mouth like from a leaky tire. She started to tell Harry where it was from but it was obvious the pieces were falling into place without her help.

"Make sure you don't step in any of the blood. In fact, don't wander around at all. The ground is hard enough we shouldn't have to worry about footprints or anything, but there's no reason to risk it." Krista took the gun and the shirt around the back of the house. An old garden hose lay in a loose pile, one end connected to a spout sticking out of the house about two feet off the ground. She turned it on with the shirt in her hand, then soaked the fabric and washed off the dried blood that had been there for over twenty years, along with any fingerprints she might have added.

"Where the hell did that come from?" Harry's voice appeared behind her as she shut the water off.

"He kept it all these years," she said. "In a Wonder Bread bag, if you can believe that. He said it was proof that he wasn't crazy. About all that happened at Cedar Lake."

Harry observed her as she said it, and she matched his gaze. She could tell he was sizing her up, trying to figure how she was going to play this. Probably wondering if she'd pulled him out from under the shadow of a crisis only to stick him under her own thumb.

She stood and held the gun up for him, holding it by the barrel with the shirt she'd wiped it down with.

The blood was gone.

He instinctively reached out for the gun, but Krista pulled it back and shook her head. "I can't imagine they're going to bother looking for fingerprints on this, but that doesn't mean we have to leave any."

Harry nodded.

They went back out front and finished their work. Harry held Krista's phone light over Jake's body as she maneuvered around the blood to get the newly cleaned gun next to his hand.

They worked mostly in silence, save for a few muttered suggestions or directions.

Satisfied they'd left nothing identifiable or suspicious behind, they each walked to their cars. Any tire tracks they might leave would be driven over and mixed in with those of whoever found the body. Krista was pulling her driver's side door open when Harry spoke.

"Krista, thank you."

She stood for a second before answering. The crickets had returned, scrubbing away the eerie silence of the dark with the sound of their tiny violin legs.

"I didn't do this for you," Krista said. "I did this for every person you're going to help from this point forward. As a congressman. *As governor.* And, after you continue to do exactly what I tell you to do, as president. And you best remember that."

Chapter Thirty-Three

Krista waded through the crowd standing on the checkerboard floor in front of the stage at First Avenue. It was their former intern Emily Kohan's idea to hold their announcement at Minneapolis's legendary rock club, and it worked. The room was packed with supporters, many of whom were in the eighteen-to-thirty-four demographic that would carry them in the election. The young woman had a bright future ahead of her, and Krista had already reserved a permanent staff position for her upon graduation.

She'd decided against a podium, for both practical reasons and optics. Traditional politicians used podiums, and Harry Leonard wasn't a traditional politician. He was young, full of fresh ideas, and a clean break from the divisive politics of the past. Besides, the stage was already set up for the bands that would follow the announcement, and getting a podium on and off posed some logistic difficulties. They'd pulled together a strong who's who of the Minnesota music scene, all of whom were happy to throw their voices (and influence within a coveted demographic) behind Harry.

Krista looked up at the huge *LEONARD FOR GOVERNOR* banner draped on the back of the stage and smiled. They were still thirty minutes from officially announcing his candidacy, but preliminary polls already had Harry with a commanding lead over the field.

Publicly turning down the vice presidential slot so he could *focus on effecting real change in my home state* had been extremely well received by Minnesotans.

She spotted their new press secretary backstage talking with a couple of campaign volunteers under a six-foot black speaker. Krista walked over to check in, making sure everything was in order.

"You ready for this?" Krista asked. Maggie Wander had been hired a few months ago, but this was her first major public event as press secretary, and it came in her hometown in front of a lot of former coworkers.

"No problem," Maggie said. "I talked to the manager, and we're going to move the postspeech press conference over into the 7th Street Entry instead of that room upstairs. We've just got too many people."

Krista smiled. "Good problem to have."

"It's pretty dark in there, but they say they've got some stage lights we can use that'll work for TV. They'll do their stand-ups outside on the sidewalk. The stars painted on the side of the club will make a good local backdrop," Maggie said. "They were out there twenty minutes ago jockeying for position in front of Prince's."

Harry popped out of a tiny dressing room behind them.

"I want a picture in front of Prince's star," he said, straightening his purple tie. "For my office."

"That can be arranged," Maggie said. She reached behind him and flattened the collar of his suit jacket. "The *Star Tribune* wants a one-on-one after the press conference. I told them you'd be delighted."

"Throwing a bone to the old team, eh?"

"Matt Szafranski is a good reporter, and it can't hurt to make him feel respected. A little access can go a long way."

Harry laughed and put his hands up in mock surrender.

"I was just kidding," he said. "That's totally fine. Whatever you feel helps the cause, I'm there."

Maggie went over a few details about the press availability after his speech and reminded Harry of their main talking points before heading out to wrangle a few photographers in front of the stage.

The first band had appeared from the bowels of the old rock club and massed around Harry in the wings of the stage. Krista smiled as he obliged multiple selfie requests, hoping they'd show up on the band's Instagram account soon.

"You want to introduce them?" Krista asked Harry.

"Sure," he said, looking over at the band. "If you guys don't mind."

The band said they'd be honored, and Harry dutifully insisted that as big a fan as he was, the honor was all his. *Fan* might have been an overstatement, but Krista had downloaded songs from each band that would play that afternoon to Harry's phone so he'd be familiar with their music. Courting the youth vote was important, but you had to be careful. Politicians had pandered to them for years, making them suspicious by default. Kids could spot a fake better than old people who'd been lied to their whole lives.

Krista pulled Harry aside, and the band went back to tuning their guitars.

"Take your tie off," Krista said. "You're coming out early to do this, before you were ready, because you're *that* excited about the band. You should be back practicing your speech, but screw it, you really want to see these guys because 'Who's Laughing Now' is your favorite song."

Harry didn't hesitate, pulling his tie loose and unbuttoning his collar.

"I actually do like that one." He took a step back, and Krista inspected him. He even had a knack for looking perfectly disheveled.

They went over the basics of what he'd say on stage—*how ya doing*, quick self-deprecating joke, name-drop the new album—and he was off.

They'd always been a powerful team, but in the last year, their momentum had picked up exponentially.

It wasn't just Harry; Krista's star was rising in the party as well. She'd even been approached about her own political future a few times, but politely demurred. She was satisfied being the woman behind the curtain, the one with her hands on the levers.

And with Harry, there was no doubt who was pulling the strings.

Her mind drifted back to her apartment, to the dark-blue box in the bottom of her closet. She'd thought it too perfect when it caught her eye in that little antique shop up in Grand Marais. It was in better shape than the one where Jake Nelson had hidden that bloodstained handgun all those years, and the lock on the front was silver instead of a tarnished brass, but it was remarkably similar and a fitting home for the little voice recorder she'd used those two days in southeast Minnesota.

It was only a prop the first time out, part of her reporter's ruse. She hadn't planned on using it the next day, but it caught her eye as she pulled up, and she figured it couldn't hurt to have a record of whatever Jake was going to say, so she'd slipped it into her pocket far enough the little red light was invisible.

And that's how Jake Nelson's entire story, the one implicating Congressman and Gubernatorial Candidate Harrison Leonard in the murder of DNR agent Kim Schroeder, had ended up locked away in a little blue box in Krista's bedroom.

She'd never told Harry she had it. Never had to, because since that day the power dynamic had fully shifted.

She was definitely the one pulling the levers.

The crowd erupted when Harry waltzed onto the stage, his shirt collar effortlessly unbuttoned and his hair perfectly out of place.

"Hey, all!"

Krista smiled from the side of the stage, watching Harry hit all the notes she'd wanted. Seeing him in front of a crowd was impressive, almost as good as he was one on one.

It was what was going to make them president someday.

"I'm supposed to be getting ready to talk to you guys later, but I figured since it's my announcement, I can do what I want, right? And I've been a huge fan of these guys ever since my chief of staff turned me on to them." Harry glanced offstage and motioned for Krista to join him. "Hey, Krista, come on out here and let me introduce you to a few people."

Not wanting to make an awkward moment for her candidate, Krista didn't hesitate. She stepped past a rack of guitars and waved to the crowd.

"She's the best." Harry put his arm around her shoulders to polite applause. "A couple years ago I made a road trip down to see my old high school buddy Ryan, and I listened to 'Who's Laughing Now' over and over for the entire drive."

The crowd cheered Harry's name-drop of the band's first single, but it couldn't drown out the sound of his voice echoing through Krista's brain.

The last time I saw Ryan Kelter was when we were in college.

She felt Harry's grip tighten around her, his fingers briefly—but unmistakably—digging into her shoulder.

But her expression didn't change as she stared into the brilliant stage lights. Krista put her arm around Harry and defiantly squeezed right back.

Acknowledgments

The first thank-you will always go to my agent, Abby Saul. This is the book that brought us together, and when the path took a few detours, she was the one who steered us back. Thank you for always being there to answer whatever dumb question I have, and for your keen editorial eye. You are the greatest agent in the world, and I will fight anyone who says otherwise.

I want to thank my editor Liz Pearsons for taking a second look at this book and getting it out into the world. Let's have lunch again soon.

The whole team at Thomas & Mercer is a dream to work with. Thanks to my production manager Miranda Gardner for shepherding me through the process and getting this all to come together. Big thanks to my copyeditor Alicia Lea and proofreader Elyse Lyon for patiently pointing out the same mistakes over and over. Thanks to my author liaison Darci Swanson for being there to answer any and all questions.

And a special shout-out to Sarah Shaw. Hope your new gig is going swimmingly.

Gabino Iglesias is one of the absolute best writers out there, and the fact that I got to work with him again on this book is insane. He pulled a lot out of me and made sure it was properly splattered across the page.

Thanks to David Drummond of Salamander Hill Design for the fantastic cover.

Thanks to Kirsten Lincoln, Mike Kalmbach, and Anthony Eichenlaub, who read an early draft long ago and helped me start this journey.

Thanks to my Lark Group buddies, Tara Tai, Brianna Labuskes, Elle Grawl, Meredith Hambrock, Mindy Carlson, Jason Powell, Terah Harris, Kris Calvin, Daisy Bateman, Stephanie Thérèse, Sarah James, Logan Steiner, Summer Olsen, and Carol Dunbar. Everyone should buy all their books.

Finally, I want to thank my family. There is no way I could have even attempted writing without the support of my wife, Erin, and I get inspiration from my daughters, Claire and Paige, every day.

Speaking of family, while this story is pure fiction, a lot of the settings are real. My grandparents owned a cabin on Cedar Lake, and one time when I was little, we went out to an island in the back part of the lake to explore the abandoned house that was there. My family called it Mystery Island, and while the details are lost to my memory, I'd always thought it would make a great setting for a novel. But before I started, I had to ask my parents, "That was real, right?"

They didn't know any of the details or history, just that it was indeed there. So I wrote a story about a group of kids up at the lake, similar to how Lou, Todd, Hagen, Jeff Pete, and I would go up whenever we could talk our families into letting us. We never went to Mystery Island, though. Probably for the best.

But I wonder if the house is still standing.

About the Author

Photo © *Grant Hamilton*

Tony Wirt was born in Lake Mills, Iowa, and got his first taste of publication in first grade, when his essay on *Airplane II: The Sequel* appeared in Lake Mills Elementary School's *Creative Courier*.

He's a graduate of the University of Iowa and spent nine years doing media relations in the Hawkeye Athletic Department. He's also been a sportswriter, movie-ticket taker, and Dairy Queen ice cream slinger who can still do the little curly thing on top of a soft serve cone.

He currently lives in Rochester, Minnesota, with his wife and two daughters.

His book *Just Stay Away* was released in 2023 from Thomas & Mercer.